I0637149

WINE, MEN & MOZART

by

Brigitte Downey

Grosvenor House
Publishing Limited

All rights reserved
Copyright © Brigitte Downey, 2025

The right of Brigitte Downey to be identified as the author of this
work has been asserted in accordance with Section 78
of the Copyright, Designs and Patents Act 1988

The book cover is copyright to Brigitte Downey

This book is published by
Grosvenor House Publishing Ltd
Link House
140 The Broadway, Tolworth, Surrey, KT6 7HT.
www.grosvenorhousepublishing.co.uk

This book is sold subject to the conditions that it shall not, by way of
trade or otherwise, be lent, resold, hired out or otherwise circulated
without the author's or publisher's prior consent in any form of
binding or cover other than that in which it is published and
without a similar condition including this condition being
imposed on the subsequent purchaser.

This book is a work of fiction. Any resemblance to
people or events, past or present, is purely coincidental.

A CIP record for this book
is available from the British Library

Paperback ISBN 978-1-83615-377-1
eBook ISBN 978-1-83615-378-8

With love for
Eileen and Andrew Downey
Abbeyfeale, Co. Limerick

PROLOGUE

This day will never come again. Why? Because we're in London, not Looney Land. This July morning 2008 is as normal as it gets in the metropolis with over 8 million inmates babbling away in 300 languages but all swearing in English. London motorists curse the mayor who introduced the congestion charge which didn't do a bloody thing about moving faster than horse carts in Dickensian days. It only slashed their disposable cash and upped their blood pressure. London commuters don't have the energy to curse even when they're stranded on packed platforms trying to tune out the incomprehensible mush about signal failures on the Piccadilly Line, or closures and delays on the District, Central and Circle.

Only innocent newcomers to the capital ask: 'what's he saying?'. Real Londoners enlighten them. Since the Underground opened in 1863 only the aurally gifted have understood the squawking that echoes from the p.a. system throughout all the tube stations 364 days of the year and 365 in Leap Years. It only shuts up at Christmas when the entire London public transport system closes down for 24 hours, thus driving all residents and tourists round the bend.

On the surface this is just another mundane morning in the metropolis. That's London. That's Life. Life doesn't pounce on you and bark in your ear: 'Hey babycakes, today's your turn. Be very careful what you curse or wish for.' London Life just trots on changing destinies - for better, for worse, forever. The livid driver cursing the congestion charge ends up in the morgue after that fatal heart attack. Commuters late for that vital interview lose the job. Some struggle on to brighter careers. Others end up on the vodka and gin cul-de-sac. Why? Hey, that's London Life!

It's July so London is heaving with tourists who don't curse and are nauseatingly optimistic even when the rain is bucketing down. But could they please have a few dry hours when they're not getting trench foot traipsing around fabulous London? And hurrah and halleluiah. So far this morning no rain! Today they can rent deckchairs in Hyde, Regents or St James Park and take photos to prove to the folks back home that London is still beyond weird and wonderful. But for millions of real Londoners, it's the 'same old, same old' as they stomp around their tiny back gardens and slaughter slugs. Gazing at the mashed mush they want more from life. But what? Dump the spouse, go trekking in India, move to Morocco or buy a bucket of arsenic and simultaneously solve both the spouse and slug problem? But this is not their story. Or that of so many losers or winners in London Life's Lottery.

This is the tale of three honorary Londoners: June, the former Manhattanite, Liz from Kent, and Moira from Mayo. They've been best friends for 40 years since 1968 when they first met as students in Vienna. During their student years in Vienna The Three majored in wine, men, and dance while belting out Dylan's *'The times they are a-changin"* and the Ofarims' *'I'll never grow old'*. They graduated in languages, art, history, design, business and had it all: careers, love, marriage, kids, divorce, heartbreak, world travel, success. But then their exuberant vim and wit went AWOL and The Three changed from wild sparks to old dead batteries.

Today is their Destiny Day. Why? Because Life is pissed off with The Three!

CHAPTER 1

June's Friday ritual is to play with her grandkids Grace (6) and Billy (5) who live at the other end of the world in the Australian outback. Her skype webcam is on. The call arrives. The two kids can see granny in bed under the duvet, snoring her guts out. Let the game begin!

'Granny, wake up, wake up.'

Under the duvet, June ups her snoring.

'It's my turn with the trumpet.'

'No! You woke her up last week.'

June twists and swirls like a giant serpent under the duvet. It's all part of the weekly pantomime.

BOOM BOOM WHEE WHEE – the sound of a trumpet played by a triumphant grandchild.

AAAAAHHHHHHHAHHHHH – the scream of a terrified granny erupting from the duvet, clutching her heart.

HEEE HEEEE HEEE - the sound of two giggling grandkids.

'You've got five minutes with granny. And then it's bed.'

Hearing her daughter Clare's voice, June is shafted with loneliness even though they skype regularly.

'We want to speak to granny privately.'

Speaking 'privately' to granny is also part of the game.

'Granny, you gotta come visit. **They** won't let us bring in Kylie and Mylie.'

'**They**' always meant 'the horrible parents' who wouldn't let them bring goats or vultures into the house. What animal was it this time? Wombats or dingoes they couldn't smuggle inside as easily as toads and frogs. The kids had hidden those for weeks while the parents worried about the bizarre noises, thinking maybe it was the boiler or heater in need of renewal.

'Who are Kylie and Mylie?' June asks sweetly.

'They're baby kangaroos and we want to bring them in so they can watch TV with us. But THEY won't let us. Granny, please help us, please.'

The grandkids had obviously rehearsed this.

'How?'

'Come over quick. Then YOU tell THEM you want to watch TV with Kylie and Mylie.'

'Yes, my little darlings.' June smiles sincerely.

By the time she visits, the two will have moved on from watching TV with kangaroos to flying on wild swans.

'Say goodnight to granny.'

The two blow her quick kisses and run off.

'Morning Mum, how're you doing?'

'Great.'

'I'll call you during the week. Bye.'

'Bye, love,' June says to the dark screen.

2

Later with her hair fluffed up, June is smartly dressed and ready for her next appointment of the day – a leisurely online chat with her daughter Connie who lives in Rome with Gianni her divine Italian son-in-law. Her grandkids Stef and Bianca love improving their granny's Italian online. June waits for Connie's usual opening comments on how to improve her hair, décor and diet.

'Sorry, Mum but I can't talk now.'

There's always a first. Then June remembers. They're spending July in Aci Trezza by the Sicilian Sea with Gabriela, Gianni's mother.

'Give my love to Gabriela.'

'Bye, Mum.'

June resists the urge to call her son Robert the financial whiz kid who works in one of the high rises she can see on the other side of the Thames. But he's a very busy boy and she doesn't want to disrupt his day. Instead, she chats to Martin her beloved husband whose ashes reside in 11 silver Mozart chocolate boxes in special places all over her apartment. He's been there since he died at a barbecue 10 years earlier at the age of 49. After bringing Martin up to date on all the family news, she eats her very healthy breakfast sitting outside on her favourite balcony. She has seven in her vast four-story penthouse home with its mega million-pound views of postcard London: Tower Bridge, the Gherkin, the Thames. She concentrates on the uplifting blue of Tower Bridge until her melancholy wafts away with the morning mist. She can look forward to brunch with her two oldest friends Liz and Moira in the Tate Modern. Putting down her cup June gazes at the brown age spots on her hands. She didn't have those when she first met her beloved Martin in Vienna in 1968. Martin the fiery Dubliner with the most advanced case of Mozartitis on the globe. Darling Martin with his conducting dream of knocking Karajan off his perch.

June finishes her coffee and almost feels content.

***

'Content' is a feeling Liz from Kent has forgotten how to even spell. She's sitting in a TV edit suite where her boss TT (Talentless Terence whose only claim to fame is Lady Mummy's connections) has ordered Liz to talk his pal George through editing procedures. Treating her like she's a teenage zoo volunteer introducing bananas to the baby baboon. Bonjour Talentless Terence! Liz is a veteran TV producer/director. But TT is 28, less than half her age which is all that counts in the 2008 British media.

George's Daddy is a cabinet minister, and his super rich son intends to rule the media world in six months. No way is he wasting time editing stupid footage with a boring old lady. Veteran Liz knows this. She smiles at George and mentally garrottes his arrogant gullet. What else can she do? She has a lifetime's experience in photography, filming, editing, producing, directing plus several degrees cum laude, cum everything. But at

59 on Planet TV she might as well be dead and doing something more useful like breeding maggots.

'Have you worked in TV before George?'

'Naw. Too busy gapping the globe.'

'You took lots of vids on your travels?'

'Naw.'

If Liz were an electric kettle on the boil, she'd have long since exploded. But she's a professional woman with iron control. She smiles at the puffed-up ass and shows him the edited footage of their programme on WAGS, their lifestyles and the contents of their wine cellars.

'That lot couldn't tell the difference between a shave and a chardonnay,' snorts George. 'But they'd definitely like a shag with their Chablis.'

'A wine expert. Wow!' says Liz holding back her contempt.

'Thank you,' George replies in the condescending tone he reserves for oldies. 'Any close-ups?'

Liz fast forwards to close-ups of different wine bottles.

'Boobs not bottles. You know – jugs, knockers.' George hoots with self-satisfied laughter.

'You're talking tits?'

Liz can't be bothered wasting contempt on the cretin.

'Exactly.'

'This is for an afternoon slot.'

'What a waste of hot WAGS.'

Liz wants to snarl that her generation used 'wag' in the same sentence as a dog's tail. Now WAG means the wives and girlfriends of obscenely overpaid footballers. How in hell did she end up on trash TV with WAGS? She spent a lifetime working on intelligent topics ranging from Fleming's brain, forgotten female geniuses, 20th dictators and ....

'Coffee?' George asks and brings Liz back to reality.

Liz quickly edits different endings while he's getting the coffee. During filming she grew to admire some of the women who genuinely knew and appreciated their wine. Especially Myrtle who had a nose to die for and spoke better French than Liz with her degree from the Sorbonne and married to Pierre from Paris. Myrtle's husband dumped her in a sordid way that made it to all the front pages. But brave Myrtle pawned her bling and set up her own wine business. Liz finishes the item with an upbeat Myrtle. WAG piece done and dusted.

Liz can now look forward to an intelligent brunch in the Tate Modern with The Two. Then TT storms into the edit suite and accuses Liz of making George walk off the job.

Liz excuses herself, goes to the ladies and downs a double dose of expensive blood pressure pills.

***

In Fulham at the opposite end of London, Moira from Mayo can't afford any blood pressure pills. A bitter irony. Four years ago, her business **Travels with Moira** was so successful she could have splashed out on a bath of Moët & Chandon whenever she felt like it. And look at her now. Hitting 60, in debt beyond her receding hairline, not a sniff of a man in years. She'd also be living in the gutter, not gazing at the stars, if Auntie Jessie hadn't left her this Fulham flat. She had spent her life setting up unique travel bureaus all over the globe from Paris to Buenos Aires. Whenever boredom reared its ugly head, she just changed countries. Until that morning 4 years ago in Quebec when she came down with the BBB (**BIGTIME/BURNOUT/BOREOUT**). She took a 'sabbatical' from her travel business and moved to London.

During her travel life Moira always woke up with a song in her heart. Now her only thoughts in the morning are mental murder most foul of her next-door neighbour Babs and her cat Beelzebub who looks like a cross between crushed walnuts and a bulldog's bottom. They moved in 3 months ago. Since then, Babs bangs on Moira's door every morning after she has collected the fox, cat, dog shit plus all the food, bones and human excrement that's been dumped in the communal garden during the night by their satanic neighbours. Babs lays out her 'evidence' on a large piece of plastic between their two doors. After she has completed her oeuvre, Babs takes photo 'proof' and emails them to the local policeman PC O'Reilly. Then she knocks on Moira's door. The way the crap is laid out on that piece of plastic with the cat proudly gazing at the 'evidence' always reminds Moira of lunatic art. Every morning, she thinks Poubelle Art. The innovative French call their waste bins 'poubelles' – 'beautiful poo'.

Moira stands behind her door. To open or not to open, that is the question.

'Morning, Babs.'

'They're getting worse,' Babs points to gigantic, blood-spattered bones. 'That's fox poop. But that blob is human.'

Listening to Babs' never-ending crap monologue Moira sometimes wishes London were the Wild West of 500 years ago! She could blithely shoot those bastards who deliberately threw their garbage into the garden to Kingdom Never Come Again.

'Does PC O'Reilly have any answers?'

'He's trying to convince the council to give us CCTV. Without it we'll never have any observational evidence.'

The cat sniffs the bones. Babs gently shoos it away, then deposits the rubbish into the appropriate bins.

Moira makes herself a strong coffee and tries not to remember that morning 4 years earlier in Quebec when two clients were rhapsodising about the glories of Venice. She had holes in her tongue suppressing the urge to scream out at the top of her lungs that Venice (a city she once adored) was infested with millions of fucking rats, tourists and had more pigeon shit than Paris, London and New York combined.

'The French eat horse steak. Can you imagine anything more disgusting?'

Horse eyeballs in Kazakhstan or reindeer balls in Finland she could have told them. She just kept on smiling, smiling for 30 years ... until that fateful morning when the thought of doing anything touristy made her want to vomit. Oh, if only she could have her wonderful old life back and recover from her burnout. Moira stops thinking about her glorious past and concentrates on the present. It's time to glam up, then get on the District Line for sophisticated brunch in the Tate Modern with her oldest - and only - friends in London.

***

Life is sick of The Three's whinging and whining. Brilliant June, once the life and soul of every party is now the world's unmerriest widow. Liz, with an intellect as bright as Newton's directs TV programmes a one-eyed donkey could pull off while tangoing with a giraffe. As for Moira… the world was her oyster. Now she's worse than any slimy slug. Life was so proud of them. That's why those Three are getting one last chance to stop acting like boring turtles who've had their brains sucked out of them.

The Three better be careful what they curse or wish for today. Because Life is going to oblige and make them come true.

CHAPTER 2

Entering the Tate Modern, Moira felt a surge of bile as she did a quick trot past the massive museum shop. She used to adore browsing such stores to see which countries had the most innovative way to sell cards/cups/aprons with Dada/Dali or Pig/ass cartoons. Her Mother in Mayo loved those 'originals' and down the decades they roared with laughter at the hilarious copies Moira brought home. Now instead of lapping up 'funny tourist art' she wondered how surgeons developed a fear of blood; pilots a fear of flying and why globe trotters like herself felt nauseous at the sight of anything touristy.

At the Members' restaurant Moira waited to be waved through as one of June's regular guests. But the new receptionists were checking names

'Your ID, please, Madame.'

'You need my ID?' Moira asked.

'If you wouldn't mind.'

She most certainly did mind. During her professional life she was waved through from Alma-Ata to Zanzibar. Only airport officials had to check her ID. She opened her wallet and pulled out a laminated card.

'Will this suffice?' she asked sweetly.

The receptionist returned her ID, looking as guilty as if she'd asked the queen for proof. Moira put the card back into her old wallet. 'Journalist' still worked even in these twittering, vlogging days. Her Canadian Journalist card was out of date. But if queried she had her answer on tap: she never put current cards in her purse – in case she was robbed. This was after all London.

Pleased with herself Moira trotted up to the bar and ordered a large G&T.

'Just one cube please,' Moira specified to Adriana (as per her identity tag) who didn't immediately cop on. The full scoop of ice hovered over the glass. Moira explained in Italian that she had a dodgy tooth and ice exacerbated the pain. It was nicer than saying: 'I'm paying for a real G&T and not a glass of ice.'

Moira got her specified one ice cube, told Adriana to keep the change and walked out to the Members' balcony where the sun shimmered on their reserved table. Sipping her drink Moira gazed up at the blue sky and at the young people working behind the bar and joking with one another. They reminded her of The Three when they were wild students in Vienna, each from a different country, but with one thing in common – the dream of making it.

Adriana reminded her of young Liz the brilliant photographer whose goal was to travel the globe taking award winning photos with one baby strapped to her front and another to her back while a besotted husband hauled her heavy equipment from Buenos Aires to Burma. When Viennese Handsome Hans walked out on her after 10 years of marriage and three miscarriages, Liz ditched the photography. By the time she married Pierre, the French foreign correspondent, she was way too old to have children and channelled all her energies into TV drama and serious documentaries. Down the decades Liz had educated them with thousands of her TV programme ideas from the 'history of breadmaking, forks, or garlic' to 'The Victorian penchant for stuffing humming birds and using them as ornaments'. Recently both June and Moira noticed that all Liz's new TV ideas involved medieval murders sprinkled with voodoo.

Moira had only taken a few sips of her G&T when a waitress startled her back to reality.

'You wait for person or you are lady alone?' The waitress (Swerka as per her ID tag) asked.

'My friends will be here shortly.'

Lady alone. The lone lady.

All her life she'd been on her own but rarely if ever alone – except for these reclusive London years. A lady alone. The former Man Magnet Moira! If only her mother had lived to see her like this. Mother never understood why Moira had chosen to 'waste her degree' to set up travel agencies in weird and remote parts of the world. Why couldn't Moira settle down with one of those lovely men who were always chasing her around the globe?

'I fresh your drink for you, Madame?' Swerka was back all smiles and reaching out for her half empty glass.

'Yes, thank you,' Moira said, opened her purse and handed Swerka a fiver.

'Another G&T, NO NO ice cubes and keep the change. Thanks.'

What she wanted to scream out loud was – 'I am not a Madame or lady alone … oh who gives a f**k'.

'Thank you,' Swerka said with a polite smile.

'*Bye,bye Miss American Pie*', the mobile ringtone from one of the other diners nearly made Moira drop her drink.

'*The day the music died …so .. bye, bye Miss ..*'

'*Bye, bye*' was one of Martin's favourite songs. Adorable, handsome, witty Martin. When they first met as students in Vienna, Moira considered dating Martin, the music student – but he never shut up about Mozart. Moira liked Mozart's music but had no time for a guy who couldn't get through a paragraph without mentioning Mozart. Besides when June and Martin met it was Love at first sight and forever more. Until that barbecue ten years ago by the Thames. Martin dressed up as the bat from Strauss ll Die Fledermaus. Some of his pals also wore funny costumes. When they were packing up to go home Martin gave a final performance jumping and flapping around singing the Finale to the opera. When he dramatically fell back on the strand with his arms outstretched everyone laughed and clapped. But this was also Martin's Finale. He'd smashed his head on a stone and had died laughing.

Eight months after his death, when Connie (named after Mozart's wife Constanze) married Gianni, The Three disgraced themselves at the wedding reception wailing like wounded banshees. The guests attributed their gales of sobbing to champagne overdose. They were so wrong. When there was no father of the bride's speech, The Three finally accepted that Martin was really dead and never ever coming back to them.

Four years later when Clare married Ron the Aussie farmer, they drank lashings of champagne and wept buckets. But this time it wasn't Martin they were mourning. It was themselves. When Martin died their joie de vivre had also been snuffed out.

'*The day the music died!*'

And all joy and laughter with it. Moira slowly finished her G&T and wished Martin were still alive and June her happy old self. She wanted, oh how she wished, wished, wished she could be the person she used to be – laughing, happy, raring to travel. That's when she heard the silvery bells. They sounded like ice jingling merrily in the Czech crystal carafe she gave her mother for one of her birthdays. She looked around her. Swerka was placing a fresh G&T in front of her. The jingling wasn't coming from her no-ice-cube drink.

'Where are those bells coming from?' she wanted to ask Swerka. But didn't. From the looks of it nobody else on that terrace was hearing bells. Well, sh**, f**k, and double screw. Now apart from living in Nuttersville, scraping by on nothing, she was hearing bells. And suddenly Moira wasn't having it. She didn't want this shit anymore. She knew wishing wouldn't change anything, but she kept on wishing for a new, fresh life that didn't include hearing friggin' bells.

Life was having one hell of a laugh. Good one Moira and about bloody time too.

CHAPTER 3

By the time she got out of her cab near St. Paul's Cathedral, Liz' blood pressure was back to normal because of her mental fantasies torturing TT. Gorilla dentists drilling his teeth without anaesthetic; wild bears practicing colonoscopies; hungry rats trimming his ugly ears. As she walked towards the Millennium Bridge, Liz banished all thoughts of TT by firing him from a circus canon manned by lions. As he flew over the spire of St. Paul's several slices were slashed from his arrogant bum before the numbskull disappeared totally from Liz's superior brain.

Walking across the Millennium Bridge Liz paused to gaze down into the tidal waters of the Thames. She loved this part of the river. This was where Shakespeare had been rowed across the river all his life because there was only one bridge in London until the 18th century. Liz smiled visualizing The Bard's most unusual trip in 1599 when he and his troupe of actors had been rowed across the Thames with the timber from their Theatre north of the river. The landlord had refused to renew their lease. Since the wood was legally theirs, the troupe dismantled the Theatre, rowed across the river with the bits (a 16th century IKEA!) and set up what was now known worldwide as The Globe. Today writers and actors wouldn't have to dismantle and rebuild their theatres even if creative people like Liz had to work for farts like TT.

It was low tide and Liz now mentally visualized the Mudlarks cluttering the muddy banks. In Victorian days, Mudlarks were scrawny, destitute little boys and girls who raked the mud to see if the tide had discarded anything they could sell like bits of coal or wood so they could buy something to eat. Normally Liz enjoyed dwelling on Victorian history. But today the image of famished orphans wading for hours in the open sewer of The Thames turned her stomach. She looked at the throngs of happy tourists, snapping away at the Globe and posting the fun results on Facebook. Unlike Liz who always visualized the Globe back in Shakespeare's day when the poor stood and gobbled back oysters, (known as 'the food of the poor' back then) while the rich sat in their boxes, sipped wine and ate with the recently invented forks. Theatres were open every day of the year – except when the Plague raged. When they reopened all the regular poor Globe standees (known as 'groundlings') had been wiped out while the rich were back in their boxes since they could always afford to leave Plague infested London.

Normally Liz liked to visualize the lives of Londoners during Shakespeare's era. But not today. The sky was blue, the Thames shimmered like a silver stream and its beauty drifted up and tickled Liz into a more frivolous frame of mind. She was ready to enjoy the afternoon with The Two even if she knew what they'd talk about. June would bang on about Martin and their fairy-tale years in Vienna. Moira who used to regale them with tales of the Great Wall of China, skating in Patagonia, politics in Pakistan would now update them on feral cats and fox faeces in Fulham.

Her mobile buzzed. Probably her darling Pierre asking what she fancied for dinner. Many foreign correspondents went into therapy to recover from the brutal horrors they witnessed in war zones. Her jewel of a husband went grocery shopping and cooked a gourmet meal for two. But the ***want u back now*** text was from the loathsome toad she'd shot over St. Paul's. She clutched the railings to stop herself screeching louder than all the gulls over the Thames. With clenched teeth and eyes closed she imagined she was back in a 16th century London night when men and women never left home without daggers or a sword or two. Until gaslights were invented, London by night was darker than a dungeon. Back then she could have shovelled TT off his mortal coil with one thrust of her dagger. With all the customers staggering out of the hundreds of pubs, brothels and bear pits that lined the south side of the Thames nobody would notice anything. She'd then kick TT's scummy carcass into the murky night river. Problem solved.

Liz opened her eyes and was momentarily blinded by the silver blue daylight. At the end of the bridge a group of laughing Italians took turns playing the noisy bird pipes they'd just bought from a vendor. Tourists stopped, laughed and clapped. Those pipes sounded like a pack of buzzards fornicating in the jungle. Liz wished she could spend the afternoon whooping it up like those Italians, laughing about nothing. She wished she could be the happy, fun-loving Liz she used to be when she first met June and Moira in Vienna, back when Life was hard and poor but peppered with fun and laughter. She wished she could rediscover the secret to being breezy and light-hearted and … that's when she heard the oddest ringing of bells. They sounded like Church bells pealing out the hour in a sleepy Alpine village. Liz checked her watch. It was five minutes to two. The silvery bells kept on ringing. They certainly weren't coming from St. Paul's, St. Bride's or any other City Church. Liz was an expert on bells having extensively researched the history of all City bells.

'Very odd,' Liz thought. 'I wonder where that's coming from.'

Life had won the bet. Know-it-all Liz hadn't a clue why she was hearing bells. It was a one off. But Liz had sincerely wished for a change and it was her lucky day. Life was going to oblige.

CHAPTER 4

Riding through the backstreets of Southwark always reminded June of the time she and Martin moved to London when it was like a fifth world city in comparison to her hometown Manhattan. Today London was the buzziest city on the globe and had changed beyond all recognition – except for parts of Southwark. Her cab drove along a street which hadn't changed since that fateful Summer her dad had given them two return tickets from Vienna so he could offer Martin a job in London real estate.

'Your father wants us to do real estate in London?' Martin had laughed out loud. 'He's really taking the piss.'

June didn't know. Maybe it was her dad's discreet way of saying 'honey, I know you and Martin have diddley squat. I just want to help you.' Budget airlines hadn't yet been invented and flights cost a fortune. They both leapt at the gift of a free trip to London. After 10 years in Vienna, Martin was exhausted from giving piano, violin and English lessons, trying to get work as an orchestra conductor. June was comatose with fatigue looking after the kids while trying to earn a bit of cash with her original children's clothes.

Dad had invested in some London real estate. He wanted to offer Martin (a graduate of Vienna's Music Conservatory) a job as manager. June (graduate cum laude of Vienna's prestigious University of Applied Arts) could be his assistant. In no time at all they'd be able afford their own home, a nanny and trips abroad. Dad made this offer over lunch in a ritzy restaurant. For the first time in his life Martin was speechless. Until he got back to their hotel and let it rip. Her 'darling Dad' suddenly became 'that raving old lunatic'. How could he even contemplate Martin moving to a city where the Paddies were considered lower than the sewers they had built? Not to mention all the bombs being set off by the Provo IRA terrorists. And they'd never hear a decent Mozart performance. At the mention of Mozart, June lost the plot and screamed.

'The only difference between fxxxxxing Mozart's pauper's life and ours is that at least we won't die of the Plague.'

For the second time in one day Martin was speechless. Then he burst out crying, begging her forgiveness. June started bawling and apologized. Dad had really insulted them. They would make it on their own in Vienna. Martin was still working on his dream of conducting the Vienna Philharmonic.

'Your dad is right,' Martin said as they had hugged and kissed each other better. 'I'll never make it in Vienna. I can hardly conduct traffic let alone the Wien Phil. You've sacrificed your designer dreams for us.'

They reluctantly took her dad's offer and moved to London – on a trial basis. To both their amazement,

Martin's gifts for sales and real estate coupled with his people skills and June's artistic and promotional talents resulted in almost overnight success. They set up their own real estate business. It was goodbye Vienna – except for long summer trips back to the City of Mozart, along with little breaks so they could enjoy autumn in NY or skiing in Vermont. Martin made plenty of musician friends in London who loved and knew more about Mozart than Martin himself. Yes, theirs was the perfect life until ….

'Sorry, Ma'am,' the cabbie said as the taxi swerved to the side and stopped. 'It's a wedding. Looks like they're trying to get to the Church on time.'

Half a dozen limos festooned with white ribbons and roses glided by.

'Spotting a stranger's wedding is a sign of good luck they say.'

'A nice superstition,' June replied, even though the very last thing she wanted to think about was a wedding.

Her darling son Robert had recently announced his engagement to Chloe Me and unhinged them all. Robert was Liz' godson and the only child Moira had ever liked. Their sweet boy could have had any girl. Instead, he falls for the greedy gold digger from the deepest Circle of Hell. Chloe Me with the deceptive doe eyes and the scanty designer dresses welded to her curvy frame that screamed out 'I'm hotter than radioactive lava'. The Three knew that June's millions were all that interested her. They'd only met her once when June was in bed with the spring flu. Moira and Liz were visiting her when Robert arrived with his girlfriend. Chloe Me completely ignored The Three.

She was too busy assessing every wall, ceiling and balcony like a greedy lizard.

They used to have fun with Chloe Me's name. 'Put Me down the Klo' (German for 'loo'). But when their darling Robert announced his engagement to the ferret, hag, skunk, turd, haemorrhoid their name calling had ceased. She was the woman their misguided Robert had chosen for better or for worse. June would never interfere with her son's choices. She would however make it crystal clear to Chloe Me that Martin and June's millions were earmarked for various Mozart trusts and struggling artists.

As the cab slowed down, she spotted the gigantic chimney of the Tate Modern. Time to forget her worries, put on a smile and not be gloomy for the girls. She suddenly caught a reflection of herself in the cab window practicing her happy mode. Her smile vanished immediately. She was practicing putting on a smile for her best friends. Life had brought many changes but not to the extent that she had to 'pretend happy' for The Two. She sighed and wished, … but again the cabbie interrupted her thoughts.

'Here we are, Ma'am,' he said and hopped out to open the door for her as per his doctor's advice. The sedentary cabbie life could lead to clots and DVTs. Hop out and stretch every few rides.

Walking into the Tate Modern the last thing on June's mind was 'wishing for something'. The sky was blue, the girls were waiting. Things were back to normal.

Life wanted to snarl like a tornado. Nothing pissed Life off more than a wish that went unexpressed.

CHAPTER 5

The Three were installed at their usual table with the glorious view of St. Paul's, the Millennium Bridge, and the glittering Thames.

'Can I say specials of the day?' Swerka asked.

'But first we'll have cocktails. With some nuts on the side.'

Usually at this point Liz made some gruesome reference to TT's nuts. But today there was none. June ordered a selection of olives, nuts and nibbles. She then regaled them with her Australian grandkids' kangaroo request.

'Where did they get that idea?' Liz asked.

'Their neighbour Wally trained his kangaroo to help him dig the garden and do the dishes before they watched TV together.'

'I wonder if kangaroos can be toilet trained like cats?' Moira mused.

'You've been to Australia often enough,' said Liz. 'You could have researched that for our Kangaroo Fairy Granny.'

'Bit late for that now,' said Moira gloomily.

June and Liz exchanged glances. It was a mistake to remind Moira that her glory days of travelling the globe were over. But Moira was smiling again.

'Remember that time I visited relatives in the outback? I'm sure I told you about that kangaroo sitting on the sofa watching TV,' she said.

'It's engraved on our memories,' June and Liz repeated verbatim -

The only thing missing from that kangaroo was a pair of specs and her knitting and she could have passed for Granny O'Brien any day.'

'Wonder what happened to kangaroo burgers?' Moira queried. 'I remember having one ages ago in Notting Hill. Scrumptious.'

'Weren't kangaroo burgers flavour of the week for a while?' June looked at Liz. Maybe she'd researched kangaroos for one of her TV histories of food.

'Could we leave the kangaroos alive in Skippyland?' said Liz. 'You two sound like those weirdoes who eat deep fried spiders.'

'Don't ever say anything like that when our Robert's around,' warned Moira.

'Robert?' queried June, the mom.

'You know any other Robert who used to catch spiders so he could drop them into his sisters' ears while they were asleep?' asked godmother Liz.

'Robert adored spiders,' said June laughing. 'They were the only things he could scare his big sisters with.'

'Dear God, where do the years disappear to? It seems like only last week he was collecting spiders and ....'

All Three were thinking the same thing: *and now he's marrying one.*

For the next few minutes, they bantered about young Robert scouring the London gutters in the hope of finding bugs, slugs or rats to terrify his older sisters with. But sooner or later one of them would crack and mention what was really worrying them: Robert's recent engagement to the Klo.

Swerka saved the day. She was back panting for their orders. They ordered the usual. A medium rare bacon/cheese/burger with fries for Liz who needed a break from Pierre's organic French feasts. June always ordered one of the exotic specials of the day. For Moira a hunk of rare steak since it was the only hunk she was getting these days.

Suddenly loud laughter erupted from the young couple seated nearby. Even Swerka was startled and stopped scribbling their orders. The Three kept gazing at the laughing couple, all thinking the same thing. They used to be like that carefree girl. Bursting a gut laughing, holding hands with her man, in love with life. And look at them now - three wistful old biddies. They were only on the cusp of sixty and on a good day and given the right light they could easily pass for 45. But no matter how forgiving the lighting, anyone looking at them knew their days (not to mention their nights!!!) of wine, men and roses were no more. The couple started kissing and the Three discreetly looked away.

'After Martin died, I knew I'd never have sex again,' said June.

This time Moira and Liz exchanged shocked glances. It was a record. June hadn't mentioned Martin until they'd finished their cocktails. Normally June started 97% of her sentences with 'After Martin died'. Once she started there was nothing either of them could do to haul her off the Martin Memory Lane.

'Bit sad that, isn't it?' asked June.

'Sure is,' said Moira, taking a long leisurely slurp of wine. Anyone looking at her would see a smiling woman enjoying a good vintage. But Moira was concentrating on the wine to stop herself leaning over the table and throttling the life out of June to put an end to her relentless Martin, Martin, Martin dirge.

'You just can't escape sex these days, can you?' asked June and sighed morosely.

'Forget sex.'

The words were on the tip of Moira's tongue. But that's as far as they got. Moira suddenly realized that she herself had forgotten all about sex and men. That hadn't been the plan when she moved to London to beat the hell out of her BIGTIME BURNOUT/BOREOUT. She certainly hadn't taken a holy oath never again to maul a man under the duvet.

'I just love the view from here,' said Moira instead of announcing that along with all her other problems she now had CRX (can't remember sex).

'Martin used to take the kids for walks down there when this area was still a wasteland,' said June. 'Unbelievable how the whole place has changed.'

'Unbelievable,' agreed Liz.

Beyond unbelievable! Her husband Pierre would still be working as an international reporter when he was bald, stooped and toothless. But Liz on the cusp of 60 would soon need voodoo plus supernatural powers to hold onto any TV job. Professional men acquired 'gravitas' as they aged. Professional women like Liz were passed over for younger, zestier, 'gals'! Airheads in magazines could delude themselves that 'sixty is the new thirty'. In Liz' profession it was a case of: 'Here's your grave, sis. Get in and stay there.'

Loud laughter again erupted from the young couple a few tables over.

'That's the way we used to laugh,' June thought, wistfully remembering all the decades she and Martin hooted with laughter.

She closed her eyes. 'I wish I could be like that again.' As she wished she heard the most extraordinary bell ringing as if Mozart had composed a symphony for bells.

Life was laying it on super strong.

'What were you saying?' Liz asked June. The Two looked concerned. They'd be doubly worried if she mentioned hearing a bell symphony.

'Wanna bet who's getting it regularly?' June joked for their benefit.

How beyond bizarre, Liz thought!

Sex and sarcasm were Moira's specialities. June's topics of conversation were: Martin RIP, her two daughters and sons-in-law, grandkids and Robert's recent engagement to Chloe Me. Time to smother the 'sex' topic, Liz decided.

'What's the name of that Viennese wine Martin loved?' Liz asked.

'Grüner Veltliner, groovy Gru Vee,' June replied quicker than a Russian reaching for the vodka bottle. 'More vino, girls?

She wafted an arm into the air and Swerka panted over.

Moira and Liz exchanged smiles and relaxed. June's new 'sex' topic had been squelched at birth.

Order was once more restored. Moira and Liz could concentrate on their own thoughts while June waffled away about life with Martin in magical Vienna. Martin, her fiery Dubliner with his dreams of conducting the Berlin Phil, The Vienna Phil, the Chicago Symphony. Martin, the man everyone had loved and adored and was no more.

CHAPTER 6

Moira tried to tune out June's tale about her first date with Martin in the Piaristenkeller. They'd heard it so often she and Liz could quote it verbatim.

'The waiter put us right next to the zither player. He thought it would put us off our food and get us out of there faster – just because we were students. That was the first time I ever ate deep fried mushrooms in batter. Martin ordered a carafe of red Rust from Burgenland.'

Moira tossed back half a glass of wine in one gulp. She had forgotten sex but could remember every detail of that Piaristenkeller. It was a short walk from their medieval dump of a student hovel.

'Martin told me some classical snobs hated the plinkety plink of the zither but we loved it. On our special anniversaries we went back for those mushrooms and the zither. Remember the take-away wine, girls?'

The Two nodded. When they had a few spare Shillings, they took a bottle to the Piaristenkeller and got their cheap wine straight from the gigantic wooden casks. Moira could still remember the little cherubs on top of the copper taps.... but she'd forgotten sex. A wasp buzzed around the top of the open bottle of wine and reminded her of some guy somewhere. Wine and wasps plus sex? When? Where? Who? Concentrate, Moira. She had dated men all over the globe. She could surely remember some romantic interludes.

'More wine?' Ever attentive Swerka had whisked up the bottle and was waiting for instructions.

'Pour away,' Moira told her and felt like adding *'and don't stop until I remember some real sex'*.

'Martin loved the Piaristenkeller because ......'

'Mozart ate there in a year we can't remember,' the two chanted.

'OK. OK. I get the message. F in Mozart,' said June.

The Three burst out laughing. 'F in Mozart' was one of Moira's sayings. With her Irish accent it was effin' Mozart. But all the serious music students thought she was referring to Mozart's oeuvres in F.

'I wonder if they still sell take away wine,' June mused.

She knew Liz and Moira were the last two who'd have the answer. After their Viennese 'tragedies' both had sworn never again to set foot in the city of their youth.

'You like desert?' A beaming Swerka was back.

They quickly chose the usual.

'I wonder what Robert's going to surprise us with at his birthday', said Liz.

'I remember the day he was born like it was yesterday,' said Moira.

'What were you up to that day?' asked Liz to avoid remembering where she was the day Robert was born – drunk and weeping on a bench in Parc Monceau, Paris. She had just graduated (degree nr. three) in journalism from the Sorbonne. But Liz hated her Parisian life. Nothing made any sense after Vienna, Hans and the loss of her three unborn babies. Until she got the call from June asking her to be Robert's godmother. Liz's life began to sparkle with some real meaning after that.

'I was lost in the Amazon,' said Moira.

June and Liz howled like the young girl earlier.

'Amazing how other people's near-death experience can be so amusing?' said Moira sarcastically.

But she wasn't annoyed. She had gotten a lot of mileage out of that adventure. She had been exploring the Amazon with a group of German businessmen/ jungle freaks who hadn't done their research properly. They were lucky they hadn't ended up being roasted on a very large spit.

'I love Robert's birthdays,' said Moira. 'They sure are different.'

The Three nodded in agreement. As a child Robert couldn't grasp the concept of birthday gifts. To pacify the child, June and Martin also gave Robert a little gift when his sisters had their birthdays. On his own birthday Robert made sure everyone else got a gift too. One year when Moira dropped by on her way home to Mayo from Taiwan, Robert (aged 8) pulled down a painting from the wall and gave it to her. Since Martin's death it had become a tradition to celebrate his birthday in his favourite restaurant – Steaks Galore. After Moira moved to London they had a new ritual. Robert got their original little gifties: Moira's home-made jam; unique champagne from Liz and Pierre and a funny baseball cap from his mom. After the desserts Robert then regaled them with HIS gifts.

One year it was dinner for The Three in Paris at Le Grand Véfour because Liz wondered if they still served roast pigeon à la gold leaf. Another year it was sleigh rides in Lapland because globe-trotting Moira had never seen the spectacular Northern green lights. The year of June's short-lived knitting mania he sent them on a tour of the Northern Ireland mills. They returned rhapsodising about the awesome scenery and the fun handbags made from traditional Aran sweaters. They had long since accepted Robert's extravagant presents. His birthday was just a week before the anniversary of Martin's death. It was his way of helping them all cope with their eternal grief.

'Has Robert dropped any hints where he's sending us this year?' Liz queried.

'Course not. It's a surprise,' said June.

'The little love is far too extravagant,' said Liz.

'But we wouldn't want to spoil his fun... or ours,' said June.

'How's Robert doing these days?' asked Moira.

'He's never been better,' June replied.

CHAPTER 7

'Never better' was not how Robert would describe himself. He was sitting outside 'The Slug, Duck & Swan' on the South Bank. This pub went out of its way to attract the City's young, rich and restless by offering thumping loud music, outdoor seating on the verge of the Thames and cigarette butt buckets. Normally, neither the noise nor the smoke bothered Robert. But today he wanted to chuck it all in and take a gap decade from everything. He hated London. He hated his work in finance. He didn't want to wait any longer for his best friend Henry who was always late even though his office was only four streets away.

His mobile buzzed. Hopefully it was Henry cancelling their afternoon drinks. But it was a text from Australian brother-in-law Ron. 'Yo Tarzen, stag suggestion - Bonding on Bondi.' Robert laughed out loud. Since he'd announced his engagement, Ron had sent him 'stag suggestions' from skiing with bears in Alaska to cockroach killing competitions in Manhattan. The only other person who had such a daft sense of humour was his Uncle Steven in Dublin who'd always been like a second Dad to him. It was Uncle Steven who nicknamed Dad – Madameus - because of his Mozart obsession.

He hadn't called Uncle Steven recently because he knew he'd detect the gloom in his voice no matter how hard he tried to hide it. But now that he was cheerful again, he'd call and tell him about 'the bonding in Bondi' stag suggestion. But the phone was on answer mode. Normal individuals left simple messages like: 'Please leave a message after the peep'. But Uncle Steven left a short joke which changed every week. Today the joke was about the wife who asks the husband if he'd like his dinner. The husband queries the choices on the menu. The wife replies: 'yes or no'. Robert dialled the number three times and laughed out loud each time. Maybe he should zip over to Dublin and have a heart to heart with Uncle Steven. He wanted to dump the City and finance and fulfil his dream of being a classical/jazz player and composer. His Uncle would think 'pre-wedding jitters' and ask for details of the event. But Robert himself was still in the dark about venue, catering or guests invited to his upcoming nuptials.

But he knew all about her Hen Party. Chloe Me and a battalion of her pals were spending a week in a Château spa outside Prague. Robert himself could do with a month in a spa. Maybe they could do a Stag Spa. He smiled. He knew how his bros-in-law Gianni and Ron would react to his 'stag spa suggestion'. 'Great for gals beyond boring for boys!' Gianni had been a 'normal' Italian banker until he married his eldest sister Connie and bonded with his Uncle Steven at his stag in

Dublin. After his second Guinness, Gianni discovered he was born to dance the jig. Gianni's stag was a hilarious 'bonding' event. It was forever branded in Robert's brain because it was the first time since Dad's death 8 months earlier that he'd laughed again.

The Hen party had taken place at the same time but in a different part of Ireland. Know-it-all-Connie who could hardly identify an egg let alone do anything with it, had decided that a sojourn at a cordon bleu cookery school in Connemara was too original for words. Those who didn't wish to improve their cuisine skills could walk the glorious Burren, improve their chirping skills with the rare birds or sniff the 'heritage' wildflowers. His sister Connie whose thoughtfulness normally ranked lower than that of a car crusher had also invited Gabriela, Gianni's Mamma and The Three to her foodie Hen. The Four clicked immediately. They didn't want to cook. Instead, they invented several original cocktails while perfecting jokes in Italian and English.

And that was the moment Robert had 'his brilliant idea'. For weeks he'd been trying to think of an original gift for The Three who'd seen and done it all. He'd give them the gift of a spa week in Prague. They could stay with Chloe Me and her pals, participate in the Hen events, bond, have fun and get to know one another. Robert felt a huge weight lift from him. Suddenly he was in the mood to enjoy a normal afternoon or as normal as any evening with Henry could be.

No matter how much he swore he'd be on time, Henry, the obituary writer couldn't tear himself away from his computer and the fascinating insights only he was able to unearth about the hidden lives of the illustrious dead. At Oxford his ambition in life was to win the Pulitzer Prize for political and economic journalism after a stint with the New York Times or the Washington Post. Instead, he got a top job with BBC news. He left of his own accord and took up a job writing obituaries for one of the major dailies.

'Why did you leave the BBC?' friends still asked.

Nobody would willingly leave the Holy Grail of World News.

'Boring farts drank like drains.'

This from Henry who could drink any pub dry and bored the teeth out of your jaw once he got onto a topic that annoyed him, e.g. why people kept fish in a bowl. But as a uniquely witty obit writer he had gained a world-wide internet fan base and become a legend in his own lunchtime. Robert and all his old Oxford mates had stopped trying to figure out when and why their Henry had been taken over by the obit writer Henry whose only purpose in life was to remind the world that Wing Commander X (who had fought gloriously for the Empire) was the inventor of a rectal thermometer for elephants or that Countess Y had also improved manicure techniques for water buffalos.

'I'm sorry, I'm holding this seat for my friend,' Robert apologized to the two women who had been eyeing up the empty seat in the packed outdoor section of the pub. The two lovelies scowled at Robert and gave Henry a withering look as he sat down.

'They wanted your chair,' explained Robert.

'Gee, thanks pal. Some of us are still single and searching even if you're getting hitched,' said Henry as he laid claim to Robert's pint.

'You're ok with another one of those?' asked Robert and nodded at what had been his drink.

By the time Robert returned with two fresh pints, Henry had secured several chairs and was waxing lyrical to four very attractive women.

'Meet my good friend Robert,' said Henry. 'But don't waste your time on him. He's about to clamp on the ball and chain.'

'Can I get you ladies something from the bar?' Robert asked with a genuine smile. It would help him stop wondering why he ever agreed to meet Henry for a pint. It always ended up with Henry getting rat assed and going home with a woman on each arm and half a dozen women's mobile numbers and the promise to call them when he was sober.

As he stood at the bar Robert looked over at Henry holding forth to his enchanted admirers. Why, he asked himself? Why didn't he just go home and leave Henry to flirt his way through the evening? Why didn't he chuck in that finance job he hated? Why on God's earth was he getting married and to Chloe Me of all people?

CHAPTER 8

'I'm going to pop by Pierre's office to pick up Robert's champagne,' said Liz.

'The weather's so lovely, I'm gonna stroll home,' said June.

'I'll wait 'til the worst of the rush hour is over,' said Moira.

'Kissy, kissy. Huggy, huggy', they said in unison and waved their farewells.

Liz smiled happily as she crossed the Millennium Bridge on her way to Pierre's office to pick up the special champagne for Robert's birthday. She hadn't called ahead. Pierre loved it when she popped in out of the blue - something she hadn't done in ages. After the brunch with the two, Liz always appreciated her beloved Pierre much more. She was so lucky to have her devoted husband. How would she ever survive if Pierre was killed on assignment? Wear elegant French widow's weeds and then take up welding? Move to a village in Brazil? Join a nunnery? She stopped thinking weird thoughts about losing her love. She also made a resolution.

Next time The Three met she'd take the bull by the horns and tell June that Martin was the very last person who'd want her to be the world's unmerriest widow. Martin would want June to buy a flat in Rome and a ranch in the Australian outback. She'd get to see her grandkids and taste la Vida Loca with the kids and their kangaroos. She'd do the same with Moira. Tell her to shut up about Urine Man the looney dipso who lived 2 floors up from her and peed out the window. The façade under his window was stained with rivers of smelly, yellow evidence and hundreds of bluebottle flies. But he kept denying the urine allegations. They were sick of hearing what PC O'Reilly told Moira: 'He's trying to convince us it's Superman taking a leak every time he flies over Fulham'. Enough of Moira's bellyaching about her crazy neighbours and her 'in mourning for her travel life'. She should just DO. Rent out that flat until the property prices soared again, then sell it for half a million quid. Get work as a guide or tourist expert in any city worldwide. She'd done it successfully for decades. What was holding her back?

Liz stopped thinking about her friends' problems. Who was she to give advice? For the past 20 years she had devoted all her energies to Plan A: only work on TV programmes with the intellectual depth she craved. Plan B hadn't worked out either – persuade Pierre to move out of Crouch End (otherwise known as London's Yummy Mummy land) to a more exciting city zone. She had reached the other side of the Bridge when she realized she was wrong about June. She had come up with a new topic but one totally devoid of any intellectual interest - sex. The banality of sex, Liz thought. These days it was the very last thing on her agenda even if it was still a permanent feature on Pierre's when he returned home from foreign assignments. Only yesterday on his return from Ghana he made her exquisite cod with sweet olives, capers and cabbage. Liz was willing to reward him and even enjoy 15 minutes of tame lust.

While she waited for a cab Liz gazed down Fleet Street. She had shown the other two all the secret nooks and crannies of this ancient legal and journalist area like the ancient pub Ye Olde Cheshire Cheese renovated in 1667. On bleak Winter evenings The Three sat in the small bar with a real coal fire. Moira always repeated that as a kid she had to clean out the grates and bring in buckets of coal. June always reminded them that Wynkyn de Worde set up the first printing press off Fleet St in 1500 – ages before her hometown Manhattan was first settled in 1624. Liz always got a huge thrill running her hand along the arm of the mahogany wooden bench next to the fire and thinking of the great writers from Oliver Goldsmith, Dickens, Yeats, P.G. Woodhouse who had worked and drunk in this pub. Liz ached to live in this historic part of the City of London instead of boring suburban Crouch End – a real bone of contention between herself and Pierre. He loved Crouch End because of its organic butchers and fish shops. But the suffocating sameness of its architecture gave Liz migraines.

In Pierre's office building, Jean-Christophe – JC - the grumpy security guard was on duty.

'Bonjour, Jean Christophe? Comment allez-vous?'

'Bonjour Madame.'

JC investigated the contents of her briefcase and even her wallet. JC was notorious for treating all the staff as suspect terrorists or carriers. Journos were sloppy, he said. They wouldn't notice if somebody smuggled plutonium or serpents into their briefcases when they were over juicing in a foreign bar. Liz gave JC a big smile which was wasted on him because he had already returned to his thriller about vigilant security men like himself saving the world.

It was a low-news day and most of the staff had availed of this lull in death and terror worldwide to go out and enjoy a sunny afternoon. Liz waved to the few who were holding the fort and walked into Pierre's office. He wasn't there – probably in the toilet because his laptop was still on his desk. This was the Christmas gift she'd given him 2 years ago in New York. The fun they'd had coming up with the password - 'patinage' - French for skating. During that romantic Christmas break they had skated like young lovers on the Rockefeller Center Rink.

Antoine, the economics expert, jolted her out of her Manhattan reverie.

'He left at lunchtime.'

'Thank you, Antoine.'

No need to hire detectives with Antoine on the premises.

How strange! Pierre always took his laptop to meetings. She'd have a quick look at his diary. He was punctilious about entering time, place and person for every meeting. She entered 'Patinage' and clicked on 'diary'. There was only one entry. Time - 13.00;

Place - The Savoy; Person – S. Was S code for some new story he was working on? They always discussed their work. The Savoy in London was a hotel and it was now after 5. What had he been doing all afternoon? She knew Pierre always confirmed his appointments by e-mail. And there it was. The text read: '*Our usual room at 13.00. I'm bringing champagne so prepare to be investigated thoroughly.*'

That's when Liz saw it was addressed to Suzanne – the blond, early 30's, brutally ambitious reporter known as 'smiley, slimy Suzie'. Liz almost vomited on the desk with the shock. A less controlled woman would have howled in pain and smashed his laptop to bits. Not Liz. She calmly switched off the laptop and closed it. She then opened the bottom drawer and saw only one bottle of champagne from the three Pierre told her he had brought back especially for Robert's birthday. 'Two for the birthday boy and one for his beloved.' Liz felt her blood turn to ice. He had given Robert's birthday champagne to Sleazy Susie.

Liz walked through the office with the control of a veteran TV producer/director. She waved a nonchalant au revoir to Antoine. Outside in the afternoon sunshine Liz was at a loss. What was she going to do? She had no intention of going home and listening to Pierre lying about his busy day. She walked back inside.

'Jean-Christophe could you please order me a cab and bill it to Pierre's account?'

Ten minutes later she was on her way to the five-star hotel where she booked in celebrity interviewees. She'd text Pierre to say she was pulling an all-nighter.

Then she'd switch off her mobile, sit outside on the balcony and toss back a few Margueritas.

After that she hadn't a clue what she'd do. But in every fibre of her being she knew it was all over between her and that prick Pierre.

CHAPTER 9

June strolled along humming the finale to 'Don Giovanni' while admiring the glorious canopy of pink fluffy clouds skipping across an amber sky. They reminded her of Martin entertaining the kids spinning stories about clouds that looked like dogs, foxes and eels. He also spun chilling tales about the Bankside Power Station which used to billow out ominous black smoke until 1981. Martin should have written down his stories about the giant ravens who lived inside the gigantic building which was abandoned and left empty until it was transformed into the Tate Modern. It was tragic that Martin hadn't lived to see the revitalized building that opened in May 2000 and some of the art installations in the massive Turbine Hall. He would have loved Olafur Eliasson's 'Weather Project' which was a gigantic piece of 'art sunshine' brightening the darkness of the Turbine Hall. During the Winter months of its installation, Londoners solved their SAD problems by settling down on cushions in the Turbine Hall and basking in the glow of Olafur's gigantic sun.

It had been such a pleasant afternoon, June thought. For a change Liz hadn't tormented them with the latest TV documentary ideas her over fervid imagination came up with daily. If only Liz could take a long look at her life and realize how lucky she was. She had an exciting career in TV plus a hunky French intellectual husband who adored her and was a gourmet cook. It was also a landmark that Moira hadn't once bellyached about her nutty neighbours like the husband beater with the egg fetish. Several times a month the demented battle-axe strapped her husband to the bench in the communal garden and pelted him with dozens of raw eggs. The police were only called if she started belting him with a frying pan. Ever since she moved into Auntie Jessie's flat, Moira had tormented them with stories about scrounger tenants who had spitting contests out the window or the squatter drug dealers who had changed what had once been an enchantingly elegant 3 storey flat complex into a filthy dump. Reviewing the afternoon June was also happy remembering all the ideas The Two had tossed around about the possible venue of Robert's wedding.

June stopped humming Mozart. Her beloved son was marrying that scheming Chloe Me, the greedy-guts who thought she'd get her fangs into Martin and June's vast landmark home in the most desirable part of 21st century London. When she and Martin bought the vast derelict warehouse on the Thames in 1983 it was a decrepit slum area even if Tower Bridge was within walking distance. The only reason they bought a derelict former wharf building with rooms bigger than football pitches was to accommodate Martin's future amateur orchestra and not disturb the children. June and Martin's musical home had been unique in London.

It still was. But because of the quirks in real estate today her 4-story loft residence was worth more than any building on Oxford Street. Over her dead body was that greedy panther getting her claws into Martin's Musical Heritage.

June was jostled out of her worries by two teenage girls who ran by her yelling back at their third friend to 'get her arse in gear'.

'I hate hair down there,' the third teenager said on her mobile as she strolled by June. 'Book your man in for a back, sack and crack wax.'

June burst out laughing. The Crack was the name ignorant people gave the latest Tate Modern art installation which ran the length of the immense Turbine Hall! Ms. Salcedo, the artist, said her complex fissure which looked like a widening crack in the ground was a statement about immigration, segregation and racial hatred. Some kids loved trying to outwit the guards by sticking both their legs in there. But The Three had nothing but total praise for Ms. Salcedo's amazingly original work of art. June wondered what Martin would have thought of the Tate Crack and started to cross the road without checking the lights. If the driver of the silver Volvo hadn't been a rally driver and capable of coming to a halt in half a second flat, June would have been in Martin's arms in heaven that same instant.

June hailed a black cab and was home five minutes later. As she got out of the cab the rain started. When she opened the balcony windows the rain was so thick, her stunning views were smothered in a dense grey drizzle. June suddenly felt dismal rain leaking into her heart. The piercing shaft of lonely pain shocked her. Up to that very moment, June had never felt truly alone in the home she and Martin had built together. She had decades of happy memories stored up here.

She took the silver box containing Martin's ashes off the mantelpiece and stroked it the way some lonely people petted a cat. Martin loved this 'silver' box with the raised sculpted portrait of Mozart. She had bought it as a birthday gift back in the days when they were dirt poor in Vienna. When they had spare cash they filled it with 'Mozart Kugeln' (chocolate Mozart Balls). Martin had renamed them 'Mozart's marbles'. He used to say that poor Mozart didn't live long enough to lose his marbles.

Martin and Mozart! He used to drive them all mental with his crazy Mozartitis and his dreams of conducting all of Mozart's works with the crème de la crème of world orchestras. Heartbroken Martin who only had enough talent to conduct his amateur group of musician friends. Martin's other dream ambition was to have his ashes scattered on Mozart's grave in Vienna. He'd even stipulated this as a codicil in his will.

'Not yet, love,' said June and kissed the silver box.

For ten years June had postponed taking Martin's ashes on their final trip to the St. Marx cemetery in Vienna. She needed them. Martin would have understood.

CHAPTER 10

'Red Rioja,' Swerka said as she placed the wine in front of Moira.

Sipping her Rioja she noticed the return of the wasps. There was some connection between wasps and sex. But it wasn't important. Sipping her zesty Rioja Moira smiled remembering the highlights of brunch with the girls. Amazing how some things never changed. When they met, they always reminisced about their student years in Vienna. They laughed about Martin the destitute romantic stealing a gigantic armful of tulips from the Volksgarten to impress June. Fearless Martin didn't care that in the stodgy and over-policed Vienna of 1968, such a gesture could have landed him in jail. They now laughed about all the things that drove them mental as students: the 'krantig' old ladies who snarled at their jeans; having to register their address with the local police every time they changed student hovels which were always colder than igloos. Up to May they had to go to bed wearing several sweaters, woolly caps and gloves to keep frostbite at bay.

They reminisced about Otto, Dieter, Stefan and all the others they'd dated and danced with at the Student Balls. They even romanticized the indignity of smuggling cheap bottles of wine strapped to their thighs under their ball gowns. None of their crowd could afford to pay the exorbitant price of wine at the swanky Hofburg Palace. The trick was to reserve a table, order one bottle of wine and get all the wine glasses they needed (15-20 sometimes) and drink their own cheap wine for the rest of the night. Obviously, the guys couldn't hide a bottle of Gumpoldskirchen down their pants. It was up to the girls to charm their way past the door police who knew all about the thigh smuggling wine racket but rarely asked them to hoist up their ball gowns so they could check for bottles. Moira smiled. Their Viennese past was a fairy tale place that had never existed. Its deluded romance was eternally trapped in their memories like a snowy landscape inside a paperweight.

Moira watched the sky change from a Matisse blue to a foggy El Greco grey. Suddenly two loud kids burst onto the veranda followed by two mothers pushing baby buggies. They settled in at the table next to her. Moira groaned. She had no time for kids or 'baby chat'. She proudly admitted she'd prefer to listen to the history of world sewers in 77 dead languages than endure the baby blah blah that fascinated today's Yummy Mummies. How could intelligent women waste their lives discussing organic recipes for toothless toddlers, homeopathic cures for baby's wind, or Elvis versus Bach for babies still in the womb? When she and her two brothers were maturing in their mother's womb the only 'music' they heard all day long was her mother running the old farm, cutting the grass, clucking to the chickens and milking the noisy cows before they could afford milking machines.

As far as Moira was concerned when babies turned 21 and could hold a halfway intelligent conversation – maybe then she might be interested. The only exception was Robert who even as a child entertained her with his advanced conversational skills, humour and virtuoso piano playing. Moira was about to leave when she heard the more serious looking 7/9-year-old ask:

'Mummy, what other animals are burglars and criminals like the cat?'

'Darling, I've already told you that a cat burglar is a thief climbing up to the top floor,' explained the mother.

'So the cat is a thief but not a burglar?' persisted the boy.

'What kind of ice cream do you two want?' the other mother asked.

'I want to know what other animals steal like the cat,' said the little boy.

Moira changed her mind. The kid was worth listening to. He was just like Robert at his age. June always included a 'Robert story' in her letters to Moira. Her top favourite was when he knocked on a neighbour's door and asked if he could borrow one of her magic broomsticks. He wanted to fly all over London on one. The neighbour smiled. Where did he get the idea she had magic broomsticks? Because his Mum said the neighbour was 'a real witch and probably had about a dozen broomsticks stuck in her closet'.

'Sweetie, cat burglar is just an expression.'

'But why?'

'Because cats are quiet just like burglars.'

'But burglar alarms are very loud. They screech'

'Exactly. Because burglar alarms are mechanical and not animals.'

The waitress handed menus to everyone. In today's world, Moira noted even children got their own menus.

'Mummy, why do pigeons have feathers?'

'I don't know darling. We'll ask Daddy when we go home.'

'I know,' the little girl piped up. 'It keeps them warm in Winter and they don't get sunburn in the Summer.'

Then the first fat raindrops plopped down. The mothers grabbed the buggies and ordered the two kids to follow them inside for their ice cream. Moira also ran for cover and then took the District Line to Fulham Broadway. At the over ground station in South Kensington several wasps swooped in adding that je ne sais quoi to the commuters' daily hell. Swatting off 'the beasts' suddenly brought it all back to her. There WAS a connection between insects and sex. But it wasn't wasps. It was mosquitoes.

Oskar, her wild artist boyfriend had miraculously sold his first crazy painting. They celebrated in a Heuriger restaurant in the Vienna woods. She could still taste the roast pork, duck breast, deep fried zucchini and chicken with choice of sauces – horseradish, apple, red berry. They also enjoyed a carafe too many of summer wine. Then they staggered out into the vineyards to try and find the night bus back to Vienna.

The stars shimmered and twinkled so they stopped to enjoy a spot of romantic love under the dazzling night sky. Oskar dropped his trousers and babbled about capturing that spectacular night on canvas. His future masterpiece would erase all memory of Van Gogh's The Starry Night. Moira tuned out Oskar's artistic ravings which she had already heard hundreds of times too often.

It was a truly romantic moment - until Oskar's howls of agony shattered the starry night. Every mosquito for miles around had targeted his tasty buttocks. Moira tried to swat off the buzzing invasion. Too late! Oskar's delicious derrière was a mass of huge red bites bigger than golf balls. On the night bus back to Vienna, Oskar was in such pain he couldn't sit down. But the surly bus driver insisted. He wasn't having any drunk standing or staggering all over his bus and injuring himself.

For 45 minutes Oskar squatted over the seat groaning in agony. What if the mosquitoes had attacked his crown jewels? It had happened to his friend and for weeks his balls were as big as footballs. She had lived with the passionate painter Oskar for 6 months. But after listening to all the things he was going to paint and suffering through the painting process itself Moira couldn't take any more artistic ravings. Their romance had died a natural death. Apart from the mosquitoes she couldn't remember another romantic evening. How sad was that?

But as she opened her front door Moira consoled herself. She was lucky CRX was her only mental ailment with a next-door neighbour like batty Babs who as usual was perched outside on her rat, fox and pigeon shit patrol with her binoculars dangling around her neck and her mobile welded to one hand. Given a choice between having a chat with Babs or a pack of rabid rodents – the rats always won hands down. Moira opened her door and darted inside. Home free! But not cat free. That effing menace had somehow flitted inside and was now meowing in her kitchen. Looking for what? A break from Babs' ravings? Moira hacked off a leg from the roast chicken she hadn't finished the day before, opened the door and tossed it outside. Beelzebub leapt after it. Problem solved.

Moira made herself a camomile tea, turned on the TV and lounged on the sofa thinking of that divine lunch in the Vienna vineyards. Guys all over the globe had cooked for Moira before and after sex. She closed her eyes and tried to remember a few. Instead, it was the food that floated in front of her eyeballs – pasta al forno, shrimp and lemon grass curry, empanadas.

'Stop throwing food into the garden.'

'Shut the fuck up, you old cunt.'

The nightly exchanges between Babs and TD had started early. With rare exceptions when Tim Dan disappeared for a few days – to be forcibly deloused was Moira's opinion – those two nutters repeated the same insults. She waited for the usual conclusion - the old Italian on the third floor yelling down at them in a mangled mess of English and Italian where every second word was 'shit', 'prick', 'cornuto' and 'bastardo'.

Moira increased the volume on the TV and watched a romantic comedy about rich, stressed lawyers who hopped on choppers every time they had a romantic rendezvous. Moira wished she could afford a private plane. She'd whiz off and make a dozen appointments with the world's most renowned sex psychiatrists from San Francisco to Tokyo. They'd have no problem solving her sex dementia.

CHAPTER 11

After tossing back twenty-four free gin and tonics between them, the lovelies drifted off to the toilets and never returned to re-join Henry and Robert.

'Women!' Henry said and shrugged.

Robert was torn between agreeing with him and saying that the women had to get sloshed to tune out Henry's ode to the guy who invented the scoop scalpel for eyeball surgery before anaesthesia had been invented. But at that moment women weren't very high on Robert's love list. Especially Chloe Me! He had come up with a fabulous idea about The Three joining her hen spa in Prague and she had texted back: NO WAY. U BONKERS.

'You understand the female of the species?' Henry asked – and not for the first time.

Now it was Robert's turn to shrug and scowl. Henry, his oldest friend knew the answer to that one. When it came to women, Robert understood more than most men. His two older sisters had made sure of that. Until he turned 13, Connie had ignored her little brother. Then suddenly he was of some use doing dodgy errands for her and her boyfriends. Clare, the kid in the middle, reminded him daily that he was a waste of space. At 14 she informed him in the haughtiest of tones that it 'wasn't personal, Robbie – just the balance of power'. Connie and Clare were older and therefore entitled to more privileges. But if anyone at school hurt as much as his little toenail those two were worse than avenging fire snorting dragons. Now he was the grown up who no longer needed those sisters. Wrong! When Chloe Me had scorned his brilliant Hen idea, his first instinct was to text both his sisters and ask them what was wrong with his gift idea?

Henry stood up.

'Fancy celebrating your birthday at Newmarket?' he asked before walking off towards the toilets.

Robert looked at Henry as he weaved through the crowd flashing his boyish smile at every female. On his way to the loo he'd charm a few, then get their phone numbers on the way back. He used to be a lot like Henry – up for everything. When they passed their A-levels a group of fun friends were about to 'do Europe' but Dad had died the day before they were due to fly off. When they graduated from Oxford, he and Henry were going to take a gap year and 'do the world' (i.e. have the fun they missed out on at university because of the nuisance of studying). But that coincided with Clare emigrating to Australia with Ron. Three years earlier Connie had moved to Rome with Gianni and Mum was still pining. He couldn't leave Mum alone in London to go boozing and shagging around the world with Henry.

He postponed his gap year. Henry returned after a few weeks. He was bored witless staying in smelly hostels with weirdo 'gappers' whose main topic of conversation was how cheap Pakistan, Thailand or Namibia was. Cheap, cheap, cheap! Henry was bored, bored, bored. One of the few things that still didn't bore Henry was horse racing. Robert also loved racing. As a teenager he and his dad went to Newmarket several times a month. Sometimes he and Henry went on their own which was much more fun. Even though he was used to strolling into the winners' circle and the members' area with his dad, it added a fun frisson to waltz in with Henry flashing their false members' badge.

Sipping the last of his pint Robert smiled ironically at the memory of his teenage self, strutting like a puffed-up turkey next to Henry who was never late for the races. It was an insult to the horses and jockeys, he said. You weren't a true race goer if you missed the first race. Dad held the same belief and had made this crystal clear to his Mum who was not a racing fanatic.

'Darling, it's just like going to the Opera. Overture, first act, intermission, second act, finale, applause. You'd never miss the overture, would you?'

Henry was making his way back to the table. Robert still hadn't made his mind up about Newmarket. He needed a bit of fun. But he didn't want to listen to Henry, the obit writer rhapsodising about the departed who had invented turf softener or horse shampoo/conditioner. His mobile buzzed. He read Chloe Me's text - CALL ME NOW.

'So, up for a spot of racing, tomorrow?' asked Henry.

'Why?'

'I'm thinking of going into horse training.'

Henry probably had that idea fifty seconds before he asked Robert if he wanted to go to Newmarket. By this time next week, Henry the obit writer would have metamorphosed into Henry the horse trainer. He didn't waste time dithering like Robert and his jazz dreams. His mobile buzzed again. Robert ignored it and stood up.

'Race you to the other side and ten quid says I win.'

Henry looked puzzled. He'd just told him he was no longer interested in 'the other side'. By the time the penny dropped Robert had sprinted halfway across London Bridge. It wasn't death he was referring to but the other side of the Thames. Henry started running after him. But Robert had a huge head start on him and was stopping and pulling funny triumphant faces back at him which reminded Henry of the Robert of old who was always up for a spot of fun. He sprinted after him even though he knew he could kiss goodbye to that ten quid.

CHAPTER 12

June was puzzled by the thick glossy brochure that arrived in the morning mail. An exclusive 4-day celebration on some island off the West Coast of France accessible only by helicopter and air balloons which would 'enhance the thrill' of getting there. Pages of photos of the French/German/Polish/American catering companies. Next to the music there was TBC. Was this a new artist/band she'd never heard of? She closed the brochure and only then spotted Chloe Me's and Robert's names. This farcical corporate event was the invitation to her only son's wedding. June ripped the brochure to bits and pieces.

Music TBC – to be confirmed. After years of mourning Martin, June thought she was all cried out. Now she sobbed uncontrollably remembering the months Connie and Martin spent discussing her wedding music.

'One SHORT Mozart piece. Only one piece, are you listening to me Dad? One Mozart and only cause you're paying and I love you, love you.'

Martin spent more time planning and rehearsing Connie's wedding music than Mozart had lavished on Don Giovanni, Figaro and The Magic Flute combined.

Connie's Wedding Ensemble included several of Martin's London friends, Uncle Steven, two old Dublin pals and Robert on the piano. Later at the reception, the classical ensemble would play tangos, waltzes and jigs. The tragedy was that Martin never lived to walk Connie down the aisle.

It was her fault Robert was marrying a grasping lunatic whose second name was corporate. If Martin were alive this would never have happened.

**

When Liz opened the wedding invitation, she thought it was a TV food documentary and a job offer. It reminded her of some food ideas she'd worked on: '16th century history of ships & salted cod', 'The history of Oysters - the Food of the Poor'. She herself had submitted countless historical/food orientated ideas to commissioning editors down the years from 'No eating of dried Reindeer in space' (why some foods are prohibited by certain cultures) to 'Simply Snails and Slivovitz' (a global investigation into the origins of local delicacies). She scrutinized the pages for the company's name. It died a sudden death when the penny finally dropped.

The island was off the Southwest of France. The Three could fly to Bordeaux and then drive along the coast. They could stay in cheap B&Bs and Moira wouldn't have to worry about the cost. She dialled June's number.

'Picnics and barbecues on the beach. Build our own little bonfires? Wouldn't that be a hoot?' Liz asked.

Silence. Liz waited for June to applaud her inventive thinking.

'Any thoughts?'

'I'd prefer to shoot off both my ears than do cheap with you,' thundered June.

'Excuse me,' Liz stuttered in her prim English accent.

'You're the Queen of Cheap!'

'What's wrong, June?'

'You're such a cheapskate you wouldn't even give me a photo of my own wedding. Some friend you were.'

June smashed the phone down. Robert's wedding was having an appalling effect on June, Liz thought and dialled Moira's number.

***

Moira sat at her desk re-reading excerpts from her fantasy murder sci-fi – 'Invisible Gorilla/Crocodile/Baboon Lady'. The original idea came to her one night while she was sipping her camomile tea in front of the TV, trying to drown out the nightly exchanges between Babs, the dumpers, and the cursing Italian.

That's when she had the fantasy idea. Wouldn't life be a blast if she became invisible whenever she drank camomile tea? She'd buy several animal costumes – gorilla, crocodile, baboon. Then one night while those nutters were screaming at one another she'd zip her invisible self into a gorilla costume, stroll outside and inform them that Gorilla Lady would chew to bits the next shitball who threw garbage into the communal garden. For weeks she had great fun writing about Invisible Baboon Lady strolling out and prising the mobile phone that was permanently welded to Babs' paw; Gorilla Lady chasing the dumpers around the garden and growling that the next time they scattered as much as a crumb she'd have their scrotums for a snack; Crocodile Lady pelting rotten eggs at the crazy nutter who abused her husband with eggs instead of scrambling them. The Babs character didn't change. In the novel she kept phoning PC O'Reilly to tell him that the 'communal garden' was now being destroyed by escaped baboons and gorillas who'd heard that the Fulham 'menu' was more diverse than the London and Berlin Zoo combined.

Hearing the post plopping onto the mat, Moira switched off her computer, made a fresh pot of coffee, and opened her mail. The usual: an upbeat letter urging her to invest in life insurance, so she'd have no worries after she croaked; an apology from British Gas for sending her a bill higher than the Queen's; a fat brochure selling helicopter holidays to a remote French island. She was recycling the junk mail when the phone rang. She hadn't a clue what Liz was babbling about … Robert's wedding, and barbecues on French beaches … until she retrieved the wedding invite from the recycling bag.

'She called me some ghastly names,' said Liz. 'It's this wedding stress.'

Moira was distracted by an endorsement in the wedding invite from a catering company near Schloss

Neuschwanstein - the enchanting castle that Disney had copied for his 'Sleeping Beauty'. One Summer Moira had worked as a bus tour guide to all the Bavarian castles built by Mad King Ludwig.

'What do you think?' Liz wanted to know.

'What did you say to June?'

'We could drive along the Coast and have barbecues on the beach,' said Liz and couldn't keep the hurt out of her voice.

'And?'

'She went mental. Accused me of not giving her some old photo of her wedding. Who can even remember back that far?'

'Ain't that the truth?' said Moira.

'And what would that truth be?' asked Liz coldly.

'You were the one who took all her wedding photos.'

'And?' Liz snapped. 'All of a sudden I'm a skinflint because of some old wedding photo I took half a lifetime ago?'

'It wasn't ONE photo,' Moira said calmly. 'It was ALL the photos of June's wedding. And I gotta go.'

Moira wasn't in the mood to get embroiled in any June/Liz tiff.

'What's so urgent?' Liz asked with the voice of a woman who needed to keep on talking.

'I still haven't made my unique jam for Robert's birthday. It's the day after tomorrow. You haven't forgotten, have you?' Moira asked. This was a bit rich since she herself had totally forgotten to make the special birthday jam that Robert loved.

'Of course not,' Liz lied.

She could hardly blurt out the truth. Since she had discovered Pierre's betrayal the only thing on her mind were visions of his dick being nailed to his desk and his balls being gnawed off by rabid rats.

CHAPTER 13

Liz wanted answers. Why was that prick shagging a maggoty tarantula? Why couldn't she confide her heart's torment to her oldest friends? Why was June raving about some old photograph of her Viennese wedding when everyone's name was 'cheap'? Martin and June's wedding had been cheaper than cheap. The 'reception' was held in a jazz club a pal had managed to get for free in the afternoon. Had June also forgotten that it was only thanks to her friends there was anything to eat at her wedding reception? They had all clubbed together and bought wine, beer, liver pate, bread and cheeses. They finished up the night in Cafè Antoandrezi.

Liz took a deep breath and tried to think of something else – anything – except that Cafè which had been hers and Hans' second home. Cafè Antoandrezi had witnessed all the joy and pain of her life with Hans - their love, engagement, wedding, death of their three babies, the end of their marriage and life together. But that had been in another lifetime! She had invested years clawing back her happiness. She was NOT NOT NOT going to dwell on the past.

Liz dialled June's number. She wouldn't sound upset or peeved. But please enlighten her about some old photo she'd taken? But June's number was engaged. Trying to tune out the phone's repetitive buzz, her mind strayed back to the Café with those unique dusky brown/beige walls that looked as if they hadn't been painted since the glory days of the Austro-Hungarian Empire. Most students agreed they looked as if they'd had a too close encounter with vats of cow dung. But the smug art students said Schiele used the same elusive brown hue in most of his paintings. The art schools were on the other side of Vienna. But the lovely Polish owners Antonina and Andrezej let the artsy lot display their insane 'arty' messes. They jazzed up the manure tinted walls and stopped the stodgy oldies frequenting 'their' café.

It wasn't the art that endeared Café Antoandrezi to 'their' crowd but the heating. They could study and write papers without having to wear three pairs of gloves. They could spend all day and half the night 'philosophising' over one cup of coffee, a bowl of goulash or a small glass of wine. To celebrate the end of semester Antonina and Andrezej let them bring in their favourite records and party all night long. June's sewing machine was permanently installed on a 'reserved' tiny table. This was where she ran off the ballgowns they wore to all the student Balls.

And that's when Liz remembered. Moira was right. It was a case of 'ALL the photos' that she'd taken of June and Martin's wedding day and shown them to her in the Café. June was so thrilled she even splurged on two Viertels of Grüner Veltliner wine from the money her father had sent her as a wedding present.

'If you want a few now, I'll only charge you for the paper and the chemicals,' Liz said.

June immediately dropped the photos as if they were on fire.

'Talk about cheap!' June angrily threw the photos onto the floor and stormed out without even saying hello to Moira who was on her way in. Moira helped Liz pick up the precious photos.

'She's having her period and taking it out on me,' Liz said.

Moira polished off June's wine while Liz told her what had happened.

'Give her the photos, it's her wedding.' Moira said.

'I'm making Martin and June a unique wedding album with these. I can't afford to make extra copies. D'you know how expensive photographic paper is, not to mention the price of the chemicals?'

The minute she had a bit of cash Liz was finishing her stunning wedding album for June and Martin. But by the time that happened June and Martin had moved to London and Liz's photography dream had died. Her photos were locked away in boxes in the attic. She hadn't looked at them in decades.

Liz made herself a strong espresso but never got to drink it. The sudden Niagara of tears shocked her. All these years her best friend considered her a cheapskate just because she couldn't afford things. Slumped over the table she also wept for her lost youthful photography dream. She was weeping so loudly at first she didn't hear her mobile ringing even though it was right next to her face on the table. It was June.

'I'm so sorry for what I said earlier,' said June.

'It's ok,' Liz sobbed.

'Can you forgive me? I was totally out of order.'

'It's ok.' Liz slurped again.

'I don't know what came over me.' June sounded as if she too was weeping. 'It's my fault Robert is marrying that skunk. I'm so sorry for taking it out on you.'

'It's ok,' said Liz, even if she knew that nothing would ever be ok again.

CHAPTER 14

Auntie Jessie was to blame for the 'birthday jam for Robert' tradition. As a child Robert found it so exciting to pick wild blackberries in Fulham's Bishop's Park with Auntie Jessie. He thought it even more exciting to make their own special jam together - until he became a teenager. Auntie Jessie always made him their 'special jam' for his birthday. By chance Moira had continued the jam tradition. When she first moved into Auntie Jessie's flat in Fulham Moira took long walks in the park to cope with the bleakness of her burnout. It reminded her of the happy times when she stopped over in London during her travel business decades. Auntie Jessie used to take her for a walk and a picnic in the 'secret garden' where she picked bags of wild blackberries and made Robert's special jam. Making jam was no mystery to Moira. Growing up in Mayo all summer long she had to pick bags of raspberries, blackcurrants, or blackberries. Her mother then boiled the berries, added sugar and a few hours later they had luscious jam for tea.

Summer jam also coincided with Auntie Jessie's annual visit home. As a teacher she had long Summer holidays and always returned home to Mayo for two weeks after trips to Paris, Athens, Istanbul. She thrilled

Moira with those travel tales even if Mother had no time for them. You didn't have to be a genius to realize how jealous mother was. She spent her life milking the cows and cleaning out the pigsties. The only glamour in Mother's life was putting on her feathery hat for Sunday Mass. Moira wanted to live like Auntie Jessie - get far away from mouldy Mayo, belly dance in Istanbul, tango in Buenos Aires, discuss poetry all through the night with Parisian poets, snorkel in the Fontana di Trevi. She'd done it all except the snorkelling.

Three years ago, when Moira picked those 'secret garden' blackberries and threw them into a pan with sugar it was because she missed old Mayo and wanted to be reminded of those happy days when Auntie Jessie visited and Mother made jars of jam. The ploy worked. Instead of dwelling on her devastating burnout the jam aromas whisked her back to happy childhood Summers. And giving the jam to Robert almost made him weep with happiness as he regaled them with his memories of picking times with Auntie Jessie. After that she returned to Bishop's Park and picked the early blackberries for Robert's special jam. But this year because of the awful weather the blackberries were still greener than gooseberries. Moira hightailed it over to Fulham market.

When she arrived back home with bags of blueberries, raspberries, and apricots PC O'Reilly plus several officers were watching a man drilling the lock in Bab's door. Babs was weeping into a wad of tissues while another officer gently patted her back. The locked-in cat could be heard yowling louder than a herd of heifers.

'Some lowlife sprayed liquid glue into her lock,' PC O'Reilly told Moira.

Babs had been at the dentist. While she was gone some criminal neighbour sprayed the glue into her lock. The locksmith was now drilling out the old lock before putting in a new one. The police were canvassing all the neighbours to see if anyone had seen the criminal destroying Babs' door.

'We all know who that toad is. We can't prove it – yet! But we'll get him', said PC O'Reilly.

'He's a coward and a turd,' another officer agreed. 'But he'll regret this.'

Cheered by the determination of the officers Moira went into her kitchen and set to her jam making. A quick wash of all the old jam jars and it only took her a few hours to make two dozen pots of divine jam which was even better than her mother's. The heady raspberry, blueberry, and apricot fragrance wafted around the Fulham kitchen and propelled her back to her youth when the remote Mayo village was as barren a landscape as the 19th century Wild West without the guns and cowboys. There was no such thing as 'choice' for girls. As a teenager Moira knew exactly what her choices were. Barry and Finn would take over the farm and look after their mother in her old age. Moira could apply for a job in their cousin's hotel in Manchester. The nuns had an equally boring idea. Embrace the sublime life of a nunnery! It was only thanks to Auntie

Jessie she made it to Vienna – the stepping stone to her world travel business.

The happy memories elevated her spirits no end and she began to draw funny arty jam labels of 'Wolfibeet', little Robert's favourite fluffy toy bear. When they were choosing names for the little bear, Martin tried to persuade the 3-year-old to go with either Wolfgang, Amadeus or Beethoven. Robert came up with Wolfibeet. The little bear's 'parents' varied from week. Some days the father was a fierce lion. Other weeks it was a giraffe. Wolfibeet's mother was sometimes one of the girls' dolls and they objected mightily to the insult. For years Robert's imaginative Wolfibeet's antics had them all in stitches. Wolfibeet the pirate setting fire to enemy boats and destroying Clare and Connie's bath toys. In the course of many glorious battles Wolfibeet lost all his limbs but managed to grow new ones because June was able to perform wonders in the costume sewing department. Moira sang along to her tango CDs as she drew about 50 Wolfibeet labels. The one she liked best was Wolfibeet popping a huge rat who bore a striking resemblance to Chloe Me into a meat grinder and coming out the other side as Bolognese sauce.

She no longer worried about her CRX. She even had one flashback about Abe in Chicago after she splashed her hand with boiling jam and put an ice pack on the burn. Abe was obsessed with crushed ice. Before crushed ice was delivered by pushing a button in the fridge Abe emptied a tray of ice cubes into a tea towel and whacked the cubes over the radiator until they were well and truly crushed. He then made a luscious cocktail called 'suffering bastard'. After that he made Moira suffer by dribbling the remainder of the crushed ice around her tits. Frostbite of the nipples was never going to light her fire. If he wanted her it would be strictly cocktails and sex without frostbite. Exit numbskull Abe.

Tangoing around while she waited for the labels to dry she suddenly remembered her unfinished novel about alien cooks, the one she was working on before she got distracted by her 'Invisible Gorilla/Crocodile/Baboon Lady' murder sci-fi fantasy. She'd find her alien cook manuscript and finish it. She was on a roll. Her creative inspiration was gushing like a geyser, her sketching ability was phenomenal. Success was just around the corner. She felt it in her bones. Even if she knew the only thing she could rely on at her age was arthritis. She was about to settle down and enjoy some TV but was overcome with sudden guilt. She hadn't given a thought to poor old Babs all day. She got 2 jars (raspberry and apricot) and opened her front door. Babs was there, sitting on her highchair as usual with the silent mobile in her hand. Moira walked over to her.

'Any news on who sprayed the glue into your lock?'

'Thank you so much for asking. The police have 'no observational evidence'. They can't prove that pig did it.'

She didn't sound a bit like the feisty warrior who was ready to take on all those dumpers who vandalized the garden. But spraying glue into her lock was a much more serious crime.

'I made jam. Would you like some?' Moira handed the jars to Babs.

Babs looked stunned.

'Thank you so much. I love apricots.' She looked on the verge of grateful tears as she accepted the gifts.

'My mother's recipe. I've got lots more.'

Babs beamed happily making Moira feel even guiltier.

Moira went back home to be greeted by Beelzebub. The cat's eyes were pleading and pitiful as he meowed against Moira's leg. Maybe Babs was so traumatized by the glue criminal she'd forgotten to feed it? Moira poured some milk from the fridge into a bowl, added some hot water and watched the old cat lap it up. She then opened a tin of tuna, emptied it into a saucer and put it next to the milk. Beelzebub stopped lapping the milk and moved his head up and down her leg purring his thanks before sucking back the tuna in record time.

When the cat strolled out into the night he looked his old self. Ready to kill any rat that dared do its business in Babs' garden.

CHAPTER 15

When Liz said she was 'working from home' nobody doubted her. She was too ancient to risk losing her TV job by skiving off. But Liz 'wasn't working from home'. She was trying to locate June and Martin's wedding album stored in the attic. It took her the entire morning to locate the 50 boxes labelled Vienna 1968-1978. But she no longer had the courage to open one. Instead, she went for a long walk up the hilly Park towards Alexandra Palace, commonly known as Ally Pally. Walking in parks bored Liz senseless. Today was no exception. What was the point of getting drenched in the rain and ruining her shoes? It wouldn't help her escape her present, her past and the Prick problem. She shook the rain from her coat and umbrella and went into the Phoenix Bar for a coffee.

The Phoenix! How fitting a name for this location, Liz thought. Sixteen days after it first opened in 1873 the enormous Victorian recreation complex known as 'The People's Palace' burnt to the ground. Two years later it rose from the ashes, re-opened and went on to thrill generations of visitors. In 1936 the first BBC TV transmissions were made from here. Ally Pally was on a roll until 1980 when the Great Hall, the Banqueting

Suite, the roller rink and theatre dressing rooms all burnt to the ground again. Only the Palm Court and the BBC area escaped. Yet again Alley Pally rose phoenix-like from the embers.

And she'd do the same, Liz thought. Her life had been reduced to dust and rubble once before and she had slowly clawed herself up from those ashes. But this time she wouldn't do 'slow'. She was about to order a second strong Americano when she got the text. The Algiers assignment had been a triumph. He'd finished early and was 'longing to investigate her'. Nausea surged through her body. She resisted the savage urge to text back and ask if his investigations in the Savoy had been as equally triumphant.

She was back in the attic about to open the first Vienna box when he arrived home.

'Chérie, mon amour where are you?'

Liz didn't reply. She heard the plonk of grocery bags and duty-free bottles and then his footsteps coming up the attic ladder. He expected her to rush over and cover him in a lather of kisses. He waited in vain.

'Any special requests for dinner, chérie?' he asked miming a kiss in her direction.

'Your dick on a spit,' Liz felt like yelling 'with minced balls on the side.' She'd give these to Moira as a treat for that Beelzebub cat she never shut up about.

She waved over to Pierre and gave him the sunny professional smile she'd used in thousands of boring interviews with cretins whose only goal in life was to have their fifteen minutes of TV fame.

'You chose,' she said.

In other words, 'just eff off and impale yourself on the carving knives'.

She ripped open the first box …. and there was a photo of herself laughing with her arms around Hans in Café Antoandrezi. She snapped the lid shut again. She needed a stiff drink before opening the tomb to her Viennese past. Any minute now the prick would be back with his aperitif suggestions - plain Kir, strawberry Kir, Kir Royale? She didn't want any of his wishy-washy cocktails. She needed a strong gin & tonic and she'd make it herself.

In the kitchen he was pounding the life out of what had once been a recognizable cut of meat. Liz was totally immersed in pouring herself a large G&T when he nuzzled her neck.

'I'm making you my very special Wiener Schnitzel,' he whispered.

Liz looked at the flattened cutlet and thought of another treat for Beelzebub: Pierre's prick pounded into the size of a large pizza topped with creamed testicles. But after days of gruesomely mutilating his privates, why not complete the job and murder him in the bath? He always sat with his back to the taps. One good whack of his skull on those taps and goodnight swindler!

Liz took a long gulp of her strong G&T. Whacking him to death had lost its appeal. The f**king shite wasn't worth her inventiveness. She decided to control herself, find June's wedding album, have a dozen strong G&Ts and drop into an alcoholic stupor in the guest room. The jerk would think she was sparing him her drunken snoring which disturbed him more than exploding bombs.

Back in the attic she opened the second box. Again, Cafè Antoandrezi and a photo of June, Moira, herself and three clean cut American Marines they dated. Liz remembered that night. The Marines had invited The Three to the movies - an expensive treat in those days. They'd seen Doctor Zhivago - the longest film of the sixties and interminable for the three Americans who didn't understand a word of German despite their years in Wien. To make it up to the guys, The Three invited them back to their Cafè. It was a rare honour to be invited to their special place but it didn't impress the young men who were used to higher standards in all things American from soft toilet paper to real hamburgers. Liz laughed at the perplexed expressions on the faces of the young marines. Maybe the past wasn't such a dangerous place to revisit after all. When that photo was taken, they were so young and callous they mainly dated the Marines to get loads of free American bacon, coffee, sausages and marshmallows. In the end the Marines got their own back. Their kitchen became out of bounds to The Three because they ate so much. Without the added allure of Rum and Coke on tap, free bacon and burgers it was Auf Wiedersehen Marines.

Liz was still smiling when she opened the next box. But the smile vanished the second she saw the photos of Hans selling Christmas trees in front of the Votivkirche – the huge neo-Gothic Church within a stone's throw of the University. It was their fourth Christmas together and Liz was five months pregnant.

They were the happiest couple on the globe. During the weeks leading up to Christmas, Hans sold trees from 8 to 8 in the ice, slush and snow. Every morning Liz made him a huge breakfast of eggs and toast and porridge. For his mid-morning snack, she made him a flask of soup and some of his favourite Wurstsemmels. At lunchtime she insisted he go with her to Die Mensa, the University canteen to thaw out, sit down and enjoy her home-made lunch. 'Die Mensa' was noted for its cheap Leberknödelsuppe (liver dumpling soup which consisted of 90% old bread and 10% liver) and if you were lucky you didn't get salmonella. In the evening they went to Café Antoandrezi and splurged on schnitzel and mulled wine. It was a white and magical Christmas. But that New Year's Eve she lost her first baby in an ambulance on the way to the hospital. That was the beginning of the awful end that didn't come until 6 years later.

She drained the last of her drink and carefully navigated her way down the attic ladder. In the hallway she picked up a jacket, threw her handbag over her shoulder and walked out the door. It was still bucketing down. The yummy mummy suburb of Crouch End wasn't like Paris or New York where you waved for a cab. She went into the nearest pub where the friendly barman ordered her one. In the 7 minutes it took for her cab to arrive she tossed back three more double G&Ts. She tipped the barman so much he wanted her to take it back thinking she was so crocked she didn't know what she was doing. Liz reassured him she was in complete control of her faculties.

She booked herself into the same 5-star hotel where the desk clerk was more than used to TV people staggering to their rooms with no luggage. She drank everything in the mini bar which was quite a feat since she hated those strange liquors which were more suited to drunken footballers. She didn't leave the room until it was time two days later to go to Robert's birthday dinner. She ordered several bottles of wine, had the mini bar restocked many times and ordered Robert's birthday present to be delivered to her room from the most expensive jeweller on Bond Street.

CHAPTER 16

June was basking in the Venetian sun while Martin manned the gondola and serenaded her with 'Belle Nuit, O Nuit d'Amour' – the famous barcarolle from 'The Tales of Hoffmann'. It simply didn't make sense. Martin only ever sang the German version - 'Schöne Nacht, du Liebesnacht'. It was his party piece. When he sang it with gusto in his best falsetto everyone burst a gut laughing. Why was he serenading her in French?

June jumped awake. She was stretched out on the couch clutching her book while 'Les contes d'Hoffmann' wafted around the living room from BBC radio 3. The sleeping pills she'd been taking to cope with Robert's engagement were playing havoc with her days and nights. As the barcarolle ended June remembered another Martin connection to 'Hoffmanns Erzählungen' and weddings.

'Now there was a man with major problems in the love department,' Martin used to say.

During the opera, 'Hoffmann, the Hope Man' fell madly in love with a mechanical doll, a prostitute who wanted to steal his soul and a woman with a weak heart who sang herself to death. The 'Hope Men' was what Martin called the guys who dated and maybe wanted to marry his precious daughters. Both Connie and Clare had a gift for dating the most unsuitable nerds. Most of the men Connie dated were aiming to save the world. Clare's were bent on destroying it. Some of the 'Hope Men' didn't have a spare pound. Others could have bought The British Museum. Some were funnier than a platoon of Seinfeld writers. Others were so solemn they made the Pope look wittier than Dave Allen.

When Connie or Clare introduced a potential life mate to the parents, Martin used his 'Get to know the guy' strategy – i.e. 'Let's have that pint, son.' The girls were wise to Dad's tactics and warned their boyfriends how Dad would grill them over a few bevvies. He'd ask them if they liked classical music, what football/ rugby/cricket team they supported, if they'd ever been homeless, blah, blah, blah. The guys reported back to Connie and Clare that their Dad was a hoot and he never 'quizzed' them.

None of them ever admitted that Martin showed more interest in them than their own fathers. Martin liked the little word 'why'. Why had they chosen to study medicine or history instead of economics? When had they discovered a passion for their particular field? Would they still be as passionate about their subject in 20 years? Did they know the difference between the penicillin that made bits of Roquefort turn blue and penicillin the antibiotic? Could they explain it to him in layman's terms? How many kids did they intend to have with his daughter? Did they know how linoleum was made? After the second pint Martin knew all he wanted. The young men also knew that Martin was a father who would not hesitate to impale them on the railings outside the 'Bear & Pigeons' pub if they hurt a single hair of his darling treasures.

After the girls broke up with them, the Hope Men continued to call Martin to see if he had time for a pint. Martin consoled the trail of broken hearts the girls left behind. All the 'Hope Men' turned up for Martin's funeral. June still got Xmas cards from them with photos of their lives' achievements – mountaineering up Everest, weddings, children. The girls arrogantly proclaimed the guys had never gotten over them and only wanted to prove they had moved on. But June firmly believed it was Martin who had forever touched those men's hearts.

If Martin were alive he would have little chats with Chloe Me and get to know her. He'd ask her about PR and probably joke that Robespierre hadn't done too well in the PR department. He wouldn't mock Chloe Me when she'd ask if Robespierre was a French friend? So why hadn't June put in that extra effort to get to know her future daughter-in-law? What proof did she have that the ferret was a greedy gold digger? Because Liz and June kept saying so even though they'd only met her once. They could all be wrong. Chloe Me stood to inherit wads of cash from her wealthy Daddy. For all she knew Chloe Me was Robert's soul mate.

She'd just like to be sure. Robert had dated an army of girls who came and went like the Four Seasons. But until that harpy Chloe Me got her claws into her darling son, June never had to quell the urge to ask Liz for her books on voodoo. But she hadn't given her future daughter-in-law half a chance. She hadn't even invited her for a cup of tea. Time to correct that. Robert wanted to marry Chloe Me. Mother wanted him to be happy and recapture the laugh out loud joy and exhilaration that had gone from his life since Martin's death. Would she make a supreme effort to like her future daughter-in law? Yes.

She was even ready to concede there were many similarities between Chloe Me and the young June who had left New York in '68. Her life's ambition was to study at the University of Applied Arts Vienna where her idol Klimt had also studied. But her mother wanted her to stay in Manhattan and attend the Parsons School of Design. June joined the 'burn your bra demonstrations', went wild, stayed with hippie weirdoes every night. She returned home smelling of the drink and drugs she just rubbed into her clothes. The ploy worked. She left for Vienna with Dad's blessing and a monthly cheque. Years later Dad admitted that he knew all about her fake strategies and wanted her to go to Vienna.

He had served in war-torn Europe. Post war he had travelled there extensively. He knew Vienna very well. Twenty-three years after the end of WW2 the city was duller than ditch water. His darling daughter wouldn't get involved with any mad hippie radicals. There weren't any in Vienna. Dad had used his brain. They both got what they wanted. She'd do the same with Chloe Me at Robert's birthday dinner.

This year there would be a change from the birthday baseball cap tradition. A case of out with the jaded old and in with the sparkling new.

CHAPTER 17

Walking into Steaks Galore Moira spotted Chloe Me. She had already installed herself at their reserved table and was snarling into a mobile phone. Moira didn't want to be alone with that viper. She ducked behind Sergei the tall Somali maître d' who knew her and was smart enough to immediately grasp that Moira wanted to scuttle to the toilet without being seen. They needn't have bothered. Chloe Me never paid attention to 'the help'.

The toilets had been 'refurbished' since the last time she'd been here. The wash area was now a mini-Versailles with marble sinks, gold taps and candelabras. The loos were the size of a small studio, decorated with books, paintings, ornaments plus a selection of expensive cosmetics. The toilet seat had six inches of comfortable padding. What a laugh Moira thought as she took out her mobile. She'd take a few pics for her brothers Barry and Finn. Then she'd email them suggesting this was how they could update the donkey sheds. Just add a jacuzzi and they'd have a luxurious spa for animal freaks. She was laughing and clicking away when she heard the high heels clattering across the marble tiles.

'It's like simply the ghastliest crisis.'

It was Chloe Me's snooty voice. What was the 'ghastliest crisis'? The car wash guy had overlooked a flea on her Mercedes? Moira clicked on the record button. Later The Three might have a laugh about the 'ghastly crisis'.

'He's only like invited those crumblies to my Hen.'

Crumblies? New hip London jargon? The person on the other end of Chloe Me's mobile didn't seem to understand either.

'Those three ancient losers – his Dodo mother and her zombie pals.'

Again, a short silence.

'He invites like those stupid pensioner crumblies to my Hen in like the most exclusive Chateau Spa in Europe. How unfucking believable. And his stupo mother. The billionaire who couldn't like spell pedicure.'

A brief silence while the other party probably agreed with the horrors of wealthy pensioners who didn't have pedicures.

'The Irish crumbly lives in like a stinking council estate. She's like the delusional scribbler. And like that no pedigree Wrinkly Lizzie! Tracey tells me they've been like trying to throw her out for yonks. Those crumblies are like NEVER coming to my exclusive Hen. I have my ways with Robbie baby.'

Moira heard the click of the mobile snapping shut. Chloe Me's high heels echoed like devil hooves as she left the loo. Even after listening to the recording four times, Moira still couldn't believe her ears. 'Smelly, delusional scribbler'? 'Dodo June?' The self-made tycoon who had been so many people's rock and salvation for decades. 'No pedigree Liz' with her degrees from Vienna and Paris. Crumblies! The insulting skank! Now she had proof how vile that 'like, like, like' creature was. But she couldn't march into the restaurant, play the recording and publicly humiliate Robert, June and Liz.

A woman rushed into the cubicle next to her jabbering on her mobile. They couldn't even wee without wittering into their phones. And she'd do the same. Moira dialled Robert's number.

'Chief Inspector here,' said Moira.

She heard Robert's enchanting laugh of recognition. It had been years since she'd resorted to their secret code for 'I don't want the parents to know it's me on the phone.' As a child he was chuffed to get phone calls from Chief Inspector Moira for a private chat. As an adult she used it when she was consulting him about a special gift to bring Martin and June from some remote part of the globe.

'Anything I can do for the Chief Inspector?

'When it comes to gifts you have impeccable taste, sweetie. But Vienna would be better. Besides Prague is only a train ride away and we could always pop over and join the other chickens.'

'How did you know about the Prague Hen do?'

'Not much gets past this Chief Inspector.'

Again, his enchanting laugh.

'We'd prefer Vienna.'

'You'd really prefer Vienna?' More than a touch of uncertainty in Robert's voice.

'Yes. June is finally ready for closure. Next week is Martin's tenth anniversary.'

This time there was no laughter but what sounded to Moira like a strangled sob.

'I'm so happy to hear you say that, Auntie Moira.'

She could hear the palpable relief in his voice. 'I'll change that straight away. Be with you all in about ten. Cheery bye.'

There was a new carefree and happy tone in his voice – just like the young Robert.

CHAPTER 18

Before his birthday dinner Robert always had a pint of Guinness on his own in the 'Turtle & Duck'. It was his secret tradition in memory of that first pint he'd drunk here with Dad 10 years earlier. If he'd only known it would also be the last pint they'd drink together he'd have paid more attention to Dad's waffle. But the only thing on Robert's mind that night was getting away from the parents and living it large all over Europe with Henry and their other mates.

There were two pints of Guinness on Robert's table - one symbolically for his dad. He knew it was daft but Robert liked to look at the pint and mentally chat with Dad. It was the only time he indulged in such peculiar behaviour. He had only taken his first swig when he got the call from the Chief Inspector. He had to take a few more long sips to digest it all. Vienna! Mum finally wanted to return to Vienna. Auntie Moira and Liz would help Mum scatter his dad's ashes in St. Marx cemetery. He took another long sip of his Guinness. It tasted divine. For three seconds he felt guilty about feeling so good until he could almost hear his dad – 'life is for living, son'.

'As long as I don't end up every morning snout down drunk in a ditch!'

He had repeated his dad's old warning out loud. The couple at the next table looked over at weirdo Robert. He waved to them. He felt so good he wanted to yell out: *Not barking mad. Just ecstatically happy*. Dad's ashes were finally going to the city he adored. In London Dad was a serious workaholic and never that talkative – due to the ungodly hours he put in every day. But the minute they hit Vienna for their Summer holidays Dad had a personality change. He metamorphosed into a verbal waterfall who never shut up about the glories of the 600 pieces Mozart had written in his tragically short life. He bored them witless droning on about Mozart's life and death which might also have been due to Mrs. Mozart's undercooked chicken. Robert sighed sadly. What he wouldn't give now to listen to Dad rambling on about Mozart.

He took a looooooong consoling gulp of his Guinness and remembered how Dad couldn't hide HIS boredom when Mum launched into HER Vienna. She took them on art and architecture tours and bored the eyeballs out of their skulls waffling on about Klimt, Kokoschka, Jungendstil, Secessionist, Otto Wagner, and more Klimt, Klimt, Klimt. It was a toss-up which was the more excruciating – Dad's Mozartitis or Mum's arty klimty Memory Lane.

The pain in Vienna became excruciating the Summer Connie turned 14. Out of the blue Connie suddenly exhibited a burning interest in the countless residences where Bruckner, Mahler, Shubert, Strauss, Von Suppé,

Beethoven, Vivaldi and Mozart had lived. Both parents were euphoric. They spent even more time visiting those boring arty buildings with a classical music connection – on every second street in Vienna. However, the parents' joy was short lived. Connie was only trying to impress a former 'Vienna boy chorister' whose name she had forgotten a week later.

'Zum Wohl! Dr. Weber!' Robert muttered to himself and drank his Guinness. Another ritual - but originally his dad's when they stayed in that vast house in Grinzing during their Summer holidays. Mr. and Mrs. Web were his Viennese 'grandparents'.

'Auch Zum Wohl! Frau Professor Doktor, Doktor, Doktor!'

'Zum Wohl' - Cheers! was the first German expression he learnt as a child during those Viennese vacations. They always stayed with the Webers. Every year Mrs. Web (as young Robert called her) again told them the story of how she had first met their father.

It was 1969. She was standing with her shopping bags at a tram stop when the angry young man pacing up and down the platform bumped into her. He stopped, apologized and did a low bow to Mrs. Web.

'Verzeihen Sie bitte.' Were his first words to Mrs. Web. 'Normalaweise bin ich nicht so.'

Mrs. Web was a woman who had seen the Nazis being clapped, cheered and welcomed into Vienna, her friends had died either in concentration camps, on the Russian front, or from starvation both during and after the war. She was not the kind of woman to even wonder why a babbling youth with a suitcase told her 'he didn't normally act like that'. Until Martin bowed again and said:

'Ich bin Irre.' (I'm a madman!)

Mrs. Web just nodded. Lunatics were littered all over Vienna like the ants that Orson Welles had so cruelly described in 'The Third Man'.

'Aus Irland!' (from Ireland)

Mrs. Web corrected his German. 'Irre' – two r's meant you were crazy. 'Ire' with one 'r' meant you were Irish. They laughed. She admired his command of German. But why hadn't his Austrian friends corrected him? Probably because his pals liked a laugh. Was he leaving Vienna she asked looking at his suitcases?

No, he'd been thrown out of the student house just because he had been conducting a group of mates who were brushing up their Mozart like himself. The Student House Authorities blamed Martin for massacring Mozart late into the night. He told the Authorities they couldn't even spell Amadeus. They threw him out. He was on his way into town to sleep on a friend's floor until he found another bed. She told him he was standing on the wrong side of the road if he was headed into the centre of Vienna. He laughed, thanked her, bowed again and was about to cross over to the other side when Mrs. Web's tram arrived. Martin picked up Mrs. Web's shopping to help her onto the high tram steps.

'Kommen Sit mit,' she said to the helpful Martin. 'Ich weiß wo mehrere Zimmer frei sind.'

Martin hopped onto the tram. 'Frei' meant both 'free' and 'a spare room'. She was referring to the many unoccupied rooms in the vast home she shared with her husband Prof. Dr. Weber a maths teacher who was also a violinist. Martin became his soul mate and their substitute son.

'Cheers again, doktor, doktor', Robert sipped his Guinness and smiled.

In Austria it was de rigeur to add 'doktor' in front of your name whether you graduated in history, sociology or flower picking. If they had two degrees it was a case of 'doktor, doktor' which Robert found most amusing as a child but not as hilarious as Frau Prof. Doktor, Doktor, Doktor Weber which most people called Mrs. Web who had two degrees in her own right. In Austria a wife was also granted a Dr. title if her husband had one.

The Webers didn't have any 'children' until Martin and his many musical mates moved in and formed the 'Grinzinger Knaben'- a nod to the more famous Wiener Knaben – the Vienna Boys' Choir. The Grinzies were a cross section of nationalities – Hungarians, Germans, Americans and Austrian and half were women. The Grinzies had one thing in common – a pulsating passion for classical music and working their way through university.

After broken hearted Martin left Vienna to move to London with his young family, he always kept in touch with the Webers and stayed with them on their long summer vacations. For many years the kids thought it was a Viennese variation of a huge B & B. After the Webers died they thought it was a musicians' home. Which it was – because they had left the house to Martin to thank him for decades of youthful spirits and music – not to mention all the painting, papering and repairs he and the students had done down the decades. Later Martin set up a trust and rented it out for free to struggling musicians. They called it the Webshaus.

'Nochmals Zum Wohl, Mrs. Web,' Robert said and drained the last of his Guinness with relish.

He looked at the other full pint. The couple at the next table were trying not to stare at him. He'd probably been talking to himself in German while he drank his pint. Suddenly he didn't care. He reached over and picked up the other pint.

'Zum Wohl, Cheers Dad,' he said out loud and laughed as he downed a third of the pint in one long luscious swallow.

He then pulled out the three cards, erased Prague and substituted Vienna.

CHAPTER 19

Sergei the welcomer/maître d' in the exclusive Steaks Galore was a gifted film director/actor/opera singer who should be working all over the globe. But there weren't that many roles for an operatic Paul Robeson double in London. For months he'd been 'resting', getting older and going nowhere. But Steaks Galore always hired him when the going got tough. When he knew he was in for a bad evening Sergei rehearsed an imaginary role of operating the guillotine during the French Revolution. He had no problem getting into that role. All he had to do was look at the braying line of people who lied about non-existent reservations and blamed him for getting their names wrong. Sergei was so wrapped up in his guillotine fantasies the bag lady had already wafted by him with a wide smile and a cheery wave.

'Madame! Madame. Arrêtez, s'il vous plaît,' he said breaking into his first language.

The over poshed people in line thought the bag lady looked like a Dickensian 'Madame' who ran a shedload of prostitutes. They were all stunned when the woman stopped and offered Sergei her hand.

'Je m'excuse, Sergei.' Liz then told Sergei she didn't want to disturb him.

Sergei beamed and shook Liz' outstretched hand. The waiting line were slack jawed to see the two laughing like old friends. This was a 4-star restaurant. But they couldn't know how well Sergei and Liz knew each other from the days they worked together in TV dramas. Sergei apologized for not recognizing her because of the costume she was wearing.

'Costume'? said Liz.

'Let me guess,' said Sergei looking at her old jeans, crumpled stained shirt and greasy hair. 'You had a re-enactment and one of the extras let you down.'

'Yes,' Liz lied. Easier than saying she'd been drunk for days and had forgotten to change her clothes.

'They lost your clothes and now they're in a crate in the costume department?'

'Précisement.'

'Remember that time I was playing a devil and they lost all my clothes and expected me to go home wearing nothing but my horns, hooves and tail?'

They both laughed.

'That was some re-enactment,' said Liz.

He was about to ask what drama she was working on when Robert walked by them.

'Good evening, Sergei,' he said and waved.

He hadn't recognized Liz. But then how could he, Sergei thought? Robert had never seen Liz during a period re-enactment where she was more than willing to pitch in as an ugly old witch or axe murderer if it kept the budget under control. Liz was legendary for her use of budget. The money spent was always visible on the screen and the actors were extremely well paid. It was a crying shame she didn't get further in film or TV drama. She oozed talent. But drama was a dog maul dog industry and Liz was a soft hearted, loveable puppy.

'Je peux passer, Monsieur?' Liz asked Sergei with a fun twinkle in her eyes.

'Bien sûr, Madame,' said Sergei and bowed dramatically. Liz wafted into the dining room leaving a distinct air of old booze behind her. Sergei attributed this to her role in a re-enactment scene. A modernized version of Oliver Twist where she had to play a prostitute/gin addicted extra?

As Liz walked towards their usual table, she saw the viper sitting next to Robert and mentally shoved her face into the ice bucket. But Robert had finally recognized her and waved. Walking over to them Liz watched as Chloe Me texted on one mobile. She counted 6 more mobile phones ranging in colour from white, red, polka dot, black and purple on the table in front of her. What clown needed 7 mobiles?

Chloe Me caught a whiff of something she was on most intimate terms with – old booze. But the fumes were coming from a bag lady and not from one of her posh friends. She wrinkled her nose then snapped her fingers.

'Lady, the exit is over there,' Chloe Me said dismissively. She then haughtily beckoned a staff underling to remove the smelly tramp.

When the alcoholic stench lingered, she raised an outraged face and saw Robert embracing the bag lady.

Later she'd text Tracey and bring her up to date on what her tramp drunk 'boss' thought she could wear in a 4-star restaurant.

CHAPTER 20

VIENNA?

NO! NO! NO!

NEVER!

Moira was in a full-blown panic, pacing to and fro in the loo, waiting for the others to arrive and trying to find the courage to call Robert and ask him to please, please go back to his Prague idea. She could tell Robert she'd had a bit of a brain snap. Closure in Vienna, my eye! They all knew June would never part with Martin's ashes. Liz never wanted to set foot in Vienna again. As for Moira herself. It wasn't her busy travel schedule that had prevented her from returning to Vienna for the past 30 years. The truth had a name – Count Hugo, her former fiancé.

She turned on the cold water. But more splashing wouldn't help. She had dug the Vienna hole all on her own because of her quick temper and Martin's Mozartitis. Why in God's earth did he want his bloody ashes scattered in that bleak St. Marx graveyard? Not even a piece of Mozart's dust was there anymore. Down their student years she had told Martin she didn't give a rat's ass where Mozart was buried or if Mrs. Mozart had put arsenic in his beer. She also repeated she didn't want to clutter up her brain with details of which Viennese fiddler had been exhumed and transferred from a decrepit grave to a fancier one. If Martin had lived to see CSI NY or CSI Miami, she knew he'd be waffling on about CSI Vienna 1888 – the year Beethoven and Schubert had been exhumed from the cemetery of their choice (Währing) and moved into more flashier graves in the Zentralfriedhof where the three Strausses, Brahms, and Margarete Schütte-Lihotzky, were also buried. Moira stopped splashing. She could remember the full name of Margarete the Austrian architect who designed the first fitted kitchen in the '20's. But she still couldn't remember sex. And didn't give a shit! Her main priorities were saving Robert from that scuzz bucket and her friends from more pain if they were forced to return to Vienna.

She looked out the door. Robert was sitting at their table. She'd order him to go back to his Prague idea. Once she started talking something original would come to her. But Liz's arrival wrecked that idea. Moira blinked several times to make sure she wasn't hallucinating. Liz looked like the carefree student they'd all known back in the days before she became Mrs. Uptight Frenchie with every hair in place. As a student Liz's thick, curly hair had been the bane of her life. She used to iron it to try and lose the jungle look. When she cut it short it looked even worse. Her nickname was Frizzie Lizzie.

June arrived and gaped aghast at Liz' outfit. As a distinguished graduate cum laude from Vienna's University of Applied Arts, June could distinguish a crêpe de chine made in 1840 from a silk woven in Lyons in the 1930's. But now she hadn't a clue what Liz was wearing. Old jeans and a torn shirt? She'd had a breakdown was the only explanation. June rushed over to help her friend.

Moira exited the loo and approached the table. A strong pong of booze wafted from Liz. She'd have to ask her what type of drink had changed her back into her wild old self? But first she'd have to endure a meal with the deceiver from Hell who had the nerve to blow her several air kisses. She sat down and waited for Liz to explain. Why had she come to Robert's elegant dinner looking worse than a woman who'd been shat on by a flock of wild geese?

'I will say this once. Sort it out. Problem is not a word you use with me,' snapped Chloe Me and clicked her mobile shut.

The way Chloe Me arrogantly shook her locks reminded June of a Thanksgiving gobbler protesting its lot in life. If only that skank could be carted off instead of one of those birds. June made a supreme effort at retrieving her serenity and seeing a positive side to her son's fiancée.

'Such a pretty colour,' she said and picked up the cream mobile covered in gaudy diamantes.

'That's for the bridal arrangements,' Chloe Me cooed. 'I have different mobiles for different assignments. Black for office work. Polka dot for close friends. Red for semi friends.'

'Such attention to detail,' June gushed and picked up the green mobile. 'Business or friends?'

'Business,' Chloe Me radiated at the woman she had called a 'a Dodo, no pedicure stupo crumbly' only 15 minutes earlier.

'You really are amazing,' said Moira.

When Chloe Me turned to her and beamed, Moira realized she had spoken aloud the sarcastic remarks that were racing through her brain.

'Why the inaccessible island?' Liz asked picking up a copy of the fat wedding invite that was on the table under the mobiles.

'To keep the plebs away,' said Moira beaming her broadest at Chloe Me. 'Get with the programme Liz. This is an élite wedding. You turn up dressed like that, they'll think you're some punk rocker who's escaped from prison rehab.'

Liz burst out laughing. The others joined in and waited for Liz to explain why she was dressed like something that had just escaped being mauled in a zoo.

'I've been thinking, dear,' said June to Chloe Me in her new pseudo motherly voice. 'When you have a window in your hectic schedule we can sit down and discuss the Irish invites.'

'Nobody's invited from Ireland,' snapped Chloe Me.

Her polka dot mobile buzzed on the table and she beamed as she read the text – 'poor u with crumblies. Have 3x daniels'. Klo was unaware that her blunt statement had frozen four faces at the table. But before any of them could react, Bernie the manager arrived.

'Champagne all round to get the ball rolling?'

'Not yet,' said Robert.

'Not yet?' Bernie gasped.

Normally when that crowd got together, they were thirstier than camels arriving in an oasis after a 2-year trek through the desert.

'Sorry, Bernie. Of course we're ready for the champagne. But the Irish invites haven't gone out yet,' said Robert.

'No champagne for me, Bernie,' Liz piped up. 'I'll start with a gin & tonic. Thanks.'

'Double Dewers on the rocks and chill the glass beforehand,' ordered Chloe Me.

'Bien sûr, Madame,' Bernie beamed his professional smile - *Up Yours, Madame!*

'None of Martin's family is coming to the wedding?' queried Moira and looked in amazement at Robert.

'Not as yet,' said Robert.

'It's my fault,' said June to Chloe Me. 'I should have given you the names and addresses long ago. You've done an amazing job. Let's do lunch soonest and we'll discuss the Irish relatives.'

Moira bit her tongue to stop herself hollering out the truth about the evil serpent in their midst. How was she going to survive the next two hours? Why was June now grovelling to that insufferable piece of manure? Why had Liz lost the plot?

Bernie was back with two waiters. One carried a silver bucket of ice and a bottle of champagne. The second waiter placed a Dewers next to Chloe Me's mobile collection and the G&T next to Liz. Moira wondered what Bernie had said to his staff? The G&T for the one who looks like a scarecrow the sewer had coughed up and the Dewers for the mobile maniac. Moira picked up her glass of champagne.

'Happy birthday.'

They all chorused as one except for Chloe Me who had a call on her white mobile. She sucked back half the Dewers as she listened with a savage scowl.

'Remind me again – you're like getting paid to do this job? Sort it out like pronto.' She snapped her mobile shut. The scowl evaporated and was replaced by that toothy smile.

'Happy birthday, big boy.'

She didn't clink glasses with Robert. Her left hand pawed his privates under the table while every pore in her body oozed hot sex.

'Thank you all. This is great,' Robert said.

Little did he know there were 3 wily women sitting at the table whose ambition in life now and forever was to make sure that his life would always be great.

CHAPTER 21

As per tradition, Robert's 'fun' birthday gifties were placed centre stage on the table. They usually remained there until they'd finished the second bottle of champagne. But Liz couldn't wait that long and handed Robert her small gift wrapped in art deco design paper.

'It's a little change from the usual champagne,' said Liz.

'This is unbelievable,' said Robert taking out the gold watch and showing them the priceless piece.

'Dates back to the Colonial times in India when British officers played polo with Indian maharajas,' Liz told him.

'That's a Reverso.' Chloe Me snapped the watch from Robert faster than a gannet piercing a sprat.

'Designs vary but it was a very original invention to protect watches from getting smashed to bits during their polo games.' Liz retrieved the watch from Chloe Me's clutches and handed it back to Robert.

Robert put on his watch and caressed it like a child hugging his puppy.

'This morning he got the first part of his birthday giftie from me,' Chloe Me announced to the table.

'How thoughtful of you, dear.' June sipped her champagne thinking eat shit and die, you rancid pile of manure!

June took deep breaths. For a few moments she had lapsed into dreamland where she was Boudica surrounded by a battalion of warrior women discussing original tortures to destroy that bitch. The Klo wouldn't be much of a challenge for Queen Boudica and her troops who had razed Roman London to the ground in AD60. June unclenched her teeth and mentally swore she would remain serene.

'I'm sure you won't mind if we have a change from baseball caps this year,' she said to Robert.

They all looked perplexed when June handed Chloe Me two Royal Opera tickets for *L'elisir d'amore* the following day.

'I told Mum you were free tomorrow afternoon,' Robert said to Chloe Me.

'And maybe I had plans.' The snarl was out of her mouth before she could control it. 'Course I don't. Not when I can go to the Opera with your mum.'

The switch between snarl and ooze was so swift, semi blink and you'd miss it. Robert obviously had.

'They heard Pavarotti sing 'una furtive lagrima' twice,' he informed his bewildered fiancée who was still trying to decipher *L'elisir d'amore* on the ticket.

Moira and Liz exchanged worried glances. Had June completely lost the plot? *L'elisir d'amore* meant everything to her. As a surprize birthday present Martin had whisked her over to Paris to hear Pavarotti singing in *L'elisir d'amore*. La Tebaldi sat in the royal box during this performance. After the intermission the orchestra gave her a standing ovation even though she hadn't sung a note. For years afterwards Martin kept repeating how extraordinary that homage was. Parisians weren't given to clapping their pampered paws. Their response to Pav in the first act was very lukewarm intimating he'd better live up to their expectations in the second act. Which he did. Pav passed the Parisian test and they wouldn't stop clapping until he gave them an encore of 'Una furtiva lagrima'. Something unheard of in the land of opera. June and Martin repeated that tale so often that for years afterwards young Connie and Clare mercilessly pulled their legs.

'Did you know Pavarotti sang 'Una furtive lagrima' TWICE on that very night Dad took Mum to the Paris Opera for her birthday?'

'No way!'

'Oh yes! Oh way!'

'Dad genuflected to La Tebaldi.'

'Who she be?'

'She be big.'

The daughters were allowed to gently mock Dad's classical obsession and Mum's gift for repeating herself. But sharing her most treasured memories with Chloe Me? Liz and Moira again exchanged horrified glances. Moira then reached over and gently pushed the special jam towards Robert. He gasped in delight when he saw the drawings.

'They look just like my Wolfibeet. Amazing.' He sounded like a little boy crying with delight.

'You think so?' asked Moira, putting on her modest tone. 'I'm delighted!'

The jam was passed around and praise lavished on the hilarious drawings. They were all startled when Chloe Me jumped up and started taking photos on one of her mobiles.

Liz had her first lucid moment in three days. She had forgotten to bring her cameras. From the day of Robert's christening, she had taken photos and videos of all his birthdays. It was her secret project. She was to present him with the finished oeuvre on his 18th birthday. But in all that footage Martin had been the funny father. She decided to wait until they had all recovered from Martin's death. She continued recording the birthdays. Now, thanks to the Savoy betrayal, the melt down brought on by her Vienna archive there would be a yawning gap in her life's project. No camera, no mobile. She could always ask Chloe Me to loan her one. She finished her cocktail and prepared to address the woman who had taken her place as official photographer and was now snapping the birthday gathering.

But there was something odd about the angle of the mobile and the mocking cackle the others couldn't hear. Looking at the angle of the mobile Liz saw that Chloe Me was only focusing on the jam. Strange! Why not take photos of the birthday boy, her fiancé? Or take a group photo? June had preened herself in vain. She would not appear in any of those pics. The gloating look on Chloe Me's face gave her away. Liz could see right through that slug. Those shots would be forwarded to all her 'rich' friends to show what an Irish 'pauper' considered a birthday gift. What a lowlife!

'Robert could I borrow your mobile for a sec?' Liz asked.

Liz dialled her office. Shawn was on duty manning the phones in case staff needed to be called in on a breaking news story. With TT in charge, alien royalty visiting his diluted aristo relatives might make the grade as a news story. The rest of the time he just copied the BBC.

'Hi Liz, what can I do for you?'

Liz told him.

Bernie was standing behind her with two bottles of wine.

'Sauvignon or Cabernet?' he asked.

'I'll have a Badoit, Bernie. Thank you.'

CHAPTER 22

Moira also spotted the serpent taking close-ups of her jam. She'd send those photos to her posh pals. See what a 'delusional scribbler' considers a birthday present. Hearing her gloating gurgle Moira suddenly decided that returning to Vienna was a much better choice that being stuck in a hell spa with that Miststück (German for bitch) and one of Moira's favourite expletives. As students they invented English/German jokes with the word Mist (shit, manure, dung, crap). Her mother in Mayo also enjoyed those jokes because her favourite liqueur was Irish Mist. This was a huge seller which they exported to Germany without changing its name. Even her mother got the joke. She used to ask Moira if the Viennese drank 'Irish Manure'. Moira relaxed and thought of all the fun they'd have in Vienna once the other two got over the initial shock.

They were choosing the desserts when Sergei approached their table followed by a young woman carrying several heavy bags and what looked like a golf bag. The grimace on her face was that of a gargoyle. Bubbles of thick foamy spittle spewed from both sides of her mouth. It was Tracey, one of Chloe Me's dear friends who worked as a TV runner for TT. Liz got up and took one of the black bags from Tracey and put it on the floor next to her chair.

'That fakking Shaun called me. ME!'

'Shaun called you because you're officially on call tonight. Right?' Liz queried professionally and unzipped the black bag at her feet.

'Shaun's a fakking stupid ass,' she snorted.

'You're insured to carry this equipment,' said Liz coldly.

'I explained to Madame that I would willingly carry the tripod,' said Sergei. 'But that she would have to personally carry the camera herself.'

Tracey turned and snarled at Sergei.

'Just fakking can it, moppet. Go back to your ca ... ve ......'

The shrill screams that spewed out of Tracey even penetrated the steel fortress of the kitchen reminding the chefs of unhappy pigs being slaughtered. She looked as if she'd suffered from a violent fit that made her go crashing down to the floor clutching the tripod for support.

Later the friends would discover that it was Moira who had saved their evening and prevented a messy lawsuit being filed by the restaurant against a member of Liz's TV company for verbally assaulting a valued member of their staff. Moira had simply smashed both tips of her shoes into Tracey's skinny shins. It wasn't the first time she had resorted to such a ploy. In the travel business her reputation as 'No lawsuits Moira' was legendary. People associated the travel business with pretty pictures of foreign places. The reality was that some customers could destroy a business by insulting the staff, faking salmonella poisoning or smuggling tarantulas into their beds to escape paying for their trip. 'Be ever aware and prepared 'cause it's a loony a day' was the motto Moira lived by throughout her professional travel career.

Moira got up and pulled out a chair for Tracey.

'Would you like to sit down for a moment?' she asked very sweetly.

'You …..' Tracey was still struggling for breath. But there was a whisper of something that sounded like 'old cunt' to those closest to her.

Robert stood up and marched over to her.

'You'd better leave now, Tracey,' he ordered with an authority that reminded The Three of Martin.

While the others ordered their desserts, Liz set up the tripod and chatted to Sergei who always acted as her assistant director. Their birthday table was in an alcove so the filming was hidden from other diners. It had been like this for the past 10 years. It was also meant to be fun, fun, fun.

'Action.'

Robert played to the camera and showed off his new watch. Liz ordered Chloe Me not to glue herself to him. It cast a shadow and could she please sit a slight distance away.

'On the edge of the Grand Canyon' would have been Moira's suggestion.

Liz ordered Moira to stand behind Robert and place the jam under Robert's ears. Why? Because the best Wolfibeet drawings were on the lids and if Moira followed her instructions on how to position the jars it would look as if Robert was wearing giant Wolfibeet earrings. By the time Liz had completed her cutaways and close ups to her satisfaction the desserts were long gone. The waiters were lined up behind the alcove ready for the next step. Liz had also taken close ups of all of them in different positions.

She handed the camera over to Sergei. He knew the score. The first thing he had to film was the tray of flaming Sambucas around the birthday cake. Then he'd film Robert and the Three standing around the flaming cake, holding up their champagne glasses and smiling for the camera.

'Zum wohl!' they all chanted holding up their glasses. 'Let's all Stoß an, Stoß an.'

They burst into song with one of Strauss 11's exuberant arias.

'Trinke, Liebchen, trinke schnell. Trinken macht die Augen hell.'

Chloe Me glared at them feeling excluded from their German yodelling. She arrogantly threw her head back, stuck out her right hand and put her left index finger under her nose.

'Heil, heil, Hitler,' she shouted and laughed.

Silence fell as suddenly as night on the equator. The Klo didn't even notice and again yelled out: 'Heil, heil' and stuck her arm out.

Robert gripped it and hissed.

'Cut it out! Now!'

For a split second all was silent. Then Chloe Me's red mobile thundered out its raucous ring. She picked it up, sneered at the crumblies and the fiancé who hadn't a clue what a bit of fun meant, then staggered away to speak in private to a 'real' friend. In her blind fury she didn't notice that she swished her 'top 30 best friends' mobile from the table and into the side pocket of the open camera bag.

Robert gave his fiancée a look of complete contempt as she stumbled towards the ladies. Then he picked up the three envelopes.

'And finally,' Robert said and handed them each an envelope.

The opening of the envelopes and The Three's funny reactions to his gifts were an integral part of the filming of Robert's life. Depending on the gift The Three improvised their performances trying to make them as loony as possible. When he gave them the knitting trip to Belfast, The Three delivered a tour de force for the camera playing three knitting witches intoning the opening lines from Macbeth. When they got the tickets to Paris to taste the pigeon in Le Grand Véfour, June did a nifty impression of shooting a bird, Moira pretended to be plucking the bird while Liz rolled her eyes in ecstasy pretending to eat it.

Down the years June's first reaction after opening the envelope never changed. She clasped the envelope to her heart looking happily ecstatic while closing her eyelids for an average of 30 seconds (Liz had timed them down the years). Moira's reaction was always over the top energetic. She kissed the envelope and then did her demented Carmen dance waving the envelope around as if it were a castanet. How could Liz ever top that? She usually hugged Robert and playfully winked at the camera.

June opened the envelope and gazed at it in frozen horror. Liz was perplexed. Why was June holding the envelope like a vial of poison instead of crushing it to her heart in her usual display of delight? Moira had also opened her envelope and was gazing numbly at it. This year Moira wasn't yelping or stomping à la Carmen. This was a first. Liz opened her envelope.

Sergei caught all her reactions on film. The look of complete horror on Liz's face; how she reached out for a glass of flaming Sambuca, tossed it back; then jumped screaming to her feet yelling about being scalded and burnt. Four waiters rushed to help her.

Bernie discreetly looked at the card that had caused the unflappable Liz to give her tonsils third degree burns.

'Vacation in Vienna'

CHAPTER 23

Sergei continued filming. Liz could edit out those scenes later or scream with laughter to see herself chug-a-lugging the carafe of water and scattering ice cubes all over the table. He captured all the touching scenes of June, Moira and Robert stroking her cheeks and hair. They freed the carafe from her clenched fists and made her sip water from a glass. Liz smiled sheepishly. They all jabbered at once. Sergei couldn't hear what they were saying. But the mike recorded it all. This was one of those mishaps they'd laugh about in years to come.

'Maybe you'd like to freshen up a bit,' said June trying to guide the stunned Liz towards the loos.

'I'd say she's fresh enough already,' said Moira taking her by the other hand. 'But we could always throw a bucket of ice cubes over you to be sure.'

'I'm fine,' said Liz and rubbed her throat.

Moira gazed at Liz' drenched hair and roared with laughter.

'I've just remembered,' she announced to the table. 'The night Jörg set fire to Liz' hair.'

'I was nearly burnt to a crisp in case you've forgotten,' sniffed Liz.

'Sorry,' said Moira still spluttering with laughter. 'But I just had a flashback of you in that Robin Hood costume drenched from top to toe with all those plastic flowers sticking out of your hair.'

'It was a Maid Marion costume not Robin Hood,' June corrected her. 'You were going undercover at the Ball.'

'What are you all talking about?' Robert asked eagerly. It had been years since The Three let rip about their wild student days in Vienna.

'It was February,' said June, starting the tale.

Moira rolled her eyes to heaven.

'Cut to the chase. February isn't important.'

'February is an essential part of the story,' June snapped.

'Why?' asked Robert.

'Because February in Vienna is the peak of the Ball season,' explained June.

'And who was Jörg?' asked a bewildered Robert.

'You tell it, Moira,' said June with a defeated sigh.

'My pleasure,' said Moira.

It was the usual freezing, slush filled Viennese February. This was also the peak of the Ball season when every strata of society had their own ball - students, firemen, diplomats, The Philharmonic, and the dull Opera Ball where the boring rich swanked about. They only went to the student balls. Then one year Liz was invited to a special Ball by Jörg a guy they all hated. Liz only condescended to go because she could take photos of prominent Viennese dressed up as clowns, goats or donkeys frolicking the night away. Liz made no bones about her intentions. She wanted photographs. Jörg wanted Liz.

Andrezej and Antonina always encouraged June's artistic sewing except when she was finishing Liz' 'undercover' Maid Marion costume for the Carnival Ball. They all wondered if it offended their Polish religion the way the Irish wouldn't dream of dancing the night away dressed up as the Virgin Mary in a miniskirt. But it wasn't the joker's costume that bothered Andrezej and Antonina. It was the student Jörg who always got what he wanted. All he had to do was flash his dad's cash about. The student habitués in their Café despised Jörg about as much as themselves for accepting the endless bottles of wine and beer he bought them. Jörg knew they hated him. He enjoyed feeling superior when he watched them guzzling his wine. Jörg was a tall, blue eyed blond with perfectly chiselled features despite the scars on his right cheek.

Andrezej and Antonina never tried to hide their loathing of Jörg but it was only on the night that he set Liz's hair on fire that they discovered the reason why. He was a member of the most virulent right-wing duelling society in Vienna. He bore his duelling scars with pride. At the time The Three knew nothing about the history of duelling societies in Vienna. To them it was a medieval male sport! Men! Their sporting obsessions varied from country to country: football, baseball, golf, ice hockey, or boxing. In Austria they assumed men liked out-dated duelling. And knew nothing about Jörg's viciously anti-Semitic duelling society. Twenty-three years after the end of the war they still had photos of Hitler in the basement where they carried out their barbaric rituals and duels. In Warsaw before and during WW2, Andrezej and Antonina had personally experienced appalling Nazi savagery. The SS went from house-to-house slaughtering dissidents and Jews including their 3 and 5-year-old daughters who were in hiding with their grandparents.

The evening had started out quite normally. Jörg had bought beers and wine for everyone. Moira was enjoying the attentions of Florian (economics), Rolf (politics), and Gerhard (medicine). June had finished her sewing and Liz finally appeared in her Maid Marion costume. June twirled Liz around so that the audience could have a complete understanding of the wonders she had wrought as a seamstress and costume designer. Every male student gobbled up stunning Liz in the short costume moulded to her perfect figure. Puffing on his cigar Jörg lurched drunkenly behind Liz trying to put his arms around her to prove to everyone that 'she was his property'.

At first nobody noticed anything. June was too involved checking for any defects in her costume. Moira was miffed that her three admirers had shifted their attention to Liz's long legs. It never ceased to amaze her how one glimpse of a woman in a tight-fitting costume and men drooled like starving hounds sniffing old bones. Liz was also fully absorbed in admiring herself. Nobody noticed that Jörg's cigar had set fire to the back of Liz's hair.

'None of us knew why he was dancing around Liz singing 'Oh Tannenbaum', saying she was light up like a Christmas tree,' said Moira taking up her story again. 'Then we saw that her hair was on fire and June ran around the place screaming for water and ....'

'Who did I bump into?' June asked.

'Hans!!!'

'Suddenly this tall hunk appears out of nowhere and runs up to Liz. He grabs the vase of flowers and flings it over Liz. But they're plastic flowers with no water. The flowers stick to her hair and are about to go up in flames too. Hans smacks her hair between his hands trying to put out the flames. Then he grabs Liz, shoves her over to the sink, turns the taps on and sticks her head under the water.'

'That's how I met Hans,' said Liz sipping her water.

'He saved my costume,' 'said June.

'But the funniest part - in retrospect of course,' Moira continued. 'Liz still hadn't a clue what was happening to her. One minute she's the main attraction, sex on legs and the next minute this guy is pelting her with plastic flowers and holding her head under the taps until she's completely drenched. She's completely dazed and shaking her head like a little doggie to get rid of the excess water and ...'

'Jörg starts yelling Fido, Fido,' June added.

'And Fido was who?' asked Robert.

'Every second dog in Vienna was called Fido back then.'

'Let me get this straight,' said Robert. 'He sets fire to your hair, dances around you and calls you a dog.'

'He goes on calling her Fido, Fido,' Moira continued. 'Then Hans punches him in the face, kicks him all the way out the door. And would you believe the nerve of that bastard? He gets up and wants to come back in. But Andrezej and Antonina both stand at the door and tell him he's barred forever. They're reporting the incident to the police and no matter who his father is, he'll never set foot inside their place again. Then poor old Oskar arrives.'

'Your artist boyfriend?' Robert queried.

'Andrezej and Antonina have finally given him a wall of his own. Oskar struts in thinking his artistic dreams have finally come true. And the first thing he sees is a mad woman with plastic flowers in her hair screaming her head off and shaking water all over his masterpiece. He tells Liz to stop destroying his work.'

'Now I remember that thing!' hooted June.

The Three howled with laughter.

'What thing?' asked Robert.

'Oskar's Oeuvre,' Moira explained. 'A gigantic seascape that covered half the wall. It had real dead fish with their guts hanging out. Plus, crows and gulls with their beaks wide open and their wings nailed or glued to the canvas. Oskar was going through his *death of artistic creativity* phase.'

'But it was spectacular art - in its own way,' Liz added.

'Yeah – it stunk to high heaven,' said Moira holding her nose.

'Poor old Oskar. He hadn't quite mastered the art of stuffing dead birds and fish. When they started to decompose the stench was appalling,' June explained to Robert. 'Andrezej and Antonina blamed the drains until an art critic complimented them on their daring choice of avant-garde art portraying the stench of modern morals. Goodbye masterpiece! Poor old Oskar was devastated. D'you remember, Oskar got his first glowing review for that stinking thing?'

'He never left home without it,' said Moira.

'That sure was one hell of an evening.'

They all agreed. Robert got up and asked The Three to pose for one last photo on this most memorable birthday. He pulled out his mobile. That was when they all remembered Chloe Me. Robert took his picture, signed the check and asked The Three to retrieve his fiancée from the toilets.

CHAPTER 24

'Happy birthday, happy birthday, happy birthday'

The Three blew kisses to Robert as his cab disappeared into the rainy night. Sergei handed the film tapes to Liz.

'We certainly wouldn't want to lose those fun tapes, would we?' she said ironically.

'How's your throat feel now?'

'Numb, but don't worry, Sergei. I'll survive.'

'Goodnight Liz and cool dreams,' said Sergei as he closed the cab door for her. As always Robert had ordered and pre-paid the black cabs to take The Three to their different destinations across London.

'Crouch End, right?' the cabbie asked checking the booking.

'No, sorry, there's a slight change,' said Liz giving her office address. 'But please don't change the original booking.'

'Certainly, Ma'am,' said the cabbie and beamed as he switched on Jazz FM. She had given him 45 minutes paid free time. The trip to the office would take 7 minutes max. To Crouch End it was over an hour.

The cab sped down the eerie emptiness of Fleet Street then stopped at a red light near the gigantic dragon in front of the Courts of Justice. Any other night Liz would be remembering the Temple Gate Bar that used to span this part of the road since the 14th century. It was notorious for the display of traitors' heads on spikes and the shop nearby that rented binoculars so people could get a better view of the gruesome skulls. Tonight, Liz was only thinking of her Maid Marion costume. June had given it to her as a gift. For the next four years she got a lot of wear from that costume both at home and at many carnival balls with Hans. They both joked she'd have to skip the fifth year because their first baby was due about then. But she lost the baby before the carnival season. Liz rolled down the window to block that piercing memory. The windy rain blasted across her face and she quickly wound the window up again. She closed her eyes and thought back to that night in their café. Love at first sight … after she'd dried off and changed out of her costume, Martin on the violin, some students admiring June's designer prowess, others singing, dancing, cheering Andrezej and Antonina who kept filling up their wine glasses and ……

The cab stopped. Shaun opened the cab door and removed the camera bag and tripod. Liz helped him bring in the rest of the equipment out of the rain that was now blasting down.

'You should have taken that cab home. I can deal with these.'

'No rush,' Liz said. 'Anything new?'

'I'm still waiting to hear from Mastermind.'

Liz nodded. Shaun's dream was to be a Shakespearean actor. Like Sergei he had tried everything. Now his plan was to appear on the intelligent TV programme Mastermind. That might give him the exposure he needed.

'Which topic did you put in this time?'

'Tiles. I've just started my research,' Shaun told her solemnly as he and Liz both signed the papers attesting to the perfect condition of the equipment.

'Was it the Romans who introduced tiles to Britain?' he asked.

'Haven't a clue,' said Liz and laughed. A few hours ago, her brain would have started thinking about a documentary on the history of tiles

'You forgot your mobile,' said Shaun and handed her Chloe Me's mobile that had fallen into the bag.

It was still active. Liz pressed the text logo to find out who the owner was. The first message read: 'fuk witch crumbly is toast.' While Shaun wondered if tiles were a sufficiently dynamic topic, Liz wondered who the 'fuk witch' was. She scrolled down but stopped when she saw Robert's name. He was a 'fuk bore nada fun' in the text from Chloe Me. The more she swiped down the more she felt like vomiting.

'Is Phil around?' she asked Shaun.

'Course he is,' Shaun laughed.

Phil was the resident IT magician who slept on the couch in his 'technical empire'. The higher ups never knew or cared what went on in the basement technical area as long as the equipment was ready when they snapped their pampered fingers. Phil couldn't afford the exorbitant London rents and wasn't fussy about sleeping with the equipment and his 'little assistant'

BG, the sweetest cat in London and named after Phil's hero Bill Gates. Phil was busy burning DVDs – another of his little sidelines.

'Would you have time to do me a favour?' Liz asked.

Liz handed him Chloe Me's mobile and picked up BG who was meowing his happiness at her unexpected visit.

'I know it's probably unethical…'

'You got a shot of TT having it off with a gorilla?' Phil asked hopefully.

'You know any gorilla who'd want him?' asked Liz sitting down on the sofa/bed where she stroked and cuddled BG on her lap.

'Yeah, those gorillas are fussy eaters. Did you know they're ..

'Vegetarians?'

The 'lives of gorillas' was another Mastermind topic Shaun had studied and droned on about for months.

'Would you be able to clone this mobile for me'?

Phil's face fell.

'I'll be frank with you … '

Liz waited. Phil had a conscience?

'This isn't what you'd call a challenge.'

He reached into a drawer full of mobiles and removed one.

'You heard about Shaun's latest?' he asked Liz as he worked his technical magic on transferring the data. 'Tiles? That'll up the viewing figures!!!'

'Each to his own,' said Liz diplomatically. It was kinder than saying that everyone thought Phil was nuttier than Shaun. Especially when he boasted how he had trained BG to 'help' him put DVDs in boxes. Liz stroked BG as he lay on her lap purring happily. She always wanted a cat or two. But Pierre was allergic to cats - probably another lie.

'Done,' said Phil, three minutes later. He enjoyed showing off his technical expertise. 'A perfect identical twin. Undercover work?'

'In a way.'

'Say no more,' said Phil and beamed at her. 'You need anything else you know where we are.'

'I owe you two bigtime,' said Liz as she hugged and kissed BG goodnight.

Shaun called her a cab. Waiting in the lobby she texted Tracey: 'how u toast crumbly Liz?'

The reply was instant. Tracey would whip TT a few times. He was her slave and he'd do anything she demanded.

'The Greeks and Romans used imbrex and tegula ...'

While Shaun waffled on about the history of tiles, Liz tapped out more texts to Tracey. Chloe Me wouldn't remember sending them. She had passed out on the toilet floor before being hauled out of there by Liz and June while Moira wanted to take photos of the Miststück with her head down the Klo 'where it belonged'.

Ten minutes later Liz was back at Steaks Galore.

'The mobile fanatic will come yelping for this.' Liz gave the mobile to Sergei. 'Could you just say you found it under the table after we'd gone home?'

'My pleasure.'

As her cab zoomed back through London, Liz didn't give a single thought to the history of wheels or if Shakespeare had plucked his quills from his own turkeys, swans or geese to write his portfolios. Farewell dull past. Life was a bowl of cherries. For years she'd been dining on the pits! Auf Wiedersehen pits!

CHAPTER 25

Moira's cabbie zoomed across London. Any other night Moira would have begged the nutty driver to pleeeeeeeeeeeeeeeze slow down. She needed to get home safe, listen to that recording again and decide what to do. The Crumblies! Every time she thought of that serpent, she felt like spelling it out for Chloe Me – the march of time spared nobody. When she was a Crumbly her once pert tits would be long sausages she could tie around her neck or dance on them.

The cabbie swore and braked abruptly. Moira couldn't believe it. They were already in Fulham. The cabbie hissed and cracked his nails against the steering wheel. The lights changed but the cabbie couldn't move because drunken football supporters blocked the road. They wore the distinctive blue and white colours of the local Chelsea football team which enflamed the driver even further. He was a Liverpool supporter. His cab had several of their red flags.

'Effing wankers,' the cabbie snarled as he walloped the steering wheel. 'Oi, ye fukking wankers, get outta the road!'

The cabbie leapt out of his cab and marched over to confront the drunks who only laughed at the angry cabbie while Moira sat in the cab wondering how the driver would react if he knew his fiancée was only marrying him for his cab or if his fiancée didn't know a Nazi heil from a hail Mary. The drunks were now scoffing at the driver. Moira leaned on the horn and roared out the window.

'OIY!!! YE' DRUNK NUTTERS JUST PISS OFF THE ROAD!!!!'

The effect was electrifying and most satisfying, Moira thought. The drunks cowered away into the night. The cabbie dashed back to the loud applause of the other drivers behind him who'd also been held up by the drunks. When he stopped in front of her address the cabbie jumped out and whipped the door open for her.

'I'm so sorry for my behaviour earlier on,' he said meekly. 'It's because my wife is giving birth.'

An original excuse?

'She's having a water birth at home. Her waters burst an hour ago but the mid wife don't want me there. Says I ain't used to pain. That one should try driving a cab for a day! I've been practicing with the birthing bath for months. I have to be there before little Moira arrives.'

'You're calling her Moira?'

'It's my Mum's name.'

'Go home and start filling that birthing bath,' Moira ordered, handing him her last few notes. 'Little Moira is lucky to have a dad like you.'

'Thank you. Sorry about earlier,' he repeated as he leapt back into the cab and zoomed off into the night faster than an angel with repaired wings.

Babs and Beelzebub were on duty outside their door. Babs was her old feisty self, babbling on her mobile about the huge pack of stray cats that had been caterwauling all evening worse than herds of randy buffaloes. She smiled and waved to Moira. The cat rushed over and rubbed her head up and down Moira's leg. In the time it took Moira to open her door she knew all about Babs' evening of chasing away feral cats to stop them mating and dropping hundreds more kittens on the premises. The cat purred merrily while Moira refilled 'her' empty bowl on the floor. Watching the cat slurping back her treaties Moira noticed the red bald patches on parts of her back. They looked like old burns. She bent down to try and have a closer look but Beelzebub had finished her treaties and was drifting outside purring even louder.

Moira collapsed onto the sofa. How had she metamorphosed into this Bigtime Loser stuck in a dump with wild cats copulating a few feet from her door. Suddenly she didn't want to go back to Vienna. She'd fake a serious eye infection or anything else that would prevent her from flying. But The Two would see right through her. And what was the big deal being a crumbly temporarily living in a jungle? All her old flames in Vienna had a superb sense of humour. Oskar would reminisce how during his 'gutted fish and bird creative period' every insect and wild animal in Vienna had turned his studio into their second home. Count Hugo would go one further. During his bad luck year his castle had been flooded three times and invaded by goats, sheep and stags.

Hugo! Her lekker fiancé and the only man she had ever considered marrying. During their 6 months together, they had lived in his luxury apartment near the Hofburg Palace within walking distance of the Vienna Opera. Was he still living in cosseted luxury? Had he moved to the family castle outside Vienna, graduated as a doctor and moved to Sidney which had been their plan? She could google his name, find out if he'd sold the castle - another of their 'joint plans'. But she had locked away all memories of Hugo – until now. He was probably a grandfather, having fulfilled his awful Mother's plan for him. Produce the male heir with his aristocratic equal and not with an Irish lowlife. Poor Hugo! In a way his life of titled luxury had been another kind of prison.

But after so many decades she might be able to face Count Hugo again and catch up over a few glasses of Summer wine. Next week she'd stroll into Hugo's 'local' Café Landtmann, the plush historic café restaurant opposite her Alma Mater. The waiters always bowed to her gorgeous student Count. Next week she'd use all her charm on the oldest looking waiter and politely inquire about the elegant Graf Hugo. But those savvy waiters would give the jaded Crumbly a pitying look and guide her to the exit with directions to a homeless centre.

NO WAY!! She was NOT going back to Vienna looking like an ancient flea ridden hen. First thing tomorrow she'd hop down to her bank and get a loan. At her age turning back the years and reclaiming some of the beauty of her youth was an expensive proposition.

CHAPTER 26

When June walked into her home the silence was suffocating. She could even hear her ankles creaking as she walked into the living room. It was still raining and the drops slid silently down the vast windows. She looked at the silver box containing Martin's ashes. She knew she could keep rubbing that fake silver all night but it wouldn't alleviate the sudden bleakness. She opened the drinks cabinet. A nightcap of Calvados or Courvoisier might help? There was no risk she'd ever end up drunk as three skunks halfway down a toilet like Chloe Me.

June poured herself another generous dose of Calvados and waited for the gloom to lift. It was unbelievable that a wealthy, educated girl like Chloe Me could be so ignorant of the atrocities that had happened in her grandparents' day. Every week British TV broadcast films about WW2. Hundreds of documentaries had been made about the Holocaust, Nazi Germany and the Blitz. Every family in London had children, parents, grandparents, sisters, brothers, friends who had been killed or mutilated in WW2.

June sipped her drink thinking of a time when she too had been as ignorant as Chloe Me during their early days of wine, men and Martin in Cafè Antoandrezi. And that was the moment she remembered.

'Jan Palach,' she whispered sadly.

The ignorance of youth! The first time she heard Jan Palach's name was when some students discussed the Prague Spring uprising. They might as well have been discussing the cherry trees in Central Park. She wasn't alone in her ignorance back then. Liz was only interested in photography and Moira in travelling the world. To them the past was a bore until Liz started dating Hans who was obsessed with history.

Hans' idea of a romantic stroll around Vienna with Liz was to point out where the bombs had fallen during WW2. He explained how the Austrians had clapped and cheered Hitler and his henchmen into Vienna in 1938 but later always denied any 'welcoming'. The Viennese also had amnesia when it came to their appalling history of Kristallnacht on 9th of November when all Jewish Synagogues, Jewish homes and businesses were burnt to the ground while the Viennese and the fire brigade just looked on. Nothing but silence in Vienna about the forced exile of over 100,000 Austrian Jews and the slaughter of over 65,000 in concentration camps. There was no Austrian version of the Nuremberg Trials. No restitution of all the properties, homes, businesses stolen from Jewish Austrians. Thanks to Hans and Liz, June knew more than the Viennese about Austria's brutality towards its Jews.

She knew why Vienna had been divided into four sections after WW2 and that the last Russian had left

Vienna only 13 years before she, Liz and Moira had their first glass of wine in Cafè Antoandrezi. She knew all about the Iron Curtain and how the Prague Spring had lasted for 8 months, starting on 5 Jan and ending with the Russian tanks rolling into the city on 20 August 1968. Jan Palach, the young Czech student dissident had set fire to himself on the 16th of January 1969 in Wenceslas Square and died 3 days later.

But June could very easily have spent those years in Vienna immersed in art and costume design without learning a thing about its appalling Nazi crimes. She could have left Vienna as ignorant as those people who spend years in a foreign country without ever learning a word of its language. Topping up her Calvados June decided she would copy Hans and educate her future daughter-in-law about WW2. She would start tomorrow after they had lapped up the L'elisir d'amore in the Royal Opera House. The rain had stopped and the lights of London twinkled up at her. For the first time in a decade, June was looking forward instead of looking back.

CHAPTER 27

It wasn't the first time Robert had lifted his drunken fiancée out of a cab and deposited her in the double bed of her open plan loft. Looking down at her, Robert felt an overwhelming surge of revulsion. How could she think giving the Hitler salute was a joke? He didn't expect her to have the same level of knowledge as his dad who bemoaned man's inhumanity to man almost as often as he mentioned Mozart. He suddenly remembered when Dad had taken them to a concentration camp. He was 9 at the time and was traumatized that people the age of his Grandad had invented the gas concentration camps that killed over 6 million human beings. Because they were Jewish. For years Robert refused to take a shower because he couldn't erase the memory of those sheds where lines of innocent people walked in expecting water to flow over them but instead were brutally gassed, killed and their bodies dumped into vast holes like piles of manure. Nothing had branded itself on his brain as much as the gas sheds until he saw the little girl cowering in the toilet in 'Shindler's List'

Chloe Me let out a yonk of a snore. He had to escape from this revolting monster. Robert checked the time on his new birthday watch. It was still his birthday. He'd see what Pavel was up to. He decided to run in the rain instead of taking a taxi. He needed to forget that hideous salute. He was still puffing in the general direction of Pavel's flat when two guys staggered by him.

'Vincent and his greyhounds. Why's he always showing off about those greyhounds?'

'The way he goes on about them, you'd think he'd given birth to them.'

The two men disappeared into the foggy rain and Robert stopped running. He was drenched, sober and standing alone in front of a pub. It reminded him of a famous 40's painting of a diner in NY symbolizing the isolation of modern man. He couldn't remember the painter's name. If an artist painted this view of a dark London street steeped in foggy rain and a lone man standing outside a busy bar, they could have called it – the isolation of Robert. He shook himself like a wet dog and went inside. He gave himself another shake when he realized where he was - back in the 'Turtle & Duck'.

'I'll have a pint,' he told the barman.

'Still raining?' asked the observant barman.

'How d'you guess?' Robert smiled and wiped away the rain from his face.

'Gimme your jacket and I'll hang it up in the kitchen for you. It's warmer back there.'

'Thanks,' said Robert.

'Better empty the pockets first.'

The barman zipped into the back kitchen with the jacket leaving Robert staring at his pint.

'Bit wet for July,' said the old man sitting on a stool next to him.

'You can say that again.'

'Bit wet for July,' said the old man laughing.

Robert picked up his pint.

'Cheers!'

He noticed the old man's whiskey glass was empty.

'Care for another?' he asked politely.

'Don't mind if I do,' said the old man looking slightly shocked but pleased.

'Cheers!'

They said it in unison as they clinked glasses and then settled into a brief period of silence until the old man said:

'I knew there was something familiar about you. You look exactly like him.'

'Like who?' asked Robert wondering what the old man was rambling about.

'Amadeus.'

Definitely bonkers!

'All the lads used to call him that. His real name was Martin and many a night he used to play Mozart on that piano over there.'

Robert put his pint down. What piano? He must have said the words out loud because the old man pointed to a dark part of the pub where a battered old piano stood like a half-hidden cow in the gloaming.

'Desperately tragic how he died so young,' said the old man gazing morosely into his whiskey.

Robert stopped chugging back his pint. He knew this used to be Dad's local, the place he came for a pint after a gruelling day's work.

'I'm Robert,' he said and put out his hand to shake the old man's.

'David. And it's a pleasure to finally meet you,' said the old man losing about a decade or two as he smiled. 'How's the piano playing going? Your Dad used to say he couldn't wait for the day when he'd bring you in here and show us what a genius you were.'

'On the house,' said the barman plonking down a pint and another whiskey.

'Thank you, son,' said the old man.

'He's your son?' asked Robert.

'Who?'

'The barman?'

'Not that I know of, son,' said David with an even wider smile. 'But I got 2 girls and 4 grandsons'

As he waffled on about the wonders of grandkids Robert had time to digest the fact of his dad coming in here, playing Mozart and telling all and sundry about his 'genius' piano playing son.

'One for the road?'

But they didn't make it immediately to the road because they were joined by several other old blokes who gushed about all the times they'd enjoyed a few pints with Martin. They reminded Robert over and over that his dad was forever saying that 'his son Robert would give Mozart a run for his money with his piano playing.'

Robert didn't notice how or who pushed the old piano out of its hiding place. But suddenly there it was in the centre of the bar looking all shiny and polished. And David was escorting him to the seat.

'One of your dad's favourites was The Kerry Dances,' one of the men said.

'I don't know that one,' Robert admitted.

'Of course you do,' David insisted and hummed a few bars.

Robert played the notes. It was a distant memory, too distant to make anything of it. He began improvising. Then stopped and looked back at David.

'Anything else you'd particularly like to hear?' he asked.

'Anything jazzy will do, son,' said David.

'That's right,' echoed the group. 'Anything jazzy at all.'

They wanted jazz? He gave them jazz. They wouldn't let him stop. The whole pub was electrified with swirling dancers, men and women humming and tapping their feet to the beat and clapping, clapping as if they'd never heard such divine music before. About an hour later Robert realized he was playing a delicate rendition of 'The Kerry Dances' and a woman with a superb voice was bringing happy tears to a lot of old eyes.

'Oh, to dream of it,
Oh, to think of it
Fills my heart with joy.
Oh, the days of the Kerry dances
Gone alas like our youth too soon.'

The barman helped him into his dry jacket before opening the cab door he had very thoughtfully ordered for Robert.

'You're one hell of a player,' he said. 'Come again.'

As the cab drove away Robert remembered the painter and the name of his oeuvre: Edward Hopper's Nighthawks. But he hadn't sat alone at the bar like the lonely man in a New York bar. Looking back at the group outside the 'Turtle & Duck' cheering him off into the night Robert waved to them and laughed.

'Thanks Dad.'

The image of Martin happily massacring Mozart on that old piano was the best birthday present he'd had in years.

CHAPTER 28

The next morning Moira lingered under the shower thinking of ways The Three could annihilate that poisonous Miststück and save their darling Robert. Later when she was ready to go to the bank, she became aware of all the noise and commotion outside. But she could also hear the distinctive crackling of police radio/mobiles. Had the glue lock criminal struck again? Moira picked up her bag and went outside.

The area in front of Bab's flat was heaving with police and officers taking photographs. She spotted PC O'Reilly and darted over to him.

'What did they do to her this time?' Moira asked.

'Really gruesome. Please don't look.'

But Moira had already seen the three dead cats and a huge mound of excrement on Bab's mat. She wanted to vomit. But she sucked it back and managed to stutter.

'And Babs? Where is she? Is she OK?'

'PC Flynn drove her to the hospital, even though she didn't want to go.'

'Why didn't she bang on my door?'

'She heard you in the shower. So, she called me instead.'

'And the cat?'

'He's staying with us at the station until Babs is discharged.'

'She'd only just recovered from the glue attack. Have you arrested the disgusting bastards who did this?' Moira asked PC O'Reilly.

'The criminals who did this don't live around here. But now we have proof.'

PC O'Reilly pointed to a drawing of a cat being hung and the large hand-written note on top of the pile of excrement – YUOR DEAD NEXT.

'How can that prove anything?' Moira asked trying to suppress her rage.

'Babs didn't tell you what that gang did to Sweetie?'

'No. She only talks about all the garbage those shits throw out every night to upset her and destroy the garden. She never tells me anything,' said Moira feeling completely guilt ridden. She had never asked Babs anything.

'It was one of the cruellest things I've ever seen,' said PC O'Reilly. 'When she was living in another borough that same brutal gang tried to kill Sweetie by burning him all over with cigarettes. But Babs stopped them.'

'Oh my God! That's why he has all those bald red spots.'

'That poor creature. The vet wanted to put him down. But Babs said she'd save him and she did. Used to be the most beautiful cat in London before those bastards burnt him.'

Guilt and remorse swamped over Moira. How often had she told the Two about the horrible cat that looked uglier than a squashed walnut crossed with a baboon's butt? She had stooped so low as to call him Beelzebub.

'When Babs stopped them with her pike and spade the bastards ran away and couldn't be traced. Later my colleagues found drawings of tortured cats with YUOR NEXT on them. Babs could only be rehoused here 3 months ago.'

'And the proof?'

'Their calling card: YUOR NEXT. The idiots can't spell. But this time we have their fingerprints. Last year we didn't.'

'Poor little Sweetie. But why didn't Babs tell me about the burns?'

'Babs never wants pity. Just justice.'

'If there's anything I can do to help…'

'We know where you are,' said PC O'Reilly.

'Is Sweetie in hospital too?'

'We're all looking after him.' PC O'Reilly said with a brighter smile. 'He's not in jail – yet'

Later that morning walking into the bank, Moira tried to remember the little white lies she'd already told to get a loan to 'modernize' the flat so she could rent it out or put it on the market. This time she'd say her boiler was leaking. London was notorious for its atrocious Victorian plumbing. If Oliver, aspiring poet, was on duty he'd top up her loan with a few quick computer clicks. Oliver knew she needed money to keep going as a sci-fi writer. It was only a matter of time before he was poet laureate, and Hollywood had snapped up Moira's 'Fables of Fulham' which would become more famous than

Maupin's 'Tales of the City'. But today there was no sign of Oliver.

Moira looked at the bank's latest ad campaign: huge posters of penguins relaxing their frozen footsies in steaming Jacuzzis and sipping cocktails (cod martinis, shrimp daiquiris?). The sub-text was 'we make all our customers' dreams come true'. Yeah! If we can do this for penguins just imagine what the bank can do for you. All Moira wanted was a mini loan towards a quick makeover so some of her former beaus in Vienna might recognize the woman they had lusted after in their youth.

'Next.'

Moira sat down in front of the new officer. The name on her badge was MS GREENE. Moira handed over her card. Ms Greene picked it up without even glancing at her. Moira watched as she read all the details of her banking history on the computer screen. Ms Greene was so intent on scrutinizing the data Dracula or The Pope could have changed places with Moira. She wouldn't have noticed. All that mattered was the computer – the super machine that never made a mistake even though the data was put in by very fallible humans.

'How can I help?' Ms Greene asked and finally looked at Moira.

Very bad start, Moira thought. Not even the addition of a little personal word like 'you' – how can I help 'you'. Oliver just asked how much she needed after they'd discussed the latest BBC 'Poetry Please' programme. But Ms Greene looked like the kind of woman who would relish listening to 'programmes on skinning and grilling your customers.' Moira gave Ms Greene the benefit of her widest smile and decided to play the daft old Irish lady in need of a bit of cash. She slumped forward and began her tale of woe.

'Me boiler is giving me awful bother. If I don't get it replaced, I'll never be able to rent out a room or sell the flat. Just when me flat was ready.'

Ms Greene checked her screen, punched in several keys, read for a while then finally looked back at Moira.

'No income?'

'When me boiler is repaired, I'll have income from the rent,' said Moira in her newly acquired brogue.

Ms Greene kept clicking the keyboard and reading the screen.

'No income.'

This time it wasn't a question.

'Dreadful isn't it?' Moira moaned, wiping away an imaginary tear and sinking deeper into her pathetic old lady role. Maybe this would remind Ms Greene of her own granny – even if she looked so flinty she could have been tossed from 'Planet No Feelings' at birth.

'But the minute I have me new boiler ....' Moira's voice faded away into a sorrowful self-pitying sigh.

'I'm sorry,' said Ms Greene.

'Thank you, dear,' said Moira completely immersed in her pathetic beggar role. She upped her Mayo brogue. 'If I could repair that boiler meself, sure I'd do it. But I'll have to pay 'em to repair it. Five thousand would be grand to tide me over 'til the tenants move in.'

'I'm sorry,' Ms Greene repeated and pushed Moira's card across the desk.

'I don't understand.'

Ms Greene began reading from the screen.

'Last year a loan for a new boiler. Four thousand. Three years ago a loan for a new kitchen. Four thousand. A new bathroom – seven thousand.'

'Tenants expect stuff,' Moira protested, dropping the brogue and her old lady act.

'So does the bank,' retorted Ms Greene. 'Ability to repay your loans.'

'I own my own flat. I could sell it in the morning and make a profit.'

'Good luck with that,' said Ms Greene. 'For the past 2 years the housing market has been in the worst slump since the 80's.'

'I just need to renew my loan,' said Moira meekly.

'Sorry. You don't qualify.'

For the first time – the little word 'you'.

You, Moira do not qualify. You, Moira is what is known as the Leader Loser.

CHAPTER 29

June put on a cd of L'elisir d'amore and hummed along as she made herself a scrumptious breakfast of American pancakes with maple syrup. She'd made thousands of them when the kids were growing up. One morning know-it-all teenager Connie wanted to enlighten them how that plateful of honey/sugar, eggs and butter would increase their blood pressure, cholesterol and cause untold number of other ailments. Martin laughed and told Connie it wouldn't affect him because his insides were cleaner and stronger than a shark's crossed with a wolf.

'Gimme a break, Dad,' Connie retorted. 'Your insides are worse than a shunk's crossed with a cockroach.'

'Proof, please. Facts,' Martin said as solemn as a high court judge.

'Just read this,' said Connie handing him a magazine with a dozen articles on how organic foods would add years to your life.

'Define organic for me,' Martin asked, still adopting his solemn advocate stance.

'Pure, clean ...'

'Ludicrously expensive.'

'It's called investing in your health.'

'Case closed,' Martin said with a tone more solemn than a judge sentencing a criminal to life in a cage seething with roaches, lice, rats and all organic.

Connie smirked, thinking she'd won. But by the time Martin had finished his morning pancakes, Connie knew she'd lost. Martin leisurely explained to her how his Dublin diet had been 'organic' long before the word became synonymous with exorbitantly expensive products. Like most of Ireland, his grandmother had a vegetable garden which produced cabbage, potatoes, peas, rhubarb, and beetroot every year. As kids they helped by cutting the eyes (buds) out of potatoes so that granny could plant them and they'd have loads more potatoes. His aunt had an orchard with plum, apple and pear trees. Neighbours gave them warm eggs straight out of the hens. Every bite of food they ate was organic.

'Ok Dad, I get it,' Connie held up her hands in defeat.

But Martin was on a roll, informing her that during their Vienna years they ate tons of organic summer black/blue/loganberries, plums and cucumbers. Why? Because they were as cheap as nettles. Their takeaway wine was also organic.

She'd been so lucky, June thought to have shared so many happy decades with her beloved Martin. In comparison to Liz who had lost her three babies and was then brutally dumped by husband Hans who started out as her 'knight in shining armour'. For the first few years Liz's life with Hans had been as lively and lovely as that first encounter in Café Antoandrezi. Their fiery first date as Liz used to say.

June's first date with Martin had been anything but fiery. He wanted to take her to a very special place outside Vienna.

'Where?'

'It's a surprise. But wear 'comfortable shoes.''

June had a brainstorming session with Moira. Was this an Irish thing? Asking a date to wear comfortable shoes? In Vienna half the fun of going on a date was spending hours dressing up for it, plucking your eyebrows and putting on false eyelashes.

'Someplace outside Vienna?' Moira mused. 'MMMM! Sex in the cheap suburbs or in a vineyard.'

'How could you even think of something like that? Martin's a city Dubliner,' June protested.

'And in love with all things Austrian'

'Classical music and Mozart. Not having sex in the vineyards.'

It was a gloomy wet November day when they took that loooooong bus ride to a dull, desolate suburb. It had none of the gorgeous architecture June saw every day in the centre of Vienna. The rain drizzled down the ugly, cement buildings and turned to grey slush on the dirty pavements.

'Where are we going?' June asked.

'To St. Marx cemetery.'

After wading through mucky paths they finally stopped in front of an angel over a grave and a sign with 'Mozart'. His special surprise was to show her

Mozart's grave. This was where Mozart had been buried in a 'common grave' on a very bleak December day in 1791. It was not 'a pauper's grave' but 'a common grave'. In the 18th century Austrian Empire after ordinary human beings died and were brought into a cemetery, the bottom of their coffin was opened and the corpses tossed into 'common graves'. That way the coffin could be reused untold number of times. Only the 'rich, privileged aristocracy' got their own coffins and family graves. According to Martin some ignorant historians had invented all sorts of stupid fables about pauper Mozart to make their own dull lives a bit more exciting. Before he died Mozart was indeed up to his eyeballs in debt (not unusual for creative geniuses). But before his burial in St. Marx, Mozart lay in state in St Stefan's Cathedral – proof how much he meant to the Viennese of his day.

Martin then went on to eulogize Constanze who for decades after her husband's tragic death at 35 had promoted and preserved Mozart's masterpieces. Without her tireless work most of his compositions would have been lost and never played by every orchestra worldwide.

'Thank you for such a lovely surprise,' June was so touched she kissed Martin's cheek.

'That's not the surprise,' Martin said. 'This is.'

He showed her two tickets to that evening's performance of 'Don Giovanni'! June's first thrilling night at the glamorous Vienna Opera House.

'I'll have to go home and change,' she told Martin.

'We're in standing room. That's why you need comfortable shoes.'

June smiled at the memory of their first romantic date of strolling through a desolate graveyard and three hours standing at the Opera. It took her legs weeks to recover and almost a year to even appreciate some of 'Don Giovanni'. But standing with Martin at the opera a few times a week became an enchanting ritual. They chatted to other music students who brought their own librettos and scores and mentally practiced while listening to the greatest music and operas in the world. Martin always enlightened her about the subtleties of the score. By the time she left Vienna she was as fanatic an opera fan as those standing room habitués.

And now she was off to sit in a very comfortable and beyond expensive box seat in the Royal Opera House, London.

CHAPTER 30

For brunch Liz ordered eggs benedict and a Virgin Mary cocktail. Waiting for her order to arrive she sat on the hotel balcony gazing over at St. Bride's Church. In 1703 a local baker had looked for inspiration at its unique four-tiered spire and had invented the first tiered wedding cake. Today that spire gave Liz a laugh. She shoved Pierre's cheating arse down the spire after dressing him up as a Tudor scoundrel in a gigantic wig riddled with fleas/bugs/lice and bouffant pants buzzing with wasps. Today she was the revitalized Frizzie Lizzie. Before last night's encounter with the flaming Sambuca, she'd have sat on the balcony thinking about the 2,000-year history of St. Bride's (known as the printers and journalists' Church) with a 1st century Roman road down in the crypt. Today she smiled about the Church's myths – originally named St. Bridget after the 5th century princess from Kildare; or Brigid a Celtic goddess; or the first Irish nun; or the miracle worker who made her own booze by changing water into beer. The best myth about St. Bridie's was that the original 6th century church was built over the filthy river Fleet in the hope that the miracle-beer-making-saint would change the Fleet sewer into a brisk brewery.

Before her 'Auf Wiedersehen Pits' wakeup call Liz was convinced she would die without her work and her dreams of one day turning all her ideas into prize winning documentaries. Today she was fed up with intelligent documentaries. She was going to make her photography dream come true and concentrate on drama. Chatting to Sergei about their old drama days had reminded her what hilariously funny and creative times they'd had.

Her brunch arrived. Savouring every morsel and sip she decided how to solve all her problems: call her lawyer and consult him about getting a quick divorce; book a storage company to remove all her photo archives into a safe lockup. She wasn't worried about the cost. Most of that Crouch End house plus all the furniture was hers. That would come to 3-4 million at least and would be legally hers after she divorced him. The howling from the striped mobile startled Liz out of her divorce plans. The raucous ring tone was like the squawking of some wounded animal in the last throes of sex or death. Why was she not surprised? When she spoke in her strangulated posh English, Chloe Me sounded worse than a pig honking. It was probably Tracey calling her dear hung-over friend for a 'quick chat'. Liz could have picked up that cloned mobile and listened in to their conversation. But by the light of day things looked different. Cloning somebody else's phone was illegal. To dump or not to dump that mobile? She'd postpone that dilemma to later. She'd take it to Vienna. The Three would put their heads together and save Robert from marrying that ignorant Nazi lying ferret.

Lies! Liz sighed. Maybe in Vienna she'd have the courage to tell June and Moira about the awful lies she had told them about Hans. The truth was she had lied to her two best friends for decades.

'Hans walked out on me, moved to Hamburg and divorced me. And I never want to hear his name again.'

Since then her friends regarded Hans as the biggest betrayer and an all-time shit. The truth was she hadn't been able to take Hans' constancy, love and devotion. During their last year together, she tried to explain that every time she looked at him she only saw the end of happiness and the death of her 3 babies.

'They were my babies too, you know,' Hans reminded her.

Liz refused to believe his pain could ever match hers. They argued and fought and she threw anything she could find at him. Then they'd make up, kiss and cry themselves to sleep. The next morning Hans got up and went to work. But Liz had lost all interest in life. Her best friends had left Vienna. June was living in London with Martin and their two little girls. Moira was swimming with the whales off some Pacific Island. Their last unbearable months together got worse. Then during that sweltering July, Hans got a lucrative job offer in Hamburg. He kept saying they could leave Vienna and start a new life. Liz said he was free to go. Hans pleaded and begged her not to give up on 'them'.

'Them? Us?' Liz snorted. When was he going to get it into his thick skull there was no 'them' or 'us' anymore?

On that broiling July day she stormed out barking insults at him in English. No matter how hard he tried,

Hans couldn't master the English language. In their happier days they had laughed themselves crooked over his mangled pronunciation. But what had once been a source of fun and laughter had become Hans' Achilles' heel. It was the only time he became truly angry. He didn't hurl dishes at the wall or verbally insult her which was how Liz vented her bitterness. Han's anger was compacted into two words – 'Sprich Deutsch'.

'Learn English,' was the insult that Liz threw at him before she stormed out telling him to piss off to Hamburg. But this time Hans followed her to the Park. The beautiful Volksgarten with the benches facing rows and rows of blooming roses were packed with Viennese on their lunch break. They all noticed the crazy couple screaming insults at each other. Years later Liz admitted she must have been suffering from temporary insanity that afternoon. She accused Hans of killing her babies because he had Nazi blood in him.

'You're insane,' Hans said. He was so stunned he recoiled and addressed her in English.

Liz repeated her accusation.

They stood facing one another in the loveliest rose garden in Europe. The suffocating silence of a smouldering Summer's day hung over the Park. Suddenly explosive thunder erupted over Vienna louder than the cannonballs at Waterloo. Then came bloodcurdling lightning. Huge hailstones cascaded from the sky. Everyone raced for cover and the benches were empty in two seconds flat. Hans looked with all-consuming loathing at Liz.

'I will never forgive you for that. I loved those babies as much as you did. I will never ever forgive you,' he said. With the hailstones pelting down his face he took one step closer to her and through clenched teeth hissed – 'Das verzeih' ich Dir nie. Niemals.' He started to walk away then returned for one last time and screamed '**NIEMALS, NIEMALS, NIEMALS.**' Never, never, never.

As he walked away, Liz stood silent in the deluge wondering why some words in German were more powerful than their counterparts in English.

'Niemals!'

The thunder bellowed and blasted while the lightning burnt terrifying patterns across the sky. Liz sat alone on a bench in the deserted Volksgarten, hailstones smashing all over her body. To an artist she would have represented a woman in mourning for her life, crying herself empty while being bombarded with hail, rain, thunder and lightning. When the storm stopped, Liz felt at peace. The hailstones had pelted all pain and anger out of her. She sat on that bench until the sky was blue again and humid heat hovered over Vienna. The rosebushes were now all bare. The ferocity of the hailstones had battered all the petals onto the grass. That vast carpet of rose petals was the graveyard where she had finally buried her sorrow. She was ready to go home to Hans, beg for his forgiveness and tell him she wanted to start a new life with him in Hamburg.

But Hans had already left. She never saw or heard his voice again. A week later she got the letter from the divorce lawyer in Hamburg, signed it and enclosed a personal note informing him that she too was leaving Vienna. She wrote a short letter to June and Moira with the lie: 'Hans walked out and started a new life in Hamburg and she was doing the same in Paris'. The Two were living happy and exciting lives so their memory of Hans faded away. But it had taken her decades to forget Vienna or Hans.

The mythical magic of Paris hadn't helped. For the first year she worked in Parisian bars where she could drink all day without the risk of losing her job. She dated every man who asked her out for a coffee. 'Dated' euphemistically speaking. 'Get 'em off you now so I can forget' would be more to the point. Nothing helped. Cigarettes, booze and sex with strangers was getting her nowhere. With every ounce of self-control, she buried all memory of Hans, 3 babies, happiness, heartbreak and Vienna. She hung up her wild shoes, worked all God's hours to study journalism at the Sorbonne. The week she graduated cum laude June asked her to be godmother to Robert – the day that changed her life.

She spent the next 15 years in Paris perfecting her French soignée look. Her heart no longer throbbed with any semblance of excitement except when it came to work. She started as a runner, a TV temp, secretary, researcher producer for French TV. Her parents had no interest in her Parisian life. She had married a 'Nazi' who had dumped her and now she was working for collaborators. Despite their eternal WW2 related insults, Liz visited them every year, tried to convince her parents to come to Paris, bought them tickets.

After her dad died her mother finally admitted the real reason they didn't want to accept her free tickets to

Paris. They didn't want to 'shame her'. Liz had become such an educated posh person she wouldn't want her Parisian friends to know about their donkey farm. A huge misunderstanding. When her mother went into a home it was Liz who contacted the donkey foundation and paid them to bring little donkeys into the old people's home every week. According to the carers, it was the only thing that brought tears of joy not only to her mother but to many of the old people for whom donkeys rekindled the happiest times of their childhood summers when a donkey ride on the beach was the highlight of the year after Christmas.

Liz shook herself. What was wrong with her? It was the relentless London rain, Liz decided. Non-stop rain in May, June, and now July was enough to unhinge anyone's brain. All that weeping from the sky was playing tricks with her brain reminding her of days she hadn't thought about in decades. She remembered her resolution from the night before.

Liz ordered another espresso and stopped thinking of the past. The priority was to save her godson. But how?

CHAPTER 31

'You don't qualify,' Ms Greene repeated.

Moira looked for inspiration at the penguins in the Jacuzzi sipping cocktails. She could joke and ask Ms Greene how the penguins paid for their booze in the pricey Jacuzzis? But by the look on her flinty face Ms Greene just wanted Moira to shift her carcass so she could torture her next victim.

'I'm sorry but there's nothing I can do for you.'

'You're right, Ms Greene,' said Moira. 'I wouldn't lend to me either.'

If the penguins had leapt from the poster and offered Ms Greene a squid margarita aperitif, she couldn't have looked more stunned.

'For 30 years I set up unique travel agencies all over the world,' said Moira still staring over at the penguins in the jacuzzi. 'Independent original tours from Patagonia to Peking. Now I can hardly afford the bus to Peckham.'

Moira reached across the desk to retrieve her card. But Ms Greene's hand was locked on it.

'What happened to you?'

The robot wanted to speak to her?

'Boreout. Burnout. Bigtime!' Moira sighed. 'Thirty years of being smiley nice to clients just finished me off. I'd take groups to the Great Wall of China and they'd bitch about the Peking duck not being the same as in New Jersey. I agreed and kept on smiling.'

'But deep down you wanted to pepper the lot of them with a Kalashnikov?' Ms Greene gave her a complicit smile of understanding.

'Worse!' Moira admitted and smiled back.

'Vats of boiling oil? Tossing them into meat grinders?'

'I rather liked the fantasy of the knife throwing circus performer.'

'The one who missed?'

'All the time.'

Ms Greene laughed and Moira joined in.

'Smiling at the public every minute of your working week is enough to drive any sane person dotty,' said Ms Greene.

'But you're still doing it,' Moira told Ms Greene. 'I gave up and only have myself to blame.'

'Most people can't cope with the smiling torture for more than a few years. You hung in there for 30.'

'Thank you. I'll remember that,' said Moira sincerely. 'Know what I'm going to do? I'm going to go home, hock everything I have and get a life. I'm too young to be sitting on the scrap heap of life.'

'Hold the hocking,' said a smiling Ms Greene as she clicked on the keyboard. 'There's a way to renew your loan.'

Walking out of the bank Moira decided she needed to sit down and recover from both the morning's cat horror followed by a money miracle. She'd have a coffee and an almond croissant in Café Del before buying those new Summer clothes. But like most cafés, Moira knew it would be teeming with the Yummy Mummys and Daddys, their babies and little ones mewling, puking and yowling worse than bulldog bats. She'd go further afield. Maybe the National Gallery café with its glorious views! She knew what to expect. Tourists bellyaching about their hotels' non-organic pillows, dull vegan restaurants, no Brazilian organic coffee, etc. But the howling baby quotient would be nil.

Suddenly Moira was too depressed to go to the National Gallery. It would not help her forget the awful crime committed a few feet from her door. Luckily old Babs had lots of friends in her hour of need. And it was useless feeling guilty. She knew nothing about those bastards torturing and burning little Sweetie. Even if she had, she couldn't have stopped them killing other cats and hanging their bodies on Babs' door. She'd have a strong Americano in Café Del, then check how the police investigations were going and ask how she could help Babs and Sweetie.

CHAPTER 32

Walking through the ROH lobby June was delighted to see the throngs of hopefuls waiting for returns. How often had she and Martin stood here decades earlier waiting in line for cheap seats! After years in standing room, it was a momentous occasion when they could afford to sit down at the Opera for the first time.

'I miss standing room in Vienna,' Martin sighed wistfully every time they walked through this foyer on the way to their expensive seats.

'I miss it too,' June always agreed nostalgically.

The Vienna Opera had 567 standing room places. It also had the handkerchief tradition. You 'booked' your spot by tying a handkerchief around the railing. Standing in Vienna had also been a fun game for those students battling for the best view behind the stalls. Martin's years of hurling and rugby helped him dive, duck and lay his claim to two choice spaces in the first row, where he tied two handkerchiefs around the places he had claimed. After they marked their places they went up to the elegant Opera bar and sat down on the delicate golden chairs to save their legs until it was time to scuttle back to their 'reserved' standing spots. Watching the 'rich folk' sipping their expensive champagne, the standees longed for that day when they too could afford to sip champers and sit down at the Opera.

'Those were the days,' June sighed nostalgically.

But some things pissed off the standees in Vienna. You couldn't slip into an empty seat even if the Opera House was half empty. Back then the ushers wore military style uniforms and recognized the standees – easy to do since they all attended the Opera several times a week. If any standee dared to slide into an upmarket empty stall seat, the ushers yanked them back to standing room. Once during the skiing season Martin pretended to have a broken leg. In the 70's half the population of Vienna hobbled around on crutches during the Winter. Martin borrowed crutches from a medical pal. But even that didn't dent the armour of the steel hearted ushers. Anyone on crutches could afford to go skiing while they had to work twenty-four seven. The only time the ushers allowed the standees to slide into empty seats was at poorly attended performances of 'Die Fledermaus' at New Year performances when the wealthy were still on vacation.

June was trying to remember if they'd seen L'elisir d'amore in standing room when her mobile rang. It was Chloe Me.

'How lovely to hear from you,' said June in her newly acquired 'understanding and forgiving mode'.

'So sorry, June,' Chloe Me said in a very apologetic voice. 'I lost the tickets you gave me. Sorry, sorry.'

'No need to be,' said June.

'I'll reimburse you,' said Chloe Me.

'That won't be necessary.'

'I insist,' said Chloe Me. 'Bye.'

Snap. End of conversation. June wasn't too sure if her future daughter-in-law had an emergency of a toilet nature or if she was giving her short shrift. Either way June was annoyed with her curt dismissal. The little Madame. But then June revised her thinking. Chloe Me was probably feeling guilty about passing out the night before and losing her opera gift. June walked over to the information desk, presented her credentials and five minutes later had her duplicate tickets.

'Sorry, no cheap tickets,' said the salesman at the next desk, breaking the bad news to a tall young man. 'This Zauberflöte sold out on the day.'

'Any chance for Don Giovanni?' the young man asked hopefully.

June stopped and listened. The young man had the same intensity as Martin when they stood here in this foyer asking for standing room.

'Those tickets haven't gone on sale yet.'

'Anything at all available at a cheap price?'

June liked his gentle persistence. One way or another he'd be sitting down one day at the Opera just like herself and Martin. She dialled Chloe Me's number.

'Good news,' said June.

'Yeah?' said Chloe Me.

'I've got replacement tickets for our matinee.'

'Huh?'

'We can still go to the Opera this afternoon. I'll wait for you in the foyer.'

A bout of loud coughing was the only response from Chloe Me.

'I'm not feeling very well,' she finally said when the coughing abated.

Why am I not surprised June felt like snapping at her? After the amount of alcohol she had swilled the previous evening even a buffalo would have felt 'unwell'.

'It wouldn't be fair to you with this cough,' said Chloe Me and gave another impressive rendition of a woman coughing herself into an early grave. 'Another time?'

'Of course,' June struggled to eek out the words. That girl was a weasel of a lying rat.

'Bye then,' said Chloe Me without a trace of a cough. Click.

Every pore in June's body June surged with rage. That ferret had taken her for a complete fool. First lying about losing the tickets and then putting on a cough worse than Mimi's in La Bohème. The dirty, filthy liar and …. June slowly became aware of the look of concern on the young man's face. He was by her side holding her arm. Everyone in the foyer was staring at her. June realized she was standing in the foyer of the Royal Opera House snorting louder than a demented bull.

'Are you alright?' asked the worried young man 'Maybe you'd like to sit down?'

June took a deep breath and stopped snorting.

'Thank you. I'm fine really, just a bit of a shock. Silly!'

'You're sure?' persisted the kind young man.

'Absolutely. But there is one thing you could do for me….'

'Of course,' replied the young man.

'Would you mind sitting down with me for a few minutes?'

The young man accompanied her over to the couches in the foyer. Two people immediately jumped up and vacated the space. June realized that they too had witnessed her snorting bull performance.

'Thank you so much for your help. I'm June.'

'Alexander.'

'I know you like opera, Alexander,' June said without adding that anyone looking for standing room six months in advance was more than mildly interested.

'I love opera. I'm a music student.'

'Where? RAM? RCM? Trinity?'

'In the army.'

He couldn't afford college fees or was it his dream to play with the famous army bands?

'Alexander, you're so thoughtful, I'd like to do something for you too.'

'There's no need,' said Alexander with the smile nice young men give to women who remind them of their grannies.

'I insist,' said June and handed him the two opera tickets.

Alexander gasped. June wondered whether it was the exorbitant price of the ticket or the thrill of hearing L'elisir d'amore sitting down in a front row box seat.

'I know it's last minute. But you can cash them in if you like. They're yours.'

Alexander gazed longingly at the two tickets.

'My girlfriend doesn't like opera – yet. She's trying. But she's working this afternoon.'

'So, you go to the Opera this afternoon and give the other ticket as a return to the salesman. They're lots of people waiting.'

This time it was June who gently helped the young man back to the Opera salesman. She explained she had given the tickets to Alexander and also asked the salesman to put his full details on the data base next to hers. They were her 'guests' the next time he was looking for standing room/affordable tickets for himself and the girlfriend who was 'trying to understand opera'. As she waved goodbye to the stunned youth, June felt yet another glow. How well she understood the unknown girlfriend. For more than 50 performances in standing room in Vienna, June had lied to Martin about how much she enjoyed the music. She simply didn't get it until one evening she realized that she had fallen in love with the whole opera thing during a stunning performance of 'Don Giovanni'.

As she walked out of the Opera House June realized she had been stupid to think she could win over Chloe Me with a pair of Opera tickets. Just like Nemorino in L'elisir d'amore who thought that by drinking a 'love potion' his heart's desire would fly into his arms. Chloe Me was a liar. But how often had her own two daughters fibbed to her? June had been so proud of Clare who volunteered every Saturday afternoon in the Amnesty International book shop in West London. Until June popped into the bookstore and discovered that her daughter had indeed volunteered for Amnesty but only for two hours 6 months earlier. Had young June behaved any differently? She told her parents hundreds of little white lies. They never knew what she got up to in Manhattan or Vienna.

She would have to invest a lot more time and effort in Chloe Me. June was a woman on a mission.

CHAPTER 33

Café Del was heaving with families and football fanatics who wanted the full English breakfast before downing a few pre-match pints. The only reason Moira didn't leave was the alluring scent of real coffee and Barbara gesturing towards an empty space where a lone diner would fit as opposed to the long line of couples waiting for a bigger space. She ordered a strong Americano plus an almond croissant and tried to ignore the kid opposite her who was spitting out her freshly squeezed orange juice.

'I want chocolate. Chocolate,' the kid screamed banging her fists on the table.

The mother waved to a waitress and ordered warm chocolate with soya milk.

Moira checked if anything in the glossy supplements could distract her from the annoying kid. A DVD was still in the arts supplement – a mini miracle. Normally the first person to have coffee on a Saturday pocketed the freebie. But nobody wanted this DVD on the life of Rodin. Neither did Moira. It reminded her of one of her first projects: 'Painting in Paris with Moira' aimed at retired old ladies who wanted to be artists before they popped their clogs. It should have been painless - reading her book while the wealthy clients painted outside or inside the buildings where famous painters had lived in direst poverty (Suzanne Valadon, Cezanne, Monet, Manet). In the beginning it even appealed to Moira's vanity to escort droves of oldies (mainly Americans and Germans) around the Parisian galleries and enlighten them about the unknown defects and secrets of the 'great' painters. The tips were mega. The oldies assumed she was an art connoisseur. But she was only regurgitating what Oskar the artist had banged on about during their time together.

The oldies loved to linger in the Musée Rodin and slobber over his huge sculpture, The Kiss. Once was never enough for them. One group revisited the Rodin shrine four times during a five day 'painting holiday'. Not a single woman was interested in Moira's sad tale of Camille Claudel the more gifted sculptor who was Rodin's inspiration and lover. Oskar was a huge fan of Claudel. He kept saying that Rodin stole most of her ideas and if she hadn't been committed to an insane asylum for 30 years by her envious older brother, Camille Claudel would be more famous than all Parisian artists. Moira soon got sick of Rodin fanatics, packed her bags, left Paris and headed off to more exciting zones.

'I want that. Gimme that.'

The child grabbed the Rodin DVD and pulled it out of its cover. She then opened the cardboard DVD cover and poured her soya chocolate into the 'cap' and the rest all over the DVD. The kid tried to drink the chocolate out of the DVD cover while her horrified mother tried to separate it from her clenched teeth. The father kept apologizing to Moira thinking it was her DVD. The mother paid the bill while the kid howled about her nasty parents.

The father kept apologizing as they left.

'No worries,' Moira kept repeating.

'Have you seen the Rodins at the V&A?' he then asked.

'No,' Moira replied.

'So sorry about the DVD. But go to the V&A and see the real thing'.

Moira felt like pelting him with the mutilated DVD and screaming: 'I hate bloody Rodin. He always reminds me of my mother and millions of other women trapped by ignorance.'

But what was the use of behaving like a spoilt child? Her Mother in Mayo could have won the Nobel Prize for economics if she hadn't been doomed to a life toiling in the sodden fields, milking cows and shovelling pig manure. Her mother was a product of her time and dark Irish history. Her Daddy was one of over 133,000 Irishmen who had fought with the British Army during WW2. Her poor Daddy was then captured by the Nazis. Unfortunately, his POW camp was not liberated by the Americans but by the Russians. It was a miracle beyond anything performed in Lourdes, Knock and Fatima combined that her Daddy escaped and crawled his back home to Mayo, a skeleton of putrid skin and protruding bones. Her older brothers were petrified by the shuffling carcass who returned to them after 8 years. But Moira loved her Daddy with every atom of her being. How he ever accumulated enough energy to create Moira in 1950 was an even more miraculous event. For the rest of his short life her Daddy poured all his love into Moira.

Liz had tormented Moira about researching her father's time in a Nazi camp and then in some Siberian POW. She wanted to do a documentary about the forgotten Irish soldiers. Moira spelt it out for her. She preferred to remember the man who held her hand, took her for long country walks and showed her baby birds in their nests. Her mother kept correcting this memory. It was Moira the child who had to hold Daddy's weak hand when they went for their walks along the country lanes covered with daisies and violets. Daddy was very sick and she had to be a big girl and help Daddy. Liz had grown up in a picture postcard seaside town where she could spend her Summers riding her parents' donkeys along the beaches. Liz had never known the pain of losing the person she loved most in the world just when Elvis's fiery songs were echoing from their old radio in the kitchen and her mother had started to sing 'Love me tender'.

Moira was about to order another Americano but changed her mind when a man and a young lad sat down opposite her. The father put his Financial Times and mobile on the table. The boy opened his satchel and pulled out a copybook and coloured pencils. Moira knew what would happen next. The guy would bark non-stop into his mobile about the financial long and shorts, bulls and bears while the little boy would sketch. Modern day 'looking after the kid'.

She waved over to Barbara miming the 'bill please'. When she looked back at the two, things had changed. The father also had pencils in his hand and was drawing together with the little lad and showing him what to do. Exactly the way her Daddy had taught her how to draw cats, mice and birds. He was too weak to do any demanding farm work. He helped as much as he could by plucking ducks/chickens/pheasants and peeling potatoes. He helped Moira with her homework. When the boring school stuff was done, he told her stories about swallows, crows, bats and swifts, who could fly non-stop for weeks while dining on airborne insects and even sleeping as they flew.

Moira noticed that the little boy had stopped sketching and was looking over at her. The happy memories were making her cry. She gave the boy a wide smile and blew her nose with one of Café Del's napkins. It was her Daddy who had given her the gift of drawing. They'd have little competitions. He would sketch chickens chasing a fox, then catching it and pecking its tail until it was bald. He'd then draw the chickens clapping and laughing as the humiliated fox crawled away. Her Daddy encouraged Moira to draw swallows chasing hares, or horses dancing with another. He had encouraged her until the day he died. She had stopped drawing until she went to Vienna. When she started painting funny sketches in Café Antoandrezi some students said she should apply to art school. She told them her passion was travel not art. What had happened to all the funny animal sketches she'd drawn in Vienna?

Barbara gave her the bill and Moira ordered another Americano. She would relax, go shopping, have her face and hair done and metamorphose back into the beauty she used to be, ready to face her past in Vienna.

CHAPTER 34

Liz finally checked her mobile. Five texts from the prick - food, wine and the evening menu: scallops wrapped in prosciutto followed by grilled organic beef filet. The fifth was 'not home for dinner, off to Beirut'. Liz jumped up and did a little dance. Maybe she could ask Moira over for brunch ... and then what? Admit all the lies she'd told about Hans? Ask for her advice about the cloned phone? Tell her about the cheating shits in the Savoy? If only she could discuss her pain and dilemma with June and Moira. She looked across the London landscape searching for a solution to her problems, a bit like the baker back in 1703 solving his wedding cake problems by looking at the spire of St Bride's.

She decided to confront Pierre after Vienna. Normally she liked to tackle problems head on but working with greasy cretins like TT had weakened her iron will. She'd also submit her notice when they were in Vienna. She'd call TT and inform him she was taking 3 months paid leave. They owed her much more because of the 'free overtime' TT always demanded. If he told her she couldn't (i.e. leave him rudderless in a sea of incompetent, well-connected pals) she would tell TT to shove a rusty umbrella up his arse and open it.

Suddenly a car backfired in the streets below. The noise got louder as it echoed up to her balcony. Then came the shrieking clamour of car tyres and irate drivers honking their horns and more cars backfiring. It sounded like a battlefield. Suddenly Liz was catapulted back to the most violent days of 1968. That was the year Liz's photographic career was finally going to take off. She had sat her school finals. After years saving every pound she earned selling polaroids of adults and kids riding her parents' donkeys on the beach, she was going to exciting foreign zones to take photographs that would make the world gasp at her talent. Her original destination was Paris and the student riots. But by the end of June the student demos had ended in France. She changed to Prague. She couldn't leave in July because Mum had an accident and needed her. But by the middle of August, Mum was back with the donkeys. Liz was packed and had her new camera, passport and visa for Prague. Since January of that year the young Czechs had demonstrated all over Czechoslovakia and in Prague demanding more freedom from Russia. The movement was known as The Prague Spring. It was still going strong in August which Liz took as a good sign. She'd take stunning photographs of those exciting demonstrations.

But the day after she landed, Russian tanks invaded Prague. Liz stood in Wenceslas Square with all the other demonstrators. The terror and brutality was terrifying. Her heart thumped louder than the tanks. But she still risked her life taking photographs of young Czechs dancing on top of those Russian tanks until one wounded youth tumbled off clutching his bleeding bullet riddled chest. As she took those photos Liz felt her own blood bursting through her eyeballs. But she kept on shooting until the barrel of a gun was fully focused on her. Then she ran for her life down a cobbled alleyway.

Together with the students and demonstrators she galloped away from the tanks that trundled after them down the medieval passage. But in the screaming chaos her camera was ripped from her, the crowd stomped all over it and broke it to bits. She waited with her back against the medieval wall in the hope she could salvage the film. She was about to reach out and retrieve the shattered camera but the wheels of the tank got there first and crushed it to smithereens. When the nozzle of the tank swivelled in her direction and the shells smashed into the walls of the alley just a few inches beyond her, Liz raced towards safety. She was still standing in frozen mourning for her film at the other end of the medieval passage when a group of old women grabbed her. The brave women were searching for their own kids and trying to help the strays they found quivering with fear in the dark alleys. Three days later thanks to the amazing help of her saviour heroines she was in the boring safety of Vienna after an eight-hour bus trip.

All her life Liz wondered about the brave Czech women who had helped her that awful night when her youthful fire wouldn't have stopped her from throwing bricks at the tanks that had destroyed her dearest dream. That was why she was originally fascinated by all the old women in their 50's who sat on the benches looking at the roses in the Volksgarten. She saw them during that first week in '68 when she paced the streets of Vienna and sat in the park trying to decide what to do next. Her dilemma was solved the afternoon a 50 something year old woman sat down next to her on the bench. She proudly showed Liz a photograph of herself and a young American soldier taken after the war when Vienna was divided into four different zones. And over twenty years later, Christina was still waiting for her American lover to come back and whisk her off to a new life. One look at that old black and white photo and Liz decided it was a sign. Do it NOW, not waste decades like Christina. She stayed in Vienna. A month later she could afford to rent a camera. Back then she didn't wait until she was in her dotage like Christina to make a decision.

She picked up her mobile. She wasn't going to wait now either. She needed a quick divorce. She called her lawyers, local real estate agents and TT. She informed the jerk if a 4-month cheque plus 1,000 hours of 'free' overtime duly owed her hadn't been transferred to her bank by Monday she would upload a magnificent video of him in his best bondage doggy gear. (She'd discovered the video on the cloned phone.) She then informed him in her most professional tone that if he didn't comply with her legitimate demand, she would lodge a formal complaint with the union and he could then kiss his career goodbye. Over and out.

She called Moira and then made an appointment for them both in Daphne's - the most deluxe hair salon in London.

CHAPTER 35

'You're dressed?' Robert asked and gaped at Henry.

For the first time in years Henry was wearing a suit, shirt, tie and a HAT.

'And you're so not dressed,' Henry replied casting a disapproving glance at Robert's casual wear – smart jacket, T-shirt, jeans and loafers.

'We're going to Newmarket, remember?' asked Henry in new toff tones.

You going to work in your pyjamas and dressing gown for the past few years is what I remember, Rob wanted to remind his friend.

At the first race in Newmarket, Robert lost £35 pounds on a dead cert.

'Dead being the operative word I'd say,' said Robert tearing his tickets and looking for a recycling bin. But the disappointed punters were not avid savers of the environment. Waves of shredded paper floated downwards and upwards like large sized confetti.

'MMM,' mused Henry grinning and caressing his winning tickets. 'If you keep betting on dead certs, you'll end up dead broke.'

'You told me he was a dead cert and you bet on something else,' said Robert with more than a hint of exasperation. It wasn't the loss of 35 quid that upset him but the glow that shone from Henry's face – that happy glaze of a kid at a zoo clutching a balloon in one hand and an ice cream cone in the other while watching monkeys play. What the bloody hell was Henry's secret?

'We've been waiting for you.'

A flock of racing beauties in their crazy hats (bits of lace and fake jewels costing more than a cellar full of champers) flapped around Henry. They jostled Robert aside as if he were part of the fence until Henry linked his arm into Robert's and introduced his bestest friend to the herd of adoring females.

'Ready for a bevvy, honey?' asked the blond with the swollen lips completely ignoring the 'bestest friend'. Those puffed-up lips looked like they'd been stung by a swarm of bees, Robert thought.

Henry checked his watch, another new addition. Henry, the former obit writer, wittered incessantly about the futility of watches. When you were writing about the dead, time wasn't of the essence. His understanding friends always forgave him for being hours or even days late for an appointment.

'You're on a tight schedule?' Robert asked with more than a hint of sarcasm which the fluttering horde noted with disapproval.

'Give us ten,' Henry said to his harem of admirers. 'We'll catch up with you in the Champagne Bar. Order a few bottles on my account.'

'You don't have an account,' snapped Robert. As usual he'd end up paying. He could care less about money but occasionally he'd like the lovelies to know whose hospitality they were quaffing.

'I called ahead. Jules runs the bar now. Remember Jules?'

'Remember Jules,' said Robert and laughed out loud.

How often had Jules whipped the full glasses of champagne from their clenched teenage fists, and then tossed them and their booze out of the hospitality tent onto the grass? All through their teenage years until the joyous day they could legitimately drink the champagne they had played their 'Is Jules around?' game. Their day at the races was never complete unless they had a run-in with Jules. They used to place bets on how many sips of alcohol they could get away with before Jules spotted them. The game ended the Summer they both turned 18. To mark the occasion Jules bought them each half a Guinness. It was, he said, to line their stomachs because from what he'd witnessed down the years they had all the makings of champagne guzzlers. Both swore they would never become guzzlers.

'Appreciators of the bubbly grape,' was how Henry had put it back then.

'Isn't she just divine?' Henry asked. Robert looked around, wondering which 'lady' caused such drooling adulation. But Henry was gazing at a sleek horse that was kicking up its hooves as if to protest that the grass wasn't up to the standard of its superior legs.

'Look at those eyelashes,' Henry rhapsodized.

'Yeah, maybe she uses L'Oréal,' said Robert sarcastically.

'Well, look what the manure truck left behind?' a familiar voice boomed behind them.

Jules locked both of them in a neck stranglehold. This was the same manoeuvre he used when he hoisted the two lads out of the champagne tent in full view of all the other 'guzzlers' who applauded the elegant strength of a waiter who could throw out two gangly teenagers. Although he had both their fathers' permission to kick their asses to kingdom come, Jules just clapped their backs after he'd thrown them out and told them he was looking forward to serving them when they wouldn't be breaking the boozing law. This time too he clapped both of them on the back.

'Great seeing you, guys. It's been way too long.'

'So long one of us forgot to dress,' said Henry.

'Oh dear, dear so dated,' said Jules winking at Robert as he expertly ran his fingers over the lapels of Henry's jacket. 'But he has to save his money now he's taking that beauty home with him.'

Jules and Henry stared lovingly at the 'beauty' who was waiting to be nuzzled and pampered.

'It's as if she's talking to you,' said Jules.

Henry caressed the horse's silky neck and blew her a few kisses which made Robert wonder if Know-it-all Connie was right. Henry definitely had more than a few screws loose.

'Sorry I can't stay, lads,' Jules said and tapped his watch. 'Gotta visit Marianne in hospital. Bloody nuisance.'

'Little Marianne?' Robert and Henry echoed in unison.

Their great friend Marianne, Jules' daughter, who during their teenage years had tried to deflect Jules's eagle eyes away from them so they could sip nonchalantly to the highest count of 17.

'In hospital? Nothing serious I hope,' said Henry. They both looked shocked to the core by his 'bloody nuisance' statement.

'Baby number two. Gorgeous little guy. Saw him yesterday just after he was born. But the wife insists we gotta visit again today. I explained I had a long-standing date with you two but she wasn't buying it.'

'Congratulations,' they both said and hugged old Jules.

'But now you've bought little beauty, we'll be seeing more of you. Marianne predicts a great future and ..'

'... Marianne was never wrong,' said Henry and clapped Jules on the back.

Robert was suddenly struck how the roles were reversed. In the past it was always Jules who had patted their backs. It was Jules who had patted his back and held his hand at Dad's funeral. It was Jules who had patted Henry's back at his beloved Gran's funeral – Henry's favourite relative and known all over the racecourses as the Great Old Dane because of her many chins which quivered like jelly when she laughed which was all the time as opposed to the rest of Henry's tight-lipped clan. And now Henry was buying this filly and Marianne had two kids. Where had all those years evaporated to, Robert wondered? Had he sleepwalked through the past ten years?

CHAPTER 36

A revitalized June relaxed on her favourite balcony and smiled up at the screeching gulls. She had achieved quite a lot that afternoon. First buying and mailing Chloe Me several DVDs and the enlightening Austrian film 'Welcome in Vienna' set in 1945 Vienna. Then e-mailing her the titles of top documentaries about WW2 and the horrors of the Holocaust. She called Uncle Steven and asked him to email her the addresses of the vast Irish clan and to tell them they were all invited to the wedding. She didn't want to gloat about her mini achievements but longed to tell somebody who'd be impressed – her know-it-all daughter Connie.

June checked her watch. It was too early to call Connie. They'd all be splashing around in the brilliant blue sea with Gabriella. Eleven years earlier when she and Martin had visited Aci Trezza they had fallen in love with the entire area, the exquisite food and wine and meeting Gabriela's family. After they'd made their retirement plans, they were going to rent a little place by the sea recommended by Gabriella. Language wasn't a problem. After 30 years of singing along to Mozart their Italian was pretty good. But after the tragedy of Martin's premature death June was incapable of making any plans to buy or rent in Aci Trezza or anywhere else.

Gabriella understood. For different reasons she hadn't been able to plan her life either until recently. Her father came from a long line of fishermen. They had a huge old house by the sea in Aci Trezza and were famous for their squid which they caught by night using spears and sold off from their beach hut the next morning. Even though they owned several boats they barely made a living. But life was pretty good even if everyone and everything reeked of fish. Unfortunately, things took a turn for the worse in the 60's/70's. Like thousands of other Sicilians, Gabriella's husband had to go to Germany where he got work as a Gastarbeiter. He could only afford an annual train trip home. As the years passed he stopped writing her long love letters but kept sending money for their three kids. It was a case of 'out of sight, out of heart' Gabriella told June. She didn't resent the husband who stayed in Munich. She was working as a nurse, bringing up three kids and caring for her elderly parents.

When Gianni her youngest left for Rome she felt her job was done. She was going to relax and enjoy life. Luck was also with her. In the 90's Sicilian seaside village real estate soared in value. When she rented out her old home, she had disposable cash for the first time and was able to rent a flat in Rome close to her kids and grandkids. She had fun doing something new like in-line skating and roller blading. One glorious night she met Mario who was 7 years younger than her. They were still together and had graduated to deep sea snorkelling. June's grandkids adored Gabriella because she spoiled them rotten whenever she and Mario popped by on their way to some exciting new adventure. Gabriella had also visited London more often than June had gone in the other direction. After Vienna June decided, she'd take Gabriella up on her offer and spend a few weeks in Aci Trezza.

She went down to the lower floor of their penthouse where Martin had his music office. Nothing had changed since Martin last sat at that desk. The walls were covered with architectural drawings of his 'Play On, Mozart' project. Before they retired to Vienna, Martin was planning to turn their 4-story vast London home into lodgings plus recital rooms for needy, talented music students. It was also his homage to the memory of the Vienna Webers who had saved and enriched his own life and that of many music students.

It was ten years since June had given a thought to the 'Play On, Mozart' project. Loss and grief had frozen her into a do-nothing. Goodbye to that! The next time she met her future daughter-in-law she'd enlighten Chloe Me about all the amazing 'Play On, Mozart' plans. And when they were in Vienna she'd check out the success of Martin's first Play On project in the Webers' old Viennese home. The last time they'd been there, 7 music students were happily installed in the Webshaus and the property was run with Martin's trust fund. Permanent grief had frozen her into not checking how they'd done or how many music students were living there now. She'd make up for all that next week in Vienna.

She dialled Connie's mobile number.

'Pronto.'

'Pronto pure,' June said with a smile. 'You're probably busy but ..'

'Mum? Is everything ok? What's up?'

'Sweetheart, I just wanted to say hi.'

'Oh, thank God.'

Connie, the eternal drama queen.

'I haven't fallen down a shaft or under a bus so you can relax.'

Connie's laughter bubbled down over the phone. June could also hear people chatting and laughing and the clinking of cutlery and glasses.

'It's a little celebration.'

What else was new? Italians found something to celebrate every day of the year even if it was only a cousin 55 times removed having their haemorrhoids deflated.

'Gabriella and Mario got engaged.'

'Fantastic!

'Hang on a minute, Mom.'

Typical! One phone call at an unscheduled time and her daughter was going to tell her to call at a more convenient time. Irritated, June went on listening as the background clattering grew fainter.

'That's better,' said Connie. 'I'm outside now. You couldn't hear yourself think with that lot. I'm settled into the deckchair so go ahead and tell me all.'

June almost sobbed with gratitude. Her Connie wanted to have a long chat the way they used to in the old days when Mum was the centre of their universe.

Connie listened to her update on Robbie's future nuptials.

'I tell you Mum if Clare and I were in London we'd thump some sense into Robbie.'

'Now girls – they'll be no thumping or poking!'

Mother and daughter laughed as they repeated the old phrase together.

'I never liked the sound of her, Mum,' said Connie seriously. 'And I liked her even less that time Robbie brought her here. She's a vacuous, selfish bitch.'

'She's young,' said June the benevolent.

She didn't dare tell Connie about the Heil incident. She knew exactly what Connie would ask. 'Robbie's still speaking to that fascist pig?'

'We all miss you, Mum,' Connie said. 'Please come and visit us soon, won't you Mum. Enjoy Vienna and give my love to the other two.'

'Sure will,' said June.

'Just say the word and I'll come to Vienna too if you're really having Dad's farewell.'

How could Connie guess she had no intention of scattering Martin's ashes in a desolate cemetery when they could give her comfort every day of her life from the little silver Mozart boxes all over her home?

'Ciao Connie. Bacioni a tutti.'

CHAPTER 37

Liz and Moira sipped cocktails with Daphne in the opulent hair salon where a cut and blow dry cost more than a return trip to Miami. Liz and Daphne were old pals. When the salon was cheap and unknown Liz had used it in several TV dramas which made Daphne's famous. Whenever Liz or one of her friends needed anything in the hair or beauty zone, it was free and theirs for the asking.

An assistant handed them a drinks list that looked like an embossed menu at a Royal banquet. Clients had a choice: cafés à la mode; unusual organic teas (guaranteed to cure everything from hairy nipples to leaky ear wax). Two pages of cocktails. Even Moira the world traveller had never heard of them because they were all Daphne's invention.

'I've invented a few new ones,' Daphne said. 'But I desperately need some zingy names.'

'Bring 'em on,' Liz laughed.

The new cocktails were arranged in tiny tasting glasses. They sipped the first one.

'Any ideas?'

'Glorious, gorgeous, divine,' said Moira.

'I know that,' said Daphne. 'It's a zingy name I'm looking for'.

'Reminds me of Viennese brambles,' said Liz and burst out laughing.

'Brambles? Now that's weird,' said Daphne puzzled. 'Go on.'

'I used to date a guy who was obsessed with brambles,' Liz explained.

'Still don't get it,' said Daphne.

'Sven was a fanatic naturist I dated for a bit. He'd take me on walks all over the Vienna woods,' said Liz.

'The Vienna woods. How romantic,' Daphne sighed.

'Might have been romantic if Sven wasn't obsessed with picking every bush and field bare if it had anything wild and edible.'

'You always said he did a better job than a herd of hungry goats,' said Moira again licking her lips. 'It was great getting all that fresh free fruit and veg.'

'You didn't have to suffer like me,' Liz snapped.

'Suffer?' asked Daphne. 'Was it hard work doing all that picking?

'Sven did all the picking,' Liz paused and took another sip. 'But then he'd try to shove me into the bushes and have it off with me.'

Daphne looked horrified.

'It wasn't like that,' Liz laughed. 'Sven was a real sweet guy. His passion was the outdoors and he just wanted us to experience the joy of sex among the brambles and the bushes.'

'Now you'll never know what you missed,' joked Moira.

'At least I didn't come home covered in nettles like you did once,' Liz said.

'Nettles?' asked Daphne.

'All over. Front and back,' Moira explained. 'We didn't notice the nettles while we were picking wild strawberries.'

'Plus a bit of sex al fresco with what was his name?'

'Alex, Maxi, Beethoven - can't remember,' Moira laughed. 'But I do remember feeling hotter than Joan of Arc for a week.'

'I could call this a Wild Vienna Martini,' said Daphne.

'Or an 'SAB Martini'. Sex amongst the brambles,' said Liz. 'Cocktails have the weirdest names.'

'Good one. What d'you think, Moira?' Daphne asked.

'Yes! Definitely,' Moira replied thinking that she hadn't seen Liz this happy and relaxed in years.

Daphne handed them another sample cocktail accompanied by a mini crêpe. Liz nibbled the tiny crêpe and licked her lips like a satisfied gorilla who's just had 7 sacks of bamboo shoots.

'Reminds me of my own creperie days,' said Moira. 'Emphasis on days … only two.'

'Where?' Daphne asked

'In the swamps of Florida,' said Liz

'You set up a creperie in a swamp?' Daphne asked.

Moira explained. After years of cultural tours 'he whose name she couldn't remember' had lured her with his dreams of opening a business from his van 'Fluffy Pets & Crêpes' in sunny Florida. Moira was up for a bit of fun. But fifty million bugs had bitten her during those first few hours with … what the heck was his name? He wanted sex standing against the side of the van within sniffing distance of any crocodile taking a stroll to break the boredom of the Florida swamps. Boring, boring .. Ben! She endured his Cats & Crap Empire for less than 2 days. But at least she saw Florida before it was sucked dry to make way for all those golf courses.

'I wonder who invented the expression cocktails,' Daphne said.

'You could call yours – 'Daphne's Hentails,' said Liz.

They were ready to dive into another hentail but an assistant said they were ready for them in the salon.

'I forgot to ask you,' Liz said to Moira. 'D'you want to come to Crouch End afterwards?'

'Why?'

'Pierre made scallops and prosciutto. But he's been called to Beirut. He hates to freeze those fresh scallops and the fillet mignon is ready to be barbecued.'

'How often have I told you I want your Pierre cloned and delivered to my door – just to do the cooking,' said Daphne.

'Me too,' said Moira.

Liz gave them both a wide, wide smile thinking she'd like to see Pierre cloned as Satan's hooves hopping in flames for all eternity.

CHAPTER 38

After her hair had been trimmed, given the most expensive treatment and styled, Moira settled in under the dryer. The soothing muted background sounds of staff chatting to clients combined with the gentle humming of dryers and background music was beautifully relaxing. She sipped her exquisite cocktail from its crystal glass … remembering, remembering.

The glorious Summer of 1968 when Auntie Jessie had found her a job in London working as an 'assistant' in Mr. Marcel's Hairdressers. It was her first taste of freedom far away from the mucky Mayo fields. She had a free bed with Auntie Jessie and two other teachers in their Notting Hill flat and going to work in the morning was a thrill a minute. She hopped onto a red double decker bus, ran upstairs and smoked with the lads. At work her duties were: showing ancient clients (aged 30 to 90) to their seats; keeping the kettle on the boil in the kitchen cum toilet; making tea all day long and serving it in cups and saucers.

'Thank you, dear,' the oldies chanted to her all day long.

On her lunchtime breaks Moira strolled around the shops gazing longingly at the 'hot pants' and 'minis' she couldn't afford. Moira ached to look like those hippie London girls. And she did. With the sharpest salon scissors she sliced a foot and a half off her 'normal' clothes. Cheap purple stockings and long false eyelashes and hey presto - she was a member of London's swinging 60's.

In the evenings Auntie Jessie and her other teacher pals took Moira to their favourite pubs and films. Their top favourite film, 'Camelot' the musical was also a huge hit with the 'thank you, dear' oldies. The mushiest song 'If ever I would leave you' oozed from the radio every half hour. For Moira it was pure torment listening to the auldies chirping along. The only person with a voice was Mr. Marcel who had been a crooner during his Army days.

It was because of that mushy old song and a ferocious Summer storm that Moira lost her job. That fateful afternoon the rain lashed down and the clients rushed in dripping pools of water all over the floor. In between serving up endless pots of tea, Moira mopped the wet floor. Because of the storm, many were late for their appointments. 'Poor Mrs. Marcel' as everyone called her, was very irritated by anything that upset her strict schedule. 'Poor Mrs. Marcel' had lost her two precious boys during the war and had never recovered. That wet afternoon Dehlia O'Donnell was getting a perm from Mr. Marcel and Sheila Smith was having her perm done by 'Poor Mrs. Marcel'. Sheila kept whining and moaning about her hopeless sons who were papering her living room.

'Those two boys are absolutely useless. A few dogs could do a better job and leave less of a mess. Useless lads. Stupid sons,' Sheila kept repeating to Mrs. Marcel.

Sheila was thicker than a brick wall, because even Moira knew that the one word you NEVER mentioned was 'sons' because of Mrs. Marcel's tragic loss of her two brave soldier lads who smiled down from dozens of silver frames all over the salon. Moira was fully occupied mopping the wet floor, zipping into the kitchen to make endless pots of tea, serving the oldies and then doing the dishes. Holding the place together with his eternal smiling and singing was Mr. Marcel. 'If ever I would leave you' wafted from the radio. Dehlia O'Donnel knew all the words. For a change everyone listened to the two singing along to the radio - *'If ever I would leave you, it wouldn't be in springtime, summer, winter or fall….. no never would I leave you at all.'* At the end the oldies even applauded.

Half an hour after the singing, Dehlia and Sheila were released from their heated domes. As the two stood up their rollers started dropping off their heads. Rollers plus all their hair! By the time they reached the mirrors they were looking at two bald biddies. Then all hell broke loose. Two bald biddies screeching and screaming clutching their skulls. A horrified Mr. Marcel rushed towards them. More drama. He skidded on the linoleum, whacked his head against the mental base of a chair and passed out. Mrs. Marcel laughed and howled like a crazy banshee until one of the clients – a nurse – escorted her into the kitchen and calmed her down. As everyone would later testify to the police that was all that happened. Nobody noticed how and when Mrs. Marcel had added a deadly substance to the perm fluids. When Mr. Marcel recovered from his fall he was able to visit Mrs. Marcel in the asylum where she stayed to the end of her days. The salon closed.

Moira was disappointed at losing her first job. But she'd soon find another one in swinging London. She had a bed and a roof over her head and two weeks' salary. What else did she need? But Auntie Jessie and her mother both decided during a very expensive phone call to Mayo that Moira needed to get away from London to recover from her hairdressers' trauma. Auntie Jessie's brainwave was to have Moira join the teachers on their educational holiday to Greece. They had a spare ticket since Agnes, the maths teacher, had just become engaged and wasn't interested in the long bus and boat journey without her fiancé. Auntie Jessie would have taken Moira all the way to Greece but the bus was going through Yugoslavia and it was too late to get her the necessary visas. She would go as far as Vienna with them and stay for two weeks in a safe youth hostel that the teachers knew. It was a once in a lifetime opportunity for Moira to see all the cultural glories of Vienna. She could go to all the museums and recover from the ghastly incident in the salon.

No way! Moira wanted to stay in London. But Mother still held the strings and her young daughter was not staying alone in dangerous London. Moira slept all the way to Vienna which Auntie Jessie put down to post traumatic stress. But it was years tuning out the nuns in Mayo that saved Moira from dying of boredom before they reached Vienna.

When Moira woke up in Vienna, it was a case of love at first sight. The city was chock-a-block with drop-dead gorgeous lads. These handsome guys gazed straight into Moira's eyes and smiled. A most welcome change from Mayo where lads would 'climb over 20 naked women to get to a Guinness'. Every time she asked a young guy for directions she genuinely needed, the lads always wanted to know where she came from, what was she doing in Vienna and would she like to join them for a glass of Summer wine. And after strolling along the Ringstraße a few times Moira made the decision to stay in Vienna.

By the time Auntie Jessie returned to Vienna, Moira had enrolled at the University, moved into a student hostel, was giving English lessons to support herself and zipping through 'Sprechen Wir Deutsch.' Auntie Jessie was prouder than Punch. She told Moira she always knew she had the makings of an intellectual like herself. All she needed was the thrilling academic ambiance of Vienna. Decades later when Auntie Jessie lay dying Moira divulged the secret about the Viennese guys and the Summer wine. Auntie Jessie laughed until her face was drenched.

But when Auntie Jessie asked if she had any funny stories about why she left Vienna five years later, Moira shook her head. There was no way she was going to depress Auntie Jessie by admitting that the real reason she left Vienna was not because she now had a degree in German, geography and business.

She left because of the crater in her heart caused by that awful incident in Count Hugo's castle.

'Wakey, wakey!'

Liz and Daphne were behind Moira hauling her back to reality.

CHAPTER 39

June looked at the awful mess in her bedroom. If a gang of wild orangutans had tossed the entire contents of her wardrobes all over the place, it couldn't have looked worse. She had created the havoc because she couldn't decide which outfits to take to Vienna. Every single one had memories of Martin, like her blue silk ensemble. He always told her how it jazzed up the ubiquitous red in the Vienna Opera. June smiled wistfully. She was going to her own grave in those lovely clothes. In the end she narrowed down her outfits to 25, all of them oozing beautiful and tender memories of Martin. She packed most of her jewellery into her carry-on case. In St. Marx cemetery at Martin's scattering, she'd wear as many as she could. Martin would have wanted it like that.

She fondled one of the silver Mozart boxes with his ashes. She had already checked with the airlines to see how much ashes she could legally take on board with her. She didn't want to arrive at the airport to discover half would end up in a bin. Sitting on the side of the bed June stroked her Mozart box. Why did Martin write that 'fun will' all those years ago? Specifying that his body was to go to science so medical students could have fun learning how to slice and dice bodies before moving on to live patients. His ashes were to be taken to Vienna and scattered around Mozart's grave in St. Marx where the composer had been buried on that freezing day in December 1791.

But June needed those ashes to add lustre to her lonely life. She couldn't part with them. She picked up the framed photo of the two of them which was always the last thing she saw before putting out the light at night. She kissed it lovingly. And that's when she had a truly brilliant idea. Martin hadn't specified 'all his ashes' in his fun will.

She took the arts section from the Times, (Martin's favourite newspaper) and carefully burnt it in a frying pan until she had more than enough ashes that looked like those in their Mozart boxes. She found another jewellery box, tipped the Times' ashes into it and then very carefully added a pinch of Martin's real ashes. Problem solved. Martin, blended in with his favourite newspaper. was on his way to Vienna. She'd have a trial run this time – a 'fun run' so to speak. June suddenly had an even more exciting idea. She would make a habit of revisiting Vienna – the way they'd done all through their married life. During every visit she could leave a tiny speck of Martin's ashes in all their old haunts like the Opera House, his favourite Heurigers, on the trams. It would be thrilling. She'd pop over to Vienna, meet up with all their old friends and talk about the old days with Martin. She would revisit Mozart's grave and leave a little bit of Martin with his idol every time. By the time she too 'threw off her own mortal coil' all Martin's ashes would be blended with Mozart's remains.

It was a fantastic solution. But first things first. The 'solemn' scattering would take place next week in St. Marx with Liz and Moira. And after they had scattered 'some of his ashes' (June giggled about the 'some of his ashes' knowing how Martin would have enjoyed that private joke with her) they would celebrate Martin's Farewell Party in Cafè Antoandrezi where his musician pals would play his favourites. But just a selection. Because they would be there until Christmas if they had to play all his old favourites.

June smiled. Only she would know that by the time all of Martin's ashes were laid to rest in Vienna they'd have time to play all of Mozart's life's work several times over. What a fantastic idea it was of Robert's to take them back to Vienna.

CHAPTER 40

'Your garden is even more stunning than I remember,' said Moira as they walked into Liz' dream kitchen with its wrap around windows and a full view of her heavenly garden.

'When was the last time you were here?' Liz asked.

'Christmas three years ago.'

'And how many times have I invited you since then?'

'You know how frantic my schedule is.'

Moira gazed at the waterfalls of red, white and blue sweet peas in full bloom all over the garden. The brown cedar of the garden furniture blended with the yellow flowers on the organic squash and zucchini.

'Seems the Sémillon goes with the scallops,' Liz read from Pierre's note attached to the bottle. 'It's a crisp white! What idiot mug invented the word 'crisp' to describe a liquid?'

She opened the bottle, poured out two gigantic glasses of Sémillon.

'Wonder if this one has legs?' said Moira scrutinizing the wine.

'Definitely no arms!' Liz laughed.

'And let's not forget that some wines are creamy without any help from cows or goats.'

'Cheers!' The two sipped their wine.

'We can dine inside or alfresco,' said Liz, who had already slurped back her entire glass and was now pouring herself a second glass while Moira was on her second sip.

'Everything's done already.'

Liz tossed back the second glass as she pointed out the 2 tables laid earlier by Pierre – one inside (in case it rained) and another outside in the pergola with trellises of cascading sweet peas. Moira was suddenly envious of Liz' perfect life, her gorgeous garden, her career, her devoted journalist husband who prepared dinner and even laid out two tables before jetting off to face bullets and bombs in foreign zones. How touching for Liz to come home to see 2 place settings, a decanter plus candles ready to be light. How many hundreds of evenings had Moira put out one plate, one glass, one knife and fork but no candles? Lady alone!

Was that why Liz was tossing back so much booze? She was worried sick about Pierre. As a foreign correspondent in war-torn zones, you might or might not return to file your piece. Moira wished she could say something to comfort her friend who was now pouring out a third glass. Moira didn't feel like tossing back her wine but it was the least she could do for her worried friend. She poured herself another glass.

Now it was Liz's turn to look warily at Moira who was tossing back the rare and expensive vintage as if it were tap water. Moira like Pierre appreciated their vino. Then people changed like her deceiving shitbag husband. A Niagara of angry tears wanted to explode through her eyeballs. But she gained control by reopening the fridge and waiting until her tears were back in their bags. Then she picked up the chilled 'rare' bottle Pierre was saving for some special occasion.

'Let's see how this goes with the scallops,' said Liz. Any other freshly betrayed woman would have smashed that 'rare' bottle over the magnet of Pierre smiling at them from the fridge door. But Liz calmly handed the wine and the bottle opener to Moira.

'We'll dine al fresco near the sweet peas.' Liz said.

Later Moira couldn't decide whether the scent from the flowers was better than the aroma drifting up from the grilled filet mignon. Moira was ready to swoon at Pierre's feet and praise him for this luscious treat. By the semi glazed look on Liz' face she was probably thinking the same. Liz smiled as she watched her old friend burying her nose even deeper into the flowers like an excited sniffer dog. Liz' smile widened thinking how she would also add the cost of all the garden upgrading she had paid for down the years. It was she who had hired and paid the gardeners from her income. It was she who had spent hours making sure they got everything right. Pierre only gave orders on where he wanted his organic squash, zucchinis, cucumbers planted. By the time she had finished with that cheating shitty turd his days of filet mignons and vintage wine would be no more.

Moira opened her eyes and saw Liz beaming over at her. She was relieved to see her so happy. Liz opened the little bottle of rosé to go with their Tiramisu. She poured out two glasses and was about to toss it back, but Moira stopped her.

'You have to give it time to breathe.'

'Good wine's gotta breathe,' they both repeated in unison.

That little saying dated back to their student days when they filled up a takeaway bottle of cheap red in the Piaristenkeller. They used to laugh at the outrageous use of the word 'breathe' when applied to wine.

'Well, this one's breathing days are over.'

They were both still laughing when Moira's mobile rang.

'PC O'Reilly what's the latest?'

Moira's face changed to sadness and gloom as she listened.

'Babs asked if you'd look after Sweetie until they discharge her from hospital,' said PC O'Reilly.

'Oh god, no. She hasn't had a heart attack or worse?'

'They're keeping her in for observation. She's had an awful shock but she's tougher than nails.'

'Why did she want me above all people to look after Sweetie?'

'She says you're the only one the poor cat trusts apart from herself. She's weeping her heart out here in the station even though all the officers have been spoiling her all day.'

'Poor little Sweetie. I'd love to look after her but I'm going away to Vienna tomorrow. Let me think if I can find some kind of solution.'

'A solution for what?' Liz asked when she put the mobile down.

'I didn't want to ruin your day by telling you earlier.'

'Tell me now.'

Moira told her how the criminals had hung up three dead cats and threatened to kill Babs and Sweetie. In another part of London they tried to kill Sweetie by burning cigarettes all over her body. But Babs had rescued her by smashing the criminals with her pike and spade.

'And those scuzzbuckets have escaped for years. Unbelievable,' Liz said after digesting the tale of horror and death

'Even PC O'Reilly and his mates all over London are at a loss. And they've tried everything.'

They continued sipping their wine until Liz banged her fist on the table.

'I've just got an idea. I know someone who's a cat person.'

'Gimme a break, Liz,' Moira snorted. 'As if that's going to help anyone.'

'C'mon, get up, I'll show you.'

They first drove off to Liz's office where they picked up Mastermind Shaun, Phil and BG in his cat carrier and then onto Charing Cross Hospital. On a bench just outside the hospital PC O'Reilly was waiting for them sitting next to Babs in a wheelchair with Sweetie on her lap. Phil opened PG's carrier and the cat rushed over to Babs, stood on his hind legs and sweetly meowed. Sweetie jumped off Babs' lap and copied BG. Babs burst out laughing as she cuddled the two cats.

'Thank you all so much.'

She picked up the two cats who snuggled down on her lap and meowed happily as she stroked them.

'You're the only person she really trusts,' Babs told Moira. 'She wouldn't even let my best friends go near her after she was burnt.'

'Little Sweetie,' said Moira all gooey eyed.

'Like I told you earlier,' PC O'Reilly explained to Babs. 'Moira is going away for 2 weeks but Shaun and Phil plus kitty PG could stay in Moira's flat and look after Sweetie in your flat. We just wanted to see if the two cats liked each other, got along and if you'd agree.'

A burst of grateful sobs from Babs. She handed Phil the keys to her flat.

'My fridge/freezer is full,' she said. 'Help yourselves.'

'So is mine,' Moira laughed.

'Two flats, two cats, two full freezers,' Liz said to Phil. 'You won't miss your IT tech empire?'

'It's a bit overcrowded at the moment,' Phil said nodding over to his mate Shaun.

'My landlady evicted me because her rich cousins are visiting,' said Shaun. 'I'm dossing down with Phil and BG until I can find another room.'

'We'll help Shaun find a new place, won't we sweeties?' Babs beamed happier than a spoilt kid at Christmas.

After they left Charing Cross Hospital PC O'Reilly drove Phil and Shaun to the police station where he showed them photographs of the ghastly crimes committed by the gang in different zones of London. They'd escaped the police for over 2 years. Some of the evidence of the animal brutality they had committed on puppies, cats and kittens was so horrendous it could never be shown on TV. Babs was the only victim who had been able to rescue her beloved cat. The police still had no idea how the evil gang had been able to track her down.

While the lads were viewing the 'evidence' Moira and Liz were in Auntie Jessie's flat getting everything organized for Shaun, Phil and the two cats.

'Didn't know you cooked so much,' Liz said looking at the freezer stacked with home cooked delicacies.

'I used to dine in all the world's top restaurants.' Moira didn't want to admit she only learnt to cook while scribbling her novel about alien chefs.

'I wish we could do more to help catch those murderers.'

'I've given the lads a few suggestions,' Liz said.

'The police have been trying to catch those brutes for years.'

'And the lads and I have been working in film and TV for years.'

'And that's going to put those criminals behind bars?'

'Yes, Missy gourmet cook.' Liz checked the time of her mobile. 'Time to pick up Sergei. He's working in a new bar. We'll zip over there and ..

'Down a few. Great idea,' said Moira.

'He's organizing all the filming.'

'Of what?

'Of the cats catching those criminals.'

'I give up,' sighed Moira.

'No. You're not. You're going to be too busy clipping.'

'Your ears off?'

An hour later she had some of the answers. PC O'Reilly had organized it all. While she clipped back bits of the hedges in front of Babs' flat Liz and Sergei installed CCTV cameras. The neighbours thought it was the council gardeners fussing over bits of ancient bushes and took no notice. They were more interested in the howling police sirens on the other side of the road which PC O'Reilly had deliberately set off to make sure nobody saw the CCTV cameras being installed. While the sirens blared Phil and Shaun were also able to smuggle in the vast amount of filming equipment they'd 'borrowed' from TT. A few hours later Moira's flat had been transformed into a complex TV studio. Shaun, Phil, Sergei and PC O'Reilly had everything they needed to film, record and edit. Moira finished packing her bags and would be spending the night at Liz's.

'Any idea when they'll try to kill Sweetie?' Liz asked.

'That vile gang have spent the past 3 months hunting Babs down,' warned PC O'Reilly. 'Nothing's going to stop them now. How and when they're going to do it we haven't a clue. But this time we're nailing them.'

The TV team nodded seriously. While The Three were frolicking in Vienna, PC O'Reilly and the TV team would be on 24-hour duty seeking justice for Babs, Sweetie and all the other victims.

CHAPTER 41

'Don't you just want to throw your arms around her?' asked Henry as he kissed the snorting horse.

'I'd prefer to throw my arms around a pint.'

Henry linked arms with him and walked towards the hospitality bar blowing back kisses to his new acquisition.

Staring into his pint Robert waited for his mood to lift. But the place was so full of memories of his dad laughing with everyone he met. Dad never made any money on those horses. Henry was just like his dad although they had absolutely nothing in common except the ability to make everyone they met light up with fun and laughter. Robert had always loved them for that. But now he felt a seething anger. But why? He 'had it all' as friends and complete strangers told him to his face … and engaged to the hottest chick in the city.

After the second pint he felt slightly more relaxed. Jules had always been right. It was best to line the stomach first if one intended to have champagne. Which he didn't really want but felt obliged to quaff back when one of Henry's lovelies handed him a glass and jabbered away to him about the odds of the 16.30. The only thing Robert was interested in was to get as pissed as a newt until he passed out and woke up as the droll, happy guy he used to be.

'Your mobile is ringing.'

Robert ignored it and ordered another round of whatever everyone was having. He'd have another pint and two packets of salt and vinegar crisps.

'I've ordered something more substantial,' said Henrietta.

Trays of shrimp, caviar, foie gras, and more snacks drifted in front of Robert's eyes. He tossed back a few and ordered yet another pint. At one stage the constant ringing of his mobile pissed him off so much he pulled it out and handed it to Henrietta. She skimmed through some of the texts from Chloe Me.

'Your mother invites all your mad Irish relatives ,,, none of those crazies at my wedding.'

'Your dippy mother … like I need educating about some old war.'

'Your mad uncle Steven …. that old moron….'

At the mention of the word 'moron' in connection with his adored uncle, Robert whipped the mobile from Henrietta and dropped it into his pint. He watched with delight as it dropped through the thick brew making a few pathetic bubbles as it sank to the bottom.

'You can't drink that.' Henrietta tried to pry the pint from his fingers. But she lacked the iron finger strength of Jules. Robert downed the pint in three quick slurps to the admiration of Henry who applauded the sinking of the mobile.

Later he would vaguely remember Henrietta guiding him to the piano where he played – brilliantly according to those who couldn't distinguish genius jazz from drunken fumbling which was what the poor old piano was usually subjected to at the end of a day's racing. He was then driven to Heathrow with Henry by Henrietta's 'designated driver boyfriend' who felt more like dumping Robert into the nearest ditch instead of strapping him into the seat of Henrietta's private plane. His Uncle Steven was picking him up at the airport in Dublin. Uncle Steven – and here's his mobile number and address – will take over once they're on the ground. And here's Lord Henry's card (the other drunk) and he'll take full responsibility for all the costs if anything goes wrong.

CHAPTER 42

Man, but it felt so good to be back, Moira thought as she settled into the plush business class seats.

'I always adored business class,' she said to Liz who was seated next to her but not squashed up close - a vital distinction in business class.

'Me too, past tense,' said Liz with a smile.

June was seated across the aisle from them smiling like a happy baby. She and Martin had always flown business class – to make up for decades of travelling on ferry boats or next to the toilets on cheap smelly trains and busses. On their annual summer excursions to Vienna the kids flew economy and were only too delighted to get away from Martin refreshing his mind-numbing Mozart monologues.

June reached across the aisle and offered Liz her newest guide to Vienna.

'No thanks,' said Liz. 'I want to see it all first-hand.'

'I wonder if they gave Oskar's gallery a mention,' said Moira and eagerly reached out to grab the guidebook.

'You didn't google him?' asked Liz cynically.

'Of course I did. How else would I know he's as bald as a coot?' said Moira running her fingers through her own abundant hair. 'I'm looking forward to meeting Bella again. She's invited me to lunch, and she's got a BIG surprise for me.'

'That Bella is amazing,' said June.

'She sure is.'

In the early 80's when foreign restaurant food in Vienna was still either Yugoslavian or Greek, Oskar's long-suffering wife Bella opened a niche Italian restaurant/food store. In the 90's when their kids were growing up and bankrupting them, Bella's Bistro offered an innovative 'free dinner for the dog plus gallery tour and meet the famous artist'. But only after a three-course meal with abundant 'refreshments' of the alcoholic kind. That was probably the only time Oskar could also be relied upon to join the guests for a post prandial slivovitz. Thanks to Bella's business strategy and art promotion, Oskar became a household name and was now hot, hip and rich. Moira was looking forward to catching up with the woman who had the sang-froid and strength to love and survive decades with Oskar.

As the plane raced down the runway and then penetrated the clouds over London all three closed their eyes, sighed contentedly and relished the adventure ahead of them. By the time the first offer of champagne came around Liz was fast asleep. Moira sipped her champagne and admired the cloud formation. After a cursory glance, the guidebook held no fascination for her. On this trip she wanted to be surprised and bask in all the modern and amazing changes that had happened in the city since the days of their youth.

Moira wondered why June had refused the luscious lunch. The Tiroler Speck was divine not to mention the Gurkensalat. She relished every mouthful of the meal washed down with a Grüner Veltliner which was drinkable but nowhere as gorgeous as she remembered the real thing when Hugo used to take her out to dinner. She was not going to do a June, always dwelling on the tragic past. But as she looked out at the clouds Moira wondered why she hadn't brought Hugo out of the prison of her mind much earlier. What was the big deal? After 30 years he meant as much to her as the tiny plane flying miles away from them in the blue beyond. She declined the hostess' offer of cappuccino, frappucino, or a kleiner Brauner. She too would snooze and wouldn't burden her brain trying to remember all the guys who used to meet them at the airport in the old days because they couldn't wait until the bus or tram had delivered them back to their arms. They were like shadows from an old film - Dietrich with his brother's motorbike, Paul with his parents' VW. She drifted off thinking of Konrad, who was so crazy about Liz that he sold his body fluids plus his blood so he could afford to take her out for half a roast chicken and a Stein of beer in a Hendl restaurant.

CHAPTER 43

'I dreamt I dwelt in marble halls
with vassals and serfs at my side ...'

Robert groaned and whined in agony. What Hell had he landed in? The thumping music was slicing through his eardrums. The pain was exacerbated by two tone deaf singers shrieking *'But you loved me still the same'* accompanied by the hiss of frying sausages. The noisy clattering 'song' ended. Robert relished the silence. But the drums in his hungover skull kept battering the back of his eyeballs. The words of the song echoed through his brain – *'But you loved me still the same'*. No, he didn't. He hated and despised that Chloe Me bitch. Eerie heavy breathing and slurping echoed in stereo close to both his ears. Robert moaned in agony. The words of another song pounded in his skull *'please release me, let me go'*. His head was on the point of exploding. With his last ounce of strength, he opened his eyes.

'AAAAAAAAHHHHHHHHHHHHHH'

Three enormous dogs stopped licking his face and jumped off the bed in fright. Robert heaved himself off the bed and sat on the floor nuzzling, patting and apologizing to Uncle Steven's gorgeous dogs: Finn, Boru and Molly.

'How're you feeling?'

Like rancid raw hamburger meat that's been vomited up by a pig! But the words wouldn't come. Robert tried to make sense of what his throbbing eyes were showing him: Henry, Uncle Steven, the blue sea lapping beyond the bay window and Finn, Boru and Molly panting with excitement.

Half an hour later Robert had showered (but postponed shaving until he could feel his fingers again) and was sitting outside on the patio sipping Barry's tea and cautiously nibbling a fried sausage. To take his mind off the delicate state of his insides he focused fully on the plastic table with the torn faded yellow parasol. Thirteen years ago, he and Henry had been present at the inauguration of that 'outdoor dining facility complete with barbecue', a birthday gift for 12-year-old Lisa – Uncle Steven's love child daughter.

'I'm sorry I got so pissed,' he said.

'Boring!' said Henry and mopped up his flowing egg yolk with a chunk of friend bread.

'I'm really sorry,' repeated Robert to stop the urge to vomit at the sight of all that oozing yellow.

'For what?' asked Uncle Steven dangling the rind of a rasher over the heads of the three hounds who were now drooling for Dublin.

He threw the rind as far as it could fly towards the beach. The three hounds chased after it faster than cheetahs.

'I remember playing some old piano.'

'A jazz version of Brahms 104 - the epitome of hilarity with a soupçon of melancholia,' said Henry mopping up the rest of the fried tomatoes.

Some of it was coming back to Robert, the Nazi salute, her insulting texts.

'OK now lads,' said Uncle Steven. Robert wasn't too sure if he was referring to the two humans or the three dogs who had raced back looking for more tasty titbits.

When cousin Lisa left home and moved in with her girlfriends, the one eyed Boru (named after Brian Boru, Ireland's flawed hero who had failed to conquer the Vikings) was the first hungry stray to come clawing at Uncle Steven's door. The next was the huge scrawny puppy who also found his way into Uncle Steven's heart and onto his own bed and cushions. He called him Finn, (short for Finn McCool the mythical, benevolent giant) when he changed from gaunt to glorious. When whimpering Molly crawled onto the patio she was a starving, bleeding and flea infested carcass. The vet wanted to put her down to spare her agony. But when Boru and Finn protested and barked angrily, the vet gave Molly sleeping pills to ease her last hours. But Molly 'rose from the dead' to quote all the locals. A few weeks later, thanks to Uncle Steven's diet plus Boru and Finn's constant caring Molly became the poster pooch of the beach.

A blinding ray of sunlight fell through the tear in the parasol and landed on Robert's face. The hot glow drifted throughout his entire body and he suddenly felt himself shedding his sadness like a snake slithering out of its old skin. It was as if that one ray of sunlight had melted through the cement coils that had resided inside him since Dad's death. He laughed out loud at the three hounds who were now licking their lips and gazing at his sausages. Robert sliced the sausages and threw them as far as he could. He watched the three dogs glistening in the sun against the blue sea as they fought over the sausages.

'OK?' asked Uncle Steven wiping his mouth with the length of kitchen towel which was his variety of napkins.

'Definitely,' said Robert. He wanted to jump up, run after the hounds and yodel that he hadn't felt this good in years. He was so happy, happy, happy.

Like Finn, Boru and Molly who were now yapping, yelping and scampering along the beach chasing another dog's ball.

CHAPTER 44

The Three checked into the luxury hotel and went to their rooms. June didn't unpack. She was a woman on a mission. She was going to relive having lunch with Martin in their favourite Grinzing Heuriger. She had to resist the temptation of taking the tram all the way to Grinzing. Martin adored the trams just like she did. A cab would get her faster to their special wine garden where she and Martin spent magical evenings lingering over a quarter of wine back in the 70's. She would linger there over lunch sipping genuine Gru Vee, while mentally reliving those laughter-soaked years with Martin. It was pouring rain when she arrived so her plans of sitting alfresco had to be postponed. She walked into the wood panelled room and greeted the young waiter who was standing behind the bar checking his mobile which he immediately put aside.

'Grüss Gott, gnädige Frau,' he said with a delightful sunny smile, waving to the empty places at her disposal.

June sat down at a table next to the window and gazed out at the traditional wine garden with benches, tables but no parasols. It was so lovely to sit in their Heuriger with the pleasant hum of chatting diners who looked like happy regulars except for the ugly old man who scowled out at the rain.

'Bitte, gnädige Frau.' The young waiter placed the traditional small silver tray with a glass, a carafe of water, menus and a basket of bread on her table. 'Was darf's sein?'

For a long languorous moment June gazed up at the young man. That expression – 'was darf's sein?' (What'll you be havin' then?) was a phrase Martin and herself used to toss around in the privacy of their bedroom during their steamy youthful years when the ceiling was about the only place they hadn't managed to make torrid love.

Without even looking at the menu June ordered a Wiener Schnitzel with cucumber, yogurt and dill salad. And without any hesitation – a Viertel of Grüner Veltliner. Perhaps a quart of wine was a lot to order on an empty stomach before lunch. But she was toasting Martin and the memories of their glorious life together.

'Zum Wohl, my love!' June whispered as she took her first sip of the young wine. It was gorgeous – like liquid Summer. How divine it was to be back in wonderful Vienna. She took another sip and noticed how the lone man was now scowling over at her and not the rain. She took another sip of her wine.

'Das gibt's nicht!'

The ugly man was standing at her table, clapping his hands.

'Das gibt's nicht,' he repeated. (I do NOT believe it.)

June looked around. Where was the attentive waiter when she needed him to keep mad old guys at bay?

He kept on repeating that he couldn't believe it was her. Just who was this guy who wanted to kiss her cheeks? June recoiled, started to get up to escape him.

'June, June, June… nein.. das gibt's nicht!'

'Wolfgang! Wolfgang! …. das gibt's nicht!'

This couldn't be handsome Wolfgang, whose main claim to fame as a student was his halitosis. The Three used to say that not even with a snorkelling mask and full diving gear could they ever contemplate having an intimate leg over with Wolfgang. He was a fantastic dancer but the agony of enduring his halitosis during a waltz made everyone run in the opposite direction …… until the day he fell in love with Eugenie. For years everyone was baffled. Either Eugenie had no sense of smell or love did indeed conquer all. Whatever the answer, a few months after the wedding Wolfgang's halitosis disappeared for ever. Wolfgang and Eugenie were besotted with one another and remained so until Eugenie had been killed in that tragic avalanche 7 years earlier.

The waiter brought over June's starter, looked at Wolfgang and waited. He wasn't going to have the 'effrontery' to ask if the guy was joining the lady for lunch which would have been the first thing out of any waiter's mouth in London. Wolfgang enlightened the young man. He and Frau June went way back. June gave the young waiter the go ahead to bring over Wolfgang's wine and meal. But no wonder the young waiter looked more than surprized. And so did June.

What had happened to handsome Wolfgang? Why did he look more decrepit and depressed than those abused donkeys with suppurating sores that the RSPCA put in TV ads? Could he be suffering from some terminal illness? But his hair was thick and elegantly grey. Half the males of England over 30 would have lopped off their right arm in exchange for such healthy follicles.

'It was very short notice,' June explained. 'Robert sprang it on us.'

'Eugenie had a real soft spot for Robert. She always wanted a little boy just like Robert.'

'It's been a long time since he was a little boy.'

'Eugenie always thought Robert would be a musician. She was most surprised he went into finance.'

The waiter delivered her crunchy, crisp and golden Wiener Schnitzel. June wanted to smile down at the Schnitzel and say 'MMM, how I've missed you.'

'Eugenie totally disapproved of Schnitzel,' Wolfgang announced mournfully. 'Eugenie said it was disgraceful that the most famous Viennese dish was made with veal.'

'This isn't veal. It's a pork Schnitzel,' said June.

'Eugenie was thinking of becoming a vegetarian just before the accident.'

The three women at the next table burst into a loud roar of laughter. Slightly miffed at this sudden eruption of hilarity, Wolfgang sent a withering glance in their direction. It was just as well. Because the image that flitted through June's mind was Eugenie looking up at the avalanche thundering down the slopes towards her and thinking. 'Yes, I'm definitely becoming a vegetarian.'

'Eugenie loved cucumber but she preferred hers with sour cream,' said Wolfgang glumly.

He was putting her off the luscious Schnitzel. He started every sentence with a reference to Eugenie. Why did he have to be so tragically gloomy? After Eugenie's death June had written long letters to Wolfgang. She was in a better position than most to understand the pain and agony that he was going through.

'Eugenie always enjoyed coming here for lunch. She didn't like it in the evening when there were too many drinkers.'

June decided that Wolfgang's dirge to Eugenie was not going to spoil her first meal in their special place. She dove in with gusto just like she did that first time she and Martin had come here as starving students. June tuned Wolfgang out and concentrated on the concerto of flavours swirling around her mouth. Maybe it was the Austrian sunflower oil that made the Schnitzel so luscious. When she made it herself or ordered it in restaurants it never, ever equalled the glory of what you could get any night of the week in most Heurigers in Vienna.

'Eugenie liked a good glass of wine but was never a fan of Heuriger.'

June looked at her sunny golden glass of Grüer Veltliner, sipped a generous slurp and mentally toasted Martin.

'Eugenie …'

What was wrong with him, June thought? He couldn't start a single sentence without mentioning Eugenie which meant that all the horrible details of her tragic death came flooding back – the news footage of the avalanche, the people saved, the families weeping with joy when one of their own was rescued, the wailing of the bereft echoing across the snowy mountains at the news of their loss. Wolfgang had compiled a video of the tragic event and sent it to all their friends. June, Liz and Moira had watched it several times with more than a feeling of guilt. They liked Eugenie even if she was borderline 'barking'. They used to joke about Eugenie's belief in the 'good aliens' who were due to take over the Earth in 2222. The alien believers would be rewarded and whisked away in a spaceship to the Planet of Goodness.

'Where boredom was de rigueur and laughter outlawed on the penalty of being repatriated back to ugly planet Earth,' was Liz's saying.

When she wasn't boring them rigid with her beliefs in aliens, Eugenie was quite a pleasant pal with extensive knowledge in astrology which was how she got started with her alien beliefs in the first place. They were a well-matched pair. Wolfgang believed Eugenie was a glorious angel sent to him, a man who had been unable to get a dance, let alone any lasting intimacy because of his incurable halitosis.

'Eugenie loved summer rain,' Wolfgang said gazing out at the rain cascading down the windows and obliterating the view of the wine garden.

June hadn't intended having more wine but she badly needed that happy wine with Wolfgang depressing the life out of her by droning on about the departed Eugenie.

'Noch eins, bitte.'

She signalled to the waiter and held up the empty wine carafe. Wolfgang declined her offer of another and continued telling her how badly he had coped after the loss of Eugenie. He had gone into therapy for a few years which hadn't helped. Neither had the pills which he often felt like taking all at once. But he couldn't. Because if he did, he would never meet his Eugenie on the Planet of Goodness.

'I understand,' June said. 'Grief is a killer.'

She was about to tell him that it was in this Heuriger that Martin told her the joke about the Kerry man and the bulldog. But Wolfgang's attention was focused on his watch. He suddenly leapt up, opened his wallet, indicated to the waiter that he was paying for June's meal, handed June his business card and was gone.

June watched in stunned amazement as Wolfgang raced through the garden faster than a man on fire.

CHAPTER 45

Liz opened her umbrella and dashed the short distance from the hotel to the medieval Stephansdom. The brightly cleansed cathedral was unrecognizable from the soot soaked gloomy one where June and Martin had exchanged vows for the second time that January afternoon in '73 when the only brightness in Vienna was the newly fallen snow and the flaming fires in their young hearts. Martin's dream was to get married in the Stephansdom just like Mozart and Constanze in 1782. But June and Martin could barely afford a plate of pasta let alone getting hitched in the most historic cathedral. But they lucked out. A year after they were officially married and expecting little Connie, Fr. O'Brien made a detour via Vienna on his way to Rome to say 'hello' to cousin Martin. Just as well Fr. O'Brien had a sense of fun. If the kids wanted him to perform a second secret wedding in the ancient cathedral he would willingly oblige. Even Fr. O'Brien couldn't take the ceremony with the same earnestness as Martin who huddled the six of them around the lighted candles and as near as they could get to the 'location' of Mozart's nuptials. Liz and Hans had gone along for the fun. They had already exchanged their 'legal vows' in the registry office. Moira and - Gerhard, Alex, Johann? – also attended.

In their student days only the religious and lonely frequented the pews of that dark, creepy church. The Three had popped in a few times and couldn't get out of there fast enough. But in the new Vienna the cathedral had more tourists than the Tower of London and Westminster combined. The rain stopped and hordes of tourists who had taken refuge inside from the pelting rain now surged onto the square in front of the Cathedral.

'Tickets for ....'

Liz was accosted by a young guy dressed up as Mozart and flashing leaflets. A battalion of Mozarts seemed to have sprung out of nowhere and were cajoling tourists to buy tickets for performances all over the city. She was approached by several other Mozarts before she finally found a taxi to take her to the AKH, the hospital where she had lost her three babies.

She was going to have her own 'private closure' there. After that she'd explore this new Vienna. Looking out the cab window as it zipped along the Ringstraße she was even more stunned by this semi-bleached Vienna. She had spent years walking down these streets where war soot blackened gigantic statues glared down from the rooftops of the Natural History Museum, the Parliament, the University. Now all the 19th buildings were dazzlingly clean. They seemed to smile down on Liz as if to say to her – 'you took your time'. Liz felt like waving up to them and saying:

'Servus.' The taxi sped past the University and Liz had her first glimpse of the Votivkirche where Hans had sold his Christmas trees. Back then the entire building was blacker than a giant raven and the Christmas trees in the snow made the building look as if it were weeping with self-pity and melancholia. The renovation wasn't complete, but the change was dazzling.

The cabbie pulled up abruptly and announced they were at the Old Hospital. Liz took a deep breath and looked at the Church on the other side of the street. This was the Dreifaltigkeitskirche where in 1827 Beethoven's funeral had taken place. This was where Hans had sat and wept for hours after they told him the tragic news of his babies' deaths.

'Is everything ok?' the driver asked.

'Yes. Just drive in, please.'

She would say a final farewell to the awful place that had ended all hope of babies and happiness with Hans. She wanted to tell the friendly cabbie that it was a case of 'closure' but couldn't remember if such a word existed in Viennese.

'Sorry, I can't go any further,' said the driver.

'Only the ambulances can go in?' asked a bewildered Liz. What did normal folk do? Hobble into the A&E?

'The only ambulance in there now is a beer restaurant,' said the driver.

Only in Vienna! The old expression they used to trot out as students. 'Nur in Wien – only in Vienna.'

She walked through the vaulted entrances of the old hospital grounds. Things sure had changed. There were signs for 'Campus' all over the place. Young students were sprawled out on raincoats and plastic bags all over the wet grass. She walked past restaurants and playgrounds full of giddy kids before she spotted a sign for 'Ambulanz'. This was a beer and wine garden and somewhere around here was the building where she had lost her babies. Overcome with nausea she went inside and made straight to the loo.

Walking back outside into the now sunny garden she sat down at the nearest table. The place was quite busy because the wide parasols had kept the rain off the tables. The scent from the giant barbecue drifted over to her. She was starving and suddenly lusting for either chicken wings, Schnitzel, or maybe white sausages like the couple were eating at the table next to her. White sausages were always eaten with the sweet mustard she loved and hadn't thought about in decades. She was about to lick her famished lips and stopped in horror. How awful! This was not how she had envisaged her tragic 'closure'

A snappily dressed waitress was at her table. Formal jacket, starched shirt and dickie bow. Take off the apron and she'd be ready for a midday recital or a funeral. Where were the dirndls of old?

'Would you like a little more time?' the young waitress asked.

'Ein kleines Beer, bitte,' Liz answered with a smile.

Half a minute later the smiling waitress was back with the beer that glistened perkily in the afternoon sun. Liz admired the efficiency of the waitress. Decades earlier Hans had taken her to the Oktober Beerfest in Munich where she was amazed how women in dirndls could carry six huge Steins in both hands. The Viennese Ambulanz garden restaurant had a more modern system. The waitress tapped her electronic 'orderman' and at the same instant a colleague inside the bar got the order and poured out the beer so that by the time the waitress got to the bar it was ready and waiting.

'Was darf's sein?'

It was usually de rigeur in Vienna to eat and drink as opposed to the British custom of drink, drink, drink and have a few bags of crisps.

'I'll have the white sausages, please.'

The lovers at the next table were laughing out loud as they ate their white sausages. Liz was reminded of that evening she and Hans were going to celebrate a very special event with beer and Weisswurst which they'd put outside on the cold windowsill. They didn't have a fridge in their first flat. As students there was no need for a fridge. They rarely had enough money to buy food for the week. Students put the staples like milk, butter, yogurt, or anything that was likely to go off quickly outside on the cold windowsills. Most times during the Winter the milk then had to be defrosted.

They didn't get to celebrate with their special Weisswurst. The crows had sniffed out the white sausages that were almost glued to the windowsill. The birds pecked all their way through. When Hans held up the strips of white sausages they roared with laughter. The birds had reduced their sausages to long strips of lace. Hans insisted on celebrating in the Zwölf Apostelkeller. It wasn't every day they were going to be parents!

The jazz quartet at the other end of the wine garden returned from their short break. They started playing the Piazzolla tango music that Liz had first heard during her first dismal years in Paris. Now in the sparkling new Vienna the sounds of Piazzolla's tangos played passionately by this young Viennese group warmed her blood and made her feel like dancing. She thirstily drank back the beer and piled the sweet mustard onto the bread. That combination was as luscious as she remembered. She demolished the white sausages, the entire basket of bread and all the sweet mustard.

Liz then strolled around the grounds of the former hospital that had been transformed into a modern jewel. She would introduce the all-knowing June to this facet of Vienna which had escaped her Martin obsessed mind. Nasty, nasty, she reprimanded herself as she strolled through the small inner courts with groups of students 'studying' and chatting. She felt happy. She'd had her closure even if it wasn't what she'd expected. She exited the enormous campus and stood facing the Church where she and Hans had gone many times to mourn their little ones.

Liz walked up the church steps and entered the side aisle. It still had all those heart-breaking plaques posted during WW1 and WW2 by people praying for the return of family, friends, children all 'missing in action.' A few of those heart-breaking pleas had a postscript thanking their God for the safe return of a beloved after the war. She paused in front of Beethoven's memorial and noted that 15,000 had attended his funeral in 1827. There was also a memorial to Schubert who had composed an original piece for the inauguration of the church bells. A few months later he died at the age of 31. Leaving the church Liz again walked by the sad war memorials. She remembered Hans agreeing with her about the God question. Millions murdered by other millions every few decades. Why would any God in her/his right mind allow such appalling mayhem? Liz took a long, deep breath, remembered the recent beauty of Piazzolla and hopped on the first tram that stopped.

CHAPTER 46

'You won't change your mind?'

How often did he have to tell them he did NOT want to go the races? He couldn't endure another day with Henry and a flock of lovelies fluttering their eyelashes and pawing his pecks.

'Lisa will be so disappointed,' said Uncle Steven.

Robert hooted with laughter. First cousin Lisa would be the very last person on the globe to garrotte herself because Robert missed one of her horse races.

Back when Henry joined him for those teenage Summer breaks, they spent their time trying to get away from little Lisa who 'was such a girl' to quote Henry. No matter how often his parents reprimanded teenage Henry and Robert for being 'unkind' to Lisa, Uncle Steven always came to their defence. It didn't matter. Lisa had hundreds of friends even before she got her own pony which was a huge attraction for the local lads without a horse. One Summer Henry advised limpet Lisa (one of their many names for her) to charge those boys a few pounds if they were so eager to go riding. Lisa, the weasel, immediately told her adoring Daddy and the entire neighbourhood what awful Henry had suggested. She got all the lads on her side by letting them ride her pony on the beach if they had their parents' written and signed permission.

The two were in the doghouse – or so the poor deluded parents thought. But while perfidious Lisa showed off on the beach, Robert and Henry snuggled down in the dunes of the golf club – smoking the discarded cigarette stubs and drinking Uncle Steven's whisky which Henry had smuggled into a plastic bottle. After their delicate teenage guts had vomited up the 'forbidden fruits' they then got their excitement by slithering like snakes along the greens and tossing golf balls all over the place. The challenge was not to get caught. That game only lasted two days. They both agreed it was as boring as golf. They reverted to torturing Lisa. No way was a girl getting the better of them. But she always did.

'You're definitely sure you'll be ok?' Uncle Steven asked one last time.

'Definitely. But you'd better hop off or you'll miss the first race.'

Robert watched the dogs splashing in the sea. As teenagers he and Henry had another game. They used to go 'one, two, three' at Uncle Steven's picket fence and then race to the sea. The twist to this game was to see who could strip down to their togs the fastest, while running and whipping off sneakers, socks, t-shirts, jeans and not injure themselves in the process. Suddenly for the first time in over a decade Robert went wild. Yodelling like a lunatic he ran towards the sea stripping off all his clothes. He dived in and swam towards the dogs who jumped up on him, yapping louder than a herd of farting whales. For the next ten minutes the dogs frolicked with Robert who tried not to choke on his own laughter. With one last effort and authority he pushed the dogs off his back and staggered onto the beach where everyone was staring at the lunatic. He merrily waved to them and picked up all his clothes. When was the last time he had felt this good? And this was only the beginning.

All he had to do for lunch was open Uncle Steven's gigantic freezer which was full of delicacies cooked by Uncle Steven's army of female admirers. In this part of suburban Dublin, any woman over 60 given the choice of spending the weekend with a resurrected Elvis or his fabulous Uncle Steven ... no contest. Gimme the live one! Robert scanned the names on the containers. Janet, Pearl, Michelle, Helen and many more had made a dizzying choice of gourmet delights: 'coq au vin', 'spicey chicken', 'cod with olives'.

Robert opted for a 'super special salmon and mushroom' and microwaved it for the recommended 7 minutes. To accompany this splendid repast Robert opted for an organic chilled carrot, ginger and apple juice. It was curiosity that drew him to the tall stack of vinyl records. Because of the covers you could immediately identify them as opposed to the hundreds of CDs. Uncle Steven was keen on all modern devices but still maintained that the quality of his vinyl was superb. Robert opened the turntable, chose four records at random and put them on. He'd sit outside and let himself be pleasantly surprised – or not. Given Uncle Steven's eclectic taste he could be end up with a medley of rats and bats, an Inuit version of the Dubliners or hip-hop Bach.

He poured out three generous portions of dog food and then sat down to enjoy his lunch al fresco. Fritz Kreisler's 'Viennese dances of love's joy and love's sorrow' drifted out to him mingling with the gentle breeze and the lilting sound of the incoming tide. Finn distracted him from the music by putting his gigantic paw on his thigh. The dog gazed pleadingly up at him.

'You've already had a huge portion,' he told the dog.

As a response all three barked and then pawed their empty bowls.

'Oh, alright then! Since you got loads of exercise this morning. And this is just between us. OK?'

He refilled the dogs' bowls and added a bone on the side. He was still hungry himself and reinvestigated the freezer. He chose a 'hearty pork, apple and potato – no cinnamon – 5 minutes in microwave. Emma.' Uncle Steven was finally enjoying life to the full. His youthful ambitions to have his own band, breed a grand national winner, travel the world – to mention but a few - were put on hold because he had to race down the aisle to marry pregnant Auntie Josie at the age of 19. If ever a pair were mismatched it was Steven and Josie. After her son was born, Auntie Josie prayed all god's hours that Liam would become the first Irish Pope and maybe then the Good Lord would forgive her transgression. She was worse than a wet decade – according to the stories Robert heard. And then the husband with whom she hadn't exchanged a civil or joyous word for years went out and shamed her again by having a love child, Lisa.

But Lisa's mother wanted to emigrate to Australia and didn't want to be burdened with a baby. Uncle

Steven could have her or else she'd be adopted. Auntie Josie was not having an illegitimate bitch under her roof. So, Uncle Steven bought a run-down house on the dunes which was going for a song and moved in there with teenager Liam and baby Lisa. From what Robert always heard everyone except he and Henry adored and worshiped lovely Lisa. She had dozens of 'Mums' who spoilt her rotten. His dad used to say that Lisa was to Uncle Steven as sunlight to flowers – another thing he and Henry hooted at. Lisa was a gigantic pain in the bum.

He couldn't finish Emma's ample portion of exquisite pork. The dogs had finished their second portions and were now snoozing in the sun filled, breeze free corner. 'Beloved' a song from his mum's favourite musical 'The Student Prince' drifted out to him. His dad serenaded his mum with his rendition of 'Beloved' and had his leg pulled every time he sang the lines - 'Beloved, I'll throw the mask away.' Young Robert used to pretend to be a musketeer whenever Dad put on that record.

Connie and Clare knew the words and always mangled them as they mocked their parents' ancient taste in music! Or Dad's other favourite Mario Lanza's 'Call me Fool' and the girls yahooed – 'You're a fool! A big, fat fool!'. When they got bored with Dad's endless serenades they put on Meatloaf and yelled out that 'they'd do anything for love but' they'd never do that – i.e. sing such awful songs! Dad didn't mind. He was a fan of Meatloaf too.

Robert leaned back, closed his eyes and drifted off into a soothing snooze.

CHAPTER 47

Moira left the hotel with the umbrella kindly provided by the front desk team. 'Always be prepared for a change in weather' was one of the first precepts of a professional tour guide. She picked up the latest mini guides then put them down again. She was not on an official 'tour' assignment in Vienna. She was here to enjoy herself and to stroll down happy memory lanes. Today she was doing her 'own tour'. A quick stroll over to the Stephansdom to catch the tram that went around the Ring to her old Alma Mater. The first change she noted – apart from the throngs of pedestrians in front of the Stephansdom was the faint 'aromatic' pong in the humid hot air. She could have been back on that old farm in Mayo when Connor Ryan was disposing of cart loads of horse dung in his fields. As a child she always wondered why steam rose from that horse manure. 'Cause it just do!' her brothers used to snap.

She rounded the corner and discovered why the 'air' reminded her of Mayo horse dung. This side of the Cathedral was wall to wall with Viennese fiacres and beautiful horses. Business was brisk! Three kids had to be almost unglued from one of the horse-drawn carriages. They wanted to stay on and do it again. Quite a recommendation since kids were impossible to please.

All those horses and there wasn't a drop of manure on any of the pristine medieval streets! How did they keep the place so clean? When she couldn't spot a trace of any dung Moira had a chat with one of the women drivers who enlightened her about the Viennese 'shit bags' or 'poo bags'. She showed her the horse diapers that were legally compulsory since 2004! If those had been around in her Uni days she'd have taken one home to the brothers who'd have told her to wear it herself. She also learnt that the German for horse dung was Pferdeäpfel ('horse apples'). Over cocktails that evening Moira would drop in a few horse apple facts.

On the tram from the Stefansdom along the Ringstraße she couldn't believe how blindingly bright all the ancient historic buildings were. But her beloved Uni looked just the same and as beautiful as she remembered it. Great to see some things had remained the same. But the minute she stepped inside she saw they hadn't. The old lobby now had information desks, cloakrooms and helpful guards. As she strolled up the magnificent staircases Moira smiled. This was a building with more pomp and columns than a cathedral, but she was on her way to check out a nostalgic memory on the first floor near the spectacular library. This was the spot where she and her pals used to smoke and chat between lectures or studying in the library. But a large no-smoking sign had replaced the old tin cans nailed to the wall which they had used as ashtrays. In an age before recycling had been invented some bright spark had put those empty cans to good use. When architectural students ranted how those cheap tin cans destroyed the history and elegance of the hallowed halls Moira and her mates told them to get with the programme. Sighing nostalgically Moira took a quick look inside the glorious library. Almost the same except for all the laptops.

She walked back down the staircase and into the arcaded courtyard with 150 or more statues/busts of famous graduates. All male but not a single female! Vienna was up to date on horse shit but not on women who'd graduated here for about 100 years. She walked out into the Arkaden yard itself. It used to be a huge green space with benches where they could lounge, flirt or study. Now they had replaced most of the green with concrete and installed an outdoor café which clashed dismally with her old memories. 'Get with the programme, Moira', she told herself. She would sit outside and enjoy the latest Uni Frappuccino. But the sudden burst of rain scuppered that idea. She darted out of the Uni, crossed the Ringstraße and took dry refuge inside Café Landtmann.

Looking across at her beloved Alma Mater dripping in the rain, Moira was back on Memory Lane. If it hadn't rained that January morning, she would NEVER have met her fiancé, Count Hugo. The only reason Moira was up and out that bleak January morning was because her witch of a landlady had given her a week's notice. She waited outside the Medical Faculty that rainy dawn to meet Gert the German medical student who was returning to Hamburg. His cheap dump was available and he was going to introduce her to his landlady. But there was no sign of Gert. A drenched Moira crept into the back of the auditorium to see if he'd gone in earlier and forgotten their appointment. The screen in the vast auditorium was bigger than any cinema. For a while Moira watched slides of organs she had inside her but would never get to see this vividly. Then she nodded off, totally exhausted from traipsing around Vienna, going from dump to dump looking for a room with a bed that she could afford. Stretched out on the empty back benches of the steep auditorium she fell into a deep, deep sleep.

Not even the students' thunderous knocking on the wooden desks at the end of the lecture (banging the desks was the Viennese tradition to thank the lecturer) woke her up. Lord only knows how long she would have slept on those hard benches if Hugo hadn't noticed her on his way out. The medical auditorium was empty when Hugo shook her boots to wake her up. When she finally opened her eyes all she could see was dark wood all around her and a handsome hunk bending over her. She was in an open coffin with the Angel of Death hovering over her?

'They're going to lock the doors,' he told her.

'The doors?' (Heaven or Hell?)

'The Auditorium,' he explained.

Gert later admitted he'd spotted her snoring on the bench but didn't want to wake her and admit to his mates that he knew the sleeping weirdo. Hugo, the kind stranger, on the other hand, took her across the road and bought her breakfast in Café Landtmann. This elegant expensive Café was Hugo's special hangout the way Cafè Antoandrezi was theirs. All the waiters knew him and bowed since he was one of the élite.

'Lekker, gell?' Hugo said as she swallowed the luscious poppy seed croissant in three bites.

Moira's German was fluent by the time she met Hugo, but he was the first Austrian who used the word 'lekker' 'luscious' with such frequency. Hugo was the guy who always found the 'luscious, lekker' side to most things in life. That first morning when she explained she was a homeless student, looking for a room and that no-show Gert had promised to introduce her to his landlady, Hugo said he could help. Moira didn't think twice about a Viennese student having a gigantic flat almost inside the Hofburg Palace. The natives always had family and relatives with spare rooms. It was also the end of the Winter Semester. Moira assumed that Hugo's flatmates had either graduated or had found flats of their own. When she saw the ancient historical ten room flat within spitting distance of the University, she wanted to hug Hugo and thank the Good Lord who for a change was looking out for her. For the next six months she did a lot of the former.

She and Hugo fell madly in love. They lived in the vast flat and Moira no longer wondered if other students would show up. Instead, the only person who did visit was the Gräfin Mutti (i.e. the countess mother). Die Mutti was the only wasp in their love ointment. She was viler than any poisonous viper and lived in her own warped world. She could stay there. Hugo and

Moira had made plans to explore the big, wide world. Without mother knowing Hugo had already applied for hospital training in Australia and the US.

Twice a month they visited Mutti's castle outside Vienna. Moira tried to get out of going and pleaded everything from migraine, period pains to salmonella. She never told Hugo that during those six months his Mutti insulted Moira in private and called her everything from an ignorant Irish peasant to a gold-digging slut. But by then she was willing to accept his horrible mother. Because she loved Hugo and he loved her. He had proposed. She had accepted.

They'd have married if Moira hadn't come down with that ghastly bout of summer flu. Hugo thought this was another excuse to get out of spending time with his mother. But Moira wasn't pretending and despite feeling like death warmed over she had gone to his maggoty mother's. She had forced herself to eat the heavy Austrian lunch of greasy pig and knödels which was one delicacy Moira hated as much as Hugo's mother. She picked at dessert – another grease and cream laden mess.

'You're not used to such finesse in Ireland, are you'?

By then Moira was inured to her insults and said nothing.

'Mutti, bitte,' Hugo said weakly.

His weak and plaintive 'please, mother!' was his only fault. That was all he ever did when the serpent insulted her. If only, if only … she hadn't eaten that lunch which her sick stomach couldn't take, she wouldn't have spewed projectile vomit all over his mother and the rare Baroque armchair. She certainly hadn't aimed deliberately at his mother who was sitting opposite them. Moira was lurching for the loo when the vomit spewed out of her and she couldn't stop it. As a future doctor Hugo should have seen how ill she was and helped her to the toilet. Instead he busied himself wiping away the vomit from the banshee who shrieked about the 17th silk in the armchair being destroyed by an Irish fiend – something not even the Nazis had managed to do.

The Nazi slur was the last straw. That combined with the fact that his mother would always be in their lives like a rotten barnacle they could never get rid of no matter how far away they emigrated. Moira packed her bags and stayed with June and Martin for two weeks sobbing her heart out and licking her wounds. In between recovering from the flu and weeping her heart out, she sat her final exams. After that she packed her suitcases, found a summer job selling encyclopaedias to American soldiers stationed all over Germany. With her heart in shreds, she worked her way up through Germany and then took trains and ferries home to Mayo.

There were no phone calls from Hugo. Mother didn't have a phone but he could have called the Doyles or the village pubs. He had written all those telephone numbers in his agenda. The bitterest lesson for Moira was trying to accept that he didn't even try. Oh sure, Hugo was madly in love with the most unsuitable Moira. He adored her with all his heart. How often had he told her so? But he wasn't a Zhivago trekking across the frozen Siberian war-ravaged wastelands with frost bitten feet hallucinating about finding his Moira again. Moira put her shredded heart into the deep freeze and locked the memory of Hugo into a reinforced steel bunker.

Those were the awful lies she had told June and Liz about Hugo for the past decades.

'Was darf's sein?' the elegant waiter asked Moira as he placed the little silver tray with a glass and a carafe of water on her table.

'Pardon,' Moira muttered as she got up and dashed away from memories of yore.

CHAPTER 48

Watching Wolfgang run into the rain June was livid. He had ruined her lunch and reminded her of too many sad things. She tried hard to concentrate on one of Martin's Kerryman jokes. But Wolfgang's long lunchtime lament had filled her mind and heart with bleakness. She tried to remember one of the many, many times she and Martin had howled with laughter. Nothing. Even the other diners looked as if they'd been injected with a vial of fast acting depression. The greyness that oozed from Wolfgang had infected the whole place.

'Noch was?'

The young waiter was standing next to her and looking out at the drenched figure of Wolfgang disappearing in the dense rain.

'Poor Eugenie,' said the young barman, shaking his head sadly.

Dear God, June thought. Now I'll have to listen to the Eugenie Dirge Memoriam again.

'Yes, it was a horribly tragic way to die,' June said and meant it. 'She was much too young.'

The handsome waiter nodded.

'Couldn't agree more,' said the waiter. 'But Wolfgang won't let Eugenie go.'

June took a huge swig of wine. Any minute now this waiter would start spouting about spirits and the good aliens taking over the Earth in 2222 and whisking their believers off to the Planet of Goodness. June wasn't in the mood. She was here to enjoy herself remembering the sunny, fun filled days with Martin.

'He's gone to the graveyard now. Not even a hurricane plus a flood would stop him getting there for 14.29. That's when the avalanche started the day Eugenie died. He likes to get to the cemetery before that. Every day of the year.'

The young waiter again shook his head.

'For the first two years after the accident he spent so much time in the cemetery they offered him a job there.'

The young waiter hooted and waited for June to join in. But she was torn between understanding Wolfgang's grief and the waiter's graveyard humour.

'He turned down the offer. Told them he wanted to focus full time on Eugenie.'

The young man smiled. June looked at the healthy, toned body with the muscles visibly rippling under his T-shirt. What would he know about coming to terms with crippling grief? He was at that age when growing old or dying would only ever happen to the ancient. Later she would inform the young man he should be more tolerant of how people grieved. But now she had a more urgent call of nature to attend to.

The toilets were upstairs and as she made her way up June was also preparing a few tips for Wolfgang. Think of the happy days with Eugenie! Remember the time they had all gone to the Summer Ball when the orchestra had come down with salmonella. Remember all that frantic coming and going from the podium to the toilets. Everyone thought the orchestra was trying to be funny. The dancers found it hilarious to see the musicians yo-yoing to and fro, violinists bent in two valiantly trying to cope with flash diarrhoea and to keep playing as much as they could. They even stopped waltzing and clapped when the conductor and half a dozen flutists fled the stage clutching their bellies.

The next day it was in all the newspapers. Now that was the kind of memory that Wolfgang should be focusing on. At that ball Eugenie had worn a ludicrous cream and pink concoction with embroidered flowers which made her look like a fairy in an Xmas pantomime. Wolfgang had taken about 500 photos of her and proclaimed she was the most beautiful woman on the globe. Why not dwell on that photo instead of the avalanche video?

June had reached the toilet area on the first floor but there was another client waiting. When would the world recognize that women needed more toilets because they just couldn't whip it out and take a leak?

'Entschuldigen Sie bitte.'

June apologized to the old bent woman who was also walking towards the toilets.

'Pardon,' she repeated to the old lady.

She was so immersed in her mental pep talk for Wolfgang she hadn't noticed anyone else around. She stepped back slightly. So did the old lady.

It took several seconds for June to realize that she was looking at her own reflection in the ceiling-to-floor mirrors outside the toilets at the top of the stairs.

'Nein, nein, no!'

June recoiled in horror. It couldn't be. That dowdy old crone with a style bypass could not be the star graduate of the University of Applied Arts Vienna. The last time she had gone to the toilets in this Heuriger eleven years earlier she had been youthful, elegant and dapper. How could she now look 99, greyer in spirit and demeanour than any drizzly November twilight? That couldn't be her. She closed her eyes to dispel the awful apparition. But when she opened them again it was still there. The once radiant, elegantissima June now looked gloomier that the grey statues of weeping angels that had stood in St. Marx cemetery for centuries. June ran down the stairs and didn't stop until she found a cab to take her back to the hotel.

CHAPTER 49

The click of china cups woke him up.

'So sorry, did I wake you?'

'Oh hello, Mrs. Casey,' said Robert getting up and shaking her hand.

'It's lovely to see you looking so well, Robert.'

'And the same to you, Mrs. Casey. How's life?'

Robert knew the answer before she said it.

'I'm mad busy!'

Or to quote Uncle Steven: 'mad busybody who knows everybody's business'. The super sprightly 85-year-old was an essential part of the local seascape, a conveyor of newsy titbits and preserver of times past. She wasn't a 'gossiper' which had a touch of cruelty to it.

'Are you all excited about your Big Day?' Mrs. Casey asked as she cut a slice of walnut and coffee cake.

He could hardly shock the old lady and tell her he was more excited about the slice of cake she was handing him. He was just about to lick his lips when he spotted the three dogs all lined up in a row with the drool dripping down their jaws. Robert burst out laughing and took the cake.

'You're not getting any,' Mrs. Casey informed the dogs as she cut off a small piece for each of them.

'Your uncle tells me the festivities are all happening on a French island. Isn't that just lovely.'

From long experience Robert knew Mrs. Casey was a monologue woman who would even give Shakespeare a run for his money. He also knew that Uncle Steven never divulged a word about his life or anyone else's to Mrs. Casey. She was probably present at the exact moment his Mum had called Uncle Steven with the news of the French island. The woman had timing in her blood. All her life Mrs. Casey had always been in the right place at the right time for local gossip.

'Your mother must be ecstatic now you're finally settling down. It's lovely to know you'll be giving her grandchildren any time now. Your uncle showed me the photos of her Australian grandchildren and their pet kangaroos.'

Robert let it all wash over him like the sound of the waves drifting in. The walnut and coffee cake was even better than he remembered. He relished every crumb. Why was that he wondered? In London he could buy a far superior one any day of the week but it would be merely pleasure for the palate and not nourishment for the soul and happy blood for the heart. Yeah, he thought. A week here and I'll be loonier than the natives. He felt tempted to lick the plate but there was no need. Mrs. Casey had put another slice on his plate.

'The last time she was here your mother and I a great chat about sewing and knitting.'

The drooling dogs had shifted towards Robert, their snouts half an inch from the crumbs on his plate. Those dogs were like a circus triple act. One two three! In unison the three dogs cast pitiful glances at the plate. One two three! In unison pleading eyes looked up at Robert begging permission to lick his plate.

'Knitting has made a big come back. It started in America with knitting clubs. Isn't it just marvellous the way the Americans can have such enthusiasm for something as simple as knitting and socializing? It's still mainly for women but a lot of men have joined in too.'

As he offered the plate to the slobbering dogs Robert had to suffocate the laughter that bubbled up inside him at the idea of himself and Henry turning up at the 'Duck & Fiddle' pub with their knitting.

Suddenly the dogs leapt forward yapping and barking out a noisy welcome home to Uncle Steven, followed by Henry and why wasn't Robert surprised – a stunningly beautiful woman.

'You missed an amazing day,' Uncle Steven said to Robert. 'Thanks a million, Mrs. Casey. You know exactly the way to this man's heart'

Uncle Steven had already swallowed half a slice of cake and had tossed several chunks to the grateful hounds.

'Dad, there's at least 20 grams of saturated fats in that slice you've just swallowed. You know what the doctor said about your cholesterol.'

'Lisa, one little slice isn't going to kill me.'

Lisa was the stunning looking woman? Robert couldn't believe it. She sure had changed from the tough tomboy but still had the bossiness and that annoying habit of knowing it all – like how many saturated fats were in a slice of cake.

'Hey cousin,' he said, getting up and hugging her. 'Still riding I see?'

'Lisa won best in show,' Henry announced proudly. 'Glorious, wasn't she, Uncle Steven?'

How weird, thought Robert. Henry was not his usual arrogant self. In fact, totally alien to the Henry he'd known all his life. He was treating limpet Lisa like an injured butterfly when that same woman could swat those three huge dogs into the waves beyond with one flick of her wrist.

'Thank you, Henry. That's so sweet of him, isn't it, Dad?'

Now Lisa was simpering like a meek kitty thanking her owner for that delicious shrimp treat.

Meanwhile Uncle Steven had whipped up afternoon drinks – beers for the boys, gin & tonics for Mrs. Casey and Lisa.

'Sláinte,' Uncle Steven said happily raising his glass. 'I wasn't allowed to have a single pint with my friends.'

'Single, my eye! You've never had a single pint Dad,' Lisa said. 'When you and those rakes get together 7 is the lowest number. I want you healthy.'

'So you can see her win the Grand National,' added Henry in that new, mawkish tone. What was wrong with Henry? He looked as if a bad meat pie had melted part of his brain.

Bingo! He remembered the only other time he had seen that look on Henry's face. Years earlier he was dying from unrequited love for Clare who got a thrill out of torturing her brother's best friend. He had bored Robert senseless repeating: 'It's love, man. Love. TRUE LOVE'. Lisa was also behaving very strangely towards Henry as if his presence was electric. In a film they could have been a couple taken over by aliens. Or two who had simply fallen in love at the horse races.

Mrs. Casey sipped her G&T and smiled over at Robert. She too had spotted this exciting new development. It was only to be expected. She was always around when the important moments of life came hurtling down the turnpike.

'Do you own shares in that island?' Lisa asked Robert.

'What island?'

'The one we're all sailing to for your wedding.'

'Sailing?'

'If it doesn't conflict with my riding schedule,' said Lisa. 'You own that island?'

'Of course not! Why would I?'

'Property investment!'

'Why are you getting married there? It's like asking us to trek across the Gobi Desert without any camels,' Lisa said.

Henry hooted as if this was the funniest joke he had ever heard. Uncle Steven smiled indulgently.

'Every bride is entitled to getting what she wants on her special day.'

All eyes swivelled towards Mrs. Casey.

'Even in my day, a bride always wanted her wedding day to be a dream come true. But in my day if a couple wanted to get married underwater or jumping out of planes they'd have been carted off to the insane asylum. Weddings have changed. But brides are entitled to having whatever kind of wedding they want.'

'You're so right, Mrs. Casey,' Lisa agreed with gusto. 'Maybe I could get married after winning the Grand National. The groomsmen and bridesmaids all trotting behind me on horses. And the bishop riding up ahead of course!'

'I'd better start making a move,' said Mrs. Casey.

'Another G&T, and you're staying for supper,' Lisa ordered. She got up and stroked the old lady's shoulder before she disappeared inside.

'Such a lovely girl,' said Mrs. Casey.

'Second that,' said Henry and gazed dreamily after Lisa. 'I'll lend a hand.'

He hopped after her eager as a young rabbit chasing a butterfly.

'I've got a lovely surprize for you,' Uncle Steven said to Robert. 'You know it's Ladies' Day at the races the day after tomorrow and I've invited your fiancée to join us. She's arriving tomorrow afternoon.'

CHAPTER 50

After a glorious Viennese breakfast in bed Liz felt happier than she had in years. How could rye bread, ham, cheese, croissant, jam and coffee taste so heavenly? The Viennese were famous for their coffee tradition even if real coffee was a rarity during their student years. Except when Antonina made them her special blend and repeated yet again the story how it was due to her Polish hero Jerzy Kolczycki that Vienna had any Coffeehouses. Andrezej used to try and correct his beloved wife's memories of the Siege of Vienna in 1683. When the Ottomans fled with or without their camels Jerzy the Polish aristocrat and multilingual interpreter/spy was the only one who knew that the gigantic bags left behind didn't contain camel food but coffee beans. Liz decided to check out if their old café hangout still existed.

'I'd like to revisit the 8th district,' she told the cab driver in her perfect German. She had lived there as a student she told him and wanted to see if any of their old haunts still existed. The young cabbie kept smiling, his hand poised on the Sat/Nav.

'Straße, gnädige Frau, Straße Name bitte.'

Were they the only words he knew, Liz wondered?

'Straße, gnädige Frau, Straße bitte,' he repeated his 'name of street' plea.

Liz struggled to remember the name of the street they had all frequented for so many years.

'Cafè Antoandrezi.'

'Cafè Antoandrezi, ja, ja.'

He hadn't understood a word the ancient Madame had been waffling about when she got into his cab but one mention of 'Cafè Antoandrezi' and he was off. He activated his CD of popular waltzes and they zoomed past all the streets and avenues Liz had spent years walking along. They zipped by a leafy outdoor restaurant and the driver turned back to her.

'Neu Schanigarten,' he said smiling.

Liz smiled back. Welcome to Vienna and what the hell is a Schanigarten? As they zipped past another sidewalk café the driver again shouted back 'Schanigarten'. These sidewalk cafès semi hidden behind trellises and plants hadn't existed in her day.

The taxi screeched to a halt.

'Cafè Antoandrezi!' the smiling driver declared and pointed to his right.

It couldn't be. But there it was. It still had WW2 soot on the façade plus the famous crack next to the windows on the second floor. This was the crack that Antonina was always complaining to Andrezej about. If he didn't mend it, the building would cave in and kill them in their beds. But the scruffy Schanigarten was 'new'. Liz laughed at the 'outdoor dining zone'. How could any garden look that second hand? Not even the Chelsea Flower Show gurus could pull off that retro look in a garden. Whoever had taken over Café Antoandrezi had obviously admired and retained Andrezej and Antonina's post WW2, 'preserved in aspic' style.

Two elderly ladies walked by Liz moaning about the Schanigartens taking up so much of the sidewalk. Liz smiled. The auldies were still 'krantig!' - one of their favourites words as students. Liz looked up and down the street. On the corner was a brashly bright plumbing and heating store which hadn't been there decades earlier. In the far distance she would see the bleached spires of the Neo-Gothic City Hall. Why had nothing changed on their tiny old street? The gigantic wooden doors were open and Liz walked into Café Antoandrezi's wide entrance.

No change here either. They had even kept the thick plastic sheets that the British had hung in the entrance after WW2 to keep the cold draughts out and the heat in. Obviously, this was one place the flashy plumbing and heating co. on the corner had failed to impress. As students they always wondered what exactly the thick plastic material was made of. It was heavier than linoleum and used to whack the false eyelashes off newcomers who weren't aware what a belt those 'curtains' could give you. They, as habitués, always entered sideways. Liz paused before sliding through and blinked a few times to make sure she was seeing straight. Unbelievable! The draft defenders still had all the old graffiti they'd put there as students.

It was Oskar who had started the 'graffiti' tradition after he had inadvertently smeared paint on the 'curtains'. When he tried to wipe it away it looked even worse. Antonina was a demon for cleanliness. Oskar knew the minute she saw that multicoloured mess she'd bar him from the warmth of the Café and ask him to remove his masterpieces from her spotless walls. Oskar's brainwave was to transform that smear into a beautiful cameo painting of Antonina and Andrezej. It was one of the few recognizable portraits he ever drew. He told Antonina he wanted her to always have a fond memory of him after he graduated. Antonina was deeply touched by his gesture. After that she allowed all her 'children' to leave their mark on the defender when they graduated or said 'Auf Wiedersehen' to Vienna. Liz' own 'graduation graffiti' was still there - the entwined hearts that she and Hans had drawn enclosing their initials on that lovely day they became engaged.

Liz slid sideways through the old curtains and walked into the main entrance room. Exactly the same except for a mini change. The corner niche with four chairs, an old brown table and a small wooden divider used to have a 'reserviert' sign on it. Nobody was allowed to sit there except the quartet of the gloomiest musicians in Europe. The four looked like leftovers from the Titanic orchestra – skinny, badly dressed, half their teeth gone. They hung onto their cello, violin, and viola cases with the devotion most 'normal' men clasped their beloveds. The young students ignored them and with youthful arrogance nicknamed them The Fad Four. This 'fad' was not an abbreviated version of 'faded' but the insulting Austrian word 'fad' meaning 'beyond boring'. The cruelty of youth, Liz now thought as she remembered the world-weary musicians. To the students they were just another group of ancient, grumpies who shuffled morosely through Vienna. Martin was the only one who got up the courage to ask the dour quartet if they knew Mozart's quartet in D major. Antonina later admitted it was the first time she had heard them laugh. Being asked by a young eager Irishman if they could play a Mozart quartet was like asking Einstein if he could subtract 7 from 14. Once they started, The Fad Four kept on laughing like men who hadn't given their laughter glands a good workout in decades. It was an extraordinary turn of events like watching sour milk change into sweetest cream. Andrezej offered the quartet and Martin a free round.

It was an excellent investment. On special occasions the quartet deigned to play some of the most hauntingly glorious pieces that even moved the callous students while making Antonina and Andrezej very happy. The Four also invited Martin to play with them since it was difficult to play Schubert's String Quintet D956 without a third violinist. It was one of the most moving concerts any of them would ever hear. Four war wounded broken old men and one cheery Irish youth playing the most poignant notes ever written and appreciated by Andrezej and Antonina who had known first hand more brutal heartbreak than all the students combined. No composer dead or alive could even come close to expressing a shred of Antonina and Andrezej's eternal mourning for their lovely children brutally murdered by the Nazi SS. Being young and untouched as yet by tragedy none of them could understand why Antonina always requested the adagio to this Quintet (they thought it was because Martin was her favourite!) and why they always smiled and cried all the way through it. But when the second movement of this Quintet was played at Martin's own funeral the Three finally understood how Schubert's notes could penetrate the heart with its tragic beauty.

Gazing at the former old Fad Four's 'private enclosure' Liz smiled ironically. That Second movement! A few years before Martin's death it was the music used in films and documentaries when 'plaintive background' was called for. As opposed to ranting how Schubert was being reduced to Mindless Musak – something he did daily when it came to his hero Mozart - Martin was always thrilled to hear that Quintet no matter how banal the ad or TV film. It gave him the opportunity to remind everyone how once in Vienna he had been privileged to play this piece with members of the Vienna Philharmonic.

Now instead of a large 'RESERVIERT' sign for the Fad Four there was an ancient computer and a notice that no internet access was available. How did the new owners manage to make even that computer look as if it were a prototype produced in the 70's? It was the only nod to modern times in Café Antoandrezi. Liz looked around and checked in vain for any other changes. The brownish colour on the walls still looked like a blending of cow dung and manure. The plastic tablecloths were still a very faded 50's yellow. There were gigantic paintings on the main wall. But they lacked the weirdness and zing of Oskar's mind-boggling oeuvres. An old man sat still as a statue reading one of the newspapers supplied by the Café. In front of him the little 'silver' tray with a carafe of wine and water. Liz advanced discreetly to make sure this wasn't some kind of 'art' installation along the lines of what one came across in cafés or museums. The man rustled the paper and turned the page. But even that too could have been part of an art installation. Liz was almost relieved when the old man put the paper down and lit a cigarette. He didn't raise his eyes and look at her but immediately resumed reading his paper. She smiled at the tableau of this smoking drinker sitting under a ludicrously godawful arty mess.

But as she walked towards the adjoining room the smile vanished from her face. A gigantic old black and white photo the size of Rembrandt's 'Night Watch' covered one entire wall. She immediately recognized the two figures - herself and Hans dancing and laughing in the snow! Bile and nausea surged through her body as she stumbled towards the bar gasping for water. That photo was taken by one of Hans' friends after a student ball in the Hofburg when about 8 of them were on their way to a 'hangover breakfast' (Katerfrühstück - another post Ball tradition). Suddenly buckets of snow started to pelt down. It was magical swirling through the floppy snow laughing and waltzing with Hans and the others. Because of the snowflakes most of the photos were just a compilation of huge white blobs. Except for this one of herself and Hans. But how in hell had it ended up on the wall of Café Antoandrezi?

The old man didn't even look up at her as she staggered towards the bar to beg for water. He didn't even blink when a young woman in motorcycle gear rushed in snapping off her helmet. The influx of cool air from the swinging 'draft defenders' brought Liz a modicum of relief.

'Hans, I'm here. Hans, where the hell are you? Hans!' the young woman yelled out as she leaned over the bar.

Hans? She was calling out for 'Hans'?

A stunning tall and athletic young man appeared behind the bar. It was Hans – her handsome Hans who still looked 21.

Liz crumpled to the ground in front of Herr Meindler who finally looked up from his newspaper and rustled it indignantly. He came here because it was one of the few Kaffeehäuser in modern Vienna which wasn't packed with tourists snapping selfies with their coffees and other clowns wittering into mobiles. Was there really no place left in Vienna where a man could sip his Viertel in peace and read his newspaper without women – at least one woman singular - fainting in front of his table?

It was simply the limit.

CHAPTER 51

Moira had an hour before lunch in Bella's Bistro. She opted for a stroll around the Bermuda Triangle an area that used to be a maze of dull old streets famous for getting lost in. She could not believe how many cafés and restaurants now cluttered the tiny streets. She kept on strolling until she came to the little café with an outdoor section. She didn't need to go to the toilet but wanted to test how 'friendly' the café was – a strategy she used in her travel business days. The young waiter almost ran in front of her to show her where the loos were. She probably reminded the nice young man of his granny! But the young waiter was visibly disappointed when Moira only wanted a large Melange coffee.

'Our omelettes are scrumptious.'

'I'm sure. But I'm having lunch at Bella's Bistro.'

'A wonderful restaurant.'

'I haven't seen Oskar in 35 years,' said Moira. Thirty-five years!

'You know Oscar?' asked the young man. His breathing had become all erratic. 'He comes here sometimes.'

'To recover from his hangover and give you a free lecture on art?' asked Moira with more than a dollop of sarcasm. When they were dating he was gifted in getting free drinks in exchange for 'art tips'. After he had waffled for 5 minutes on TRUE ART most normal people thought he was either deranged or a genius. They were more than willing to pay for a few drinks before they moved away to another table 'so they could digest Oskar's pearls on the true meaning of art'. This was the Viennese code for 'shut the fuck up about the pain of painting.'

The young man laughed.

'I'm Franz, a graphic artist,' announced the young man.

'Moira. Pleased to meet you, Franz.'

'Oskar is such an inspiration. He's so kind, so funny. Just a moment.'

Franz ran back inside. Moira hoped he wasn't going to show her his portfolio. She needed to keep all her strength to cope with Oskar's latest mad arty interpretations. The young man returned with a sheaf of magazines. What a thoughtful lad! She could relax and flick through the mags and sip her Melange.

'Darf ich?' Franz asked before sitting down next to Moira. He pointed to an array of photographs in a glossy magazine.

'Aren't they amazing? So imbued with the bewilderment of the conflict between modern and ancient morals.'

Franz laughed hilariously as he showed her an article about Bella's Bistro with funny sketches on the restaurant door and windows.

'He changes the theme every few months,' the young man explained. 'This one is the mutilation of

Mozart's music and the exploitation of his genius in the name of commerce.'

In normal parlance Moira thought that would mean 'Oskar is taking the piss out of Mozart'.

The next minute Moira was also howling with laughter. How did he get away with it? '**No Mozarts allowed in here**' was the theme! The main sketch showed a huge, ugly, overweight modern-day Mozart covered by a red circle and a line through it (the universal 'no' sign). Another sketch was a band of drunken players in dirty Mozart costumes. The undeniable Oskar touch were the notes erupting from the players' bottoms and dollar signs cascading like yellow urine into the instruments. Mozart Balls had also come in for an arty battering.

'That's you, isn't it?' Moira pointed to a photograph of the young waiter.

'And Oskar!' Franz proudly pointed to the old butterball next to him.

'Oskar?'

That couldn't possibly be the handsome Oskar of her youth?

'Yes. He's the patron of our graphic arts society. I got one of the scholarships he set up.'

Oskar – a patron of the graphic arts? Now she had heard it all.

'He is such a funny person.'

No change there Moira thought. Oskar was still the fruitiest nut in the bowl.

'He's putting on a new exhibition. It's opening this Friday and Oscar sent me an invite,' Franz proudly pulled out the invitation card and handed it to her.

Moira took the card with a bright smile. The Three would go to the vernissage of Oskar's demented paintings and exchange their private reviews later over a few Viertels of Grüner Veltliner.

'Do you understand this?' Franz asked.

He pointed to the sketch on the invitation to the vernissage. It showed a bedraggled, old dog lying in front of a busking beggar violinist. The dog had its paws clamped over both ears looking as if it was trying to recover from a humongous hangover. The sign behind them read: OPER. Franz pointed to the subtext: 'F in Mozart' and Moira burst out laughing. Franz was visibly pleased with this reaction.

'It's such a dynamic portrayal of the divide between those who understand art and those who don't,' he stated. 'Because there is nothing to understand about art or music. But to FEEL. But this sketch isn't one of Oskar's.'

'It sure ain't.' Moira wanted to enlighten Oskar's young admirer.

The sketch was one of hers. Moira had often used Oskar's sketch books so she wouldn't die of boredom waiting for him to get his ass in gear before they went out for the evening. This was one of those animal sketches she'd done in Oskar's atelier while he perfected yet another 'ashpit mess' humming along to Papageno in the 'Magic Flute'. She didn't want to break young Franz's heart and tell him the drawing had nothing to do with the divide between art cognoscenti or non-cognoscenti. She drew it to distract herself from Oscar's incessant humming (mainly Mozart). You simply couldn't get away from people massacring Mozart.

'F in Mozart'

She watched as young Franz tried to alleviate the scowls of two irate tourists who wanted a coffee just like a Starbucks one.

She couldn't resist it. She walked up to their table and demurely asked in English:

'Excuse me, I'm terribly sorry to disturb you.'

The two scowlers looked relieved. At least some of the natives spoke the right language their snarling mouths signalled.

'We've just been discussing this English phrase. Do you know what it means?'

They shrugged and gave the card back to Moira. She suddenly had no interest in having a laugh and telling them that this café was not 'an F in Starbucks' because all levity would be lost on them. Leave them to stew in their own gloomy juices in one of the loveliest squares in Europe.

'Aw shit,' the woman moaned. 'Now it's raining. I told you to buy that umbrella.'

Moira paid, left a huge tip for the inspiring Franz, told him she'd see him at the vernissage. As she passed the dour duo she paused deliberately and made a huge show of opening her umbrella. She smiled. Not at them but at the thought of seeing her 'Art' again.

CHAPTER 52

June twirled gleefully in front of the full-length mirror.

'You still got it, girl. Yeah!' she told the mirror and laughed remembering how she had transformed her ancient self into this new, sparkling girl.

The evening before as arranged she went up to the rooftop terrace to join The Two for cocktails. She wanted to apologize for all the years she had tortured them with her eternal remembrances of Martin. One hour listening to Wolfgang had almost unhinged her. Her best friends had endured a much more excruciating torment for 10 long years. However, she never got around to saying how sorry she was. Moira wittered nonstop about how her old Uni should have preserved their tin can ashtrays. Liz waffled about the history of the Old Hospital and the amazing new Campus. The minute June mentioned Eugenie the two regurgitated every alien Planet joke they could think of. Moira then explained why the streets of Vienna didn't have any horse dung and Liz waffled about the tons of dung in London which lead to the Great Manure crisis of 1894. June finished her cocktail and decided to do something she hadn't done in years. She'd refresh her image and stop looking like some old dodo.

She got scissors, needles and threads from the helpful hotel staff. She then cut up her favourite outfits imbued with lifelong memories of her beloved Martin. She could almost hear Martin applauding her as she stitched the torn bits together until her opus looked more inventive than any design on a Parisian catwalk. June was thrilled with herself. The half-slashed look was the hottest style of the day. It had taken her hours to finish her masterpiece since her fingers were no longer as fast as a squirrel skipping through the Chopin Minute Waltz in 20 seconds. Before dropping into bed she attacked her lifeless hair and slashed it off front, back and sides.

After her morning shower June scrutinized her new haircut which made her look like Frizzie Lizzie's twin. She'd book an appointment and get herself a real haircut later on. Her new dress looked sensational. But the side slash went up too high. She used a few safety pins to cover up her mistake. Later today she'd go the Webshaus. It also had a creative studio where students designed and made opera costumes. She'd finish sewing her new outfit on one of their machines. Glowing with self-satisfaction she went up to the rooftop restaurant for a late breakfast and to show The Two how she had slashed 20 years off herself without Botox or other poisons. But they had already left to update memories of 'their' Vienna. Hopefully it would be more exciting than Moira wittering about horse nappies or Liz licking her lips about the Ambulanz beer and sausages.

After her rooftop breakfast June wafted through the hotel entrance waving to the staff and resisting the urge to throw kisses to her newfangled image in the hotel mirrors. Her self-adulation came to an end when she stumbled over the legs of a woman seated in the foyer surrounded by suitcases. June flopped sideways onto the sofa.

'I'm so sorry,' June stuttered.

'Non, non, it's my fault,' said the young woman with a French accent.

'I wasn't looking where I was going.'

'My legs were out too far. I was trying to put my brain back together again. I'm Jeanne.'

Jeanne, (French interpreter fluent in German, English, Spanish) was 'recovering' from high-level diplomatic meetings which had been more boring than listening to Wagner being played by farting frogs.

'That bad?' June asked.

'I love my work, but diplomats take half an hour to say what a child could say in three minutes.'

June suddenly sprang up from the sofa.

'I think I've broken something of yours. I sat on this.'

She handed Jeanne the large cardboard picture she'd sat on. It showed a photo of a sweet Jack Russell terrier holding a small sign in his mouth saying 'Nimm ein Sackerl für mein Gackerl'. It was the funniest depiction of a dog asking his owners to pick up his dog poop or else pay a huge fine if they didn't.

'I've never seen one of those before,' June said laughing at the German play-on-words.

'They're scattered all over Vienna. I found this one stuck in the grass near a wine bar in Grinzing,' Jeanne explained. 'I'm taking it back with me and creating a French version. Get those posh Parisians to stoop and scoop their own dog shit. Or else!'

June finally understood the slogan: you'd be fined €36 if you didn't pick up after your dog.

'But how do they collect the money? They can hardly ask the dog to stand and deliver.'

'The Waste Watchers do that. They can legally fine dog owners if they don't stoop and scoop and keep Vienna clean.'

'Waste Watchers!' said June. 'Does it work?'

'Their Waste Watcher plan is fabulous! Vienna has over 60,000 dogs so you can imagine how many tons of dog shit is dropped every day. They started by putting up hundreds of free poop bag containers. But some dog owners couldn't even be bothered to pull them out and use them. Then they had the brilliant Waste Watchers idea.'

'Sounds a bit unusual.'

'Non, non, non,' Jeanne protested. 'It's a fantastic organization. And they've succeeded with the help of this lovely little doggie.' Jeanne patted the large card.

'My grandkids would love one of those,' June said wondering if there were Waste Watchers for kangaroos in Australia.

CHAPTER 53

'Your cab, Sir,' Mickie Dennison hopped out of his old traditional taxi and bowed to Robert who was waiting for him outside Uncle Steven's home.

'The airport and hop on it,' Robert ordered in a 'snooty' accent.

'Yes, Sir.'

Mickie and Robert croaked with laughter as they hugged one another. 'How've you been, Mickie?

Mickie Dennison was a younger version of Mrs. Casey – a veritable tsunami of information about hurling, horses, the economy, the latest corruption scandals. After he'd delivered his news Mickie looked over at Robert waiting for his news. He waited in vain. Normally Robert loved chatting to Mickie but he was in agony trying to come up with a succinct 'shove off out of my life, Chloe Me'. All through the night he had mentally rehearsed his speech: 'Just shove off you ignorant bitch. Get out of …..'

Robert laughed. He didn't exactly want to be 'out of' Mickie's cab and tossed into the centre of the four-lane traffic leading to Dublin airport.

'D'you still enjoy driving Mickie?'

'Love it.'

'Why?'

'Put me behind the wheel of a car and I'm Lord of all I survey. Used to be open roads in most of Dublin, now it's more like the clogged arteries of an old donkey. Why d'you ask?'

'Did you ever want to do something else?'

Mickie howled with laughter.

'Course I did. Route 66, Canada, Latin America. My mother's to blame. She had this book about a woman rally driver in the 20's or 30's who drove all over the world by herself. But in the 50's you had to be rich to afford a car.'

'And you? When did her dream become your dream?'

'Dunno. But Route 66 is my dream. And when the kids are reared, I'm off. We both are – me and Siobhan. We've got it all planned.'

Robert almost blurted it out. Help me, Mickie. Help me break off this shite wedding. My whole life is a heap of dung, Mickie. Any tips? Maybe I could call Siobhan and ask her.

'Bet you can't wait to see your fiancée, eh?'

Fiancée! Robert sighed with the despair of a man about to hanged. But Mickie didn't notice. He was now fully focused on finding the right lane in the ever-expanding concrete jungle that was to be the glittering airport of Dublin future. A huge truck trundled by them with a gigantic sign which proudly proclaimed: 'We're on our way to the dump.' Teddy bears were glued all around the truck. Cast-offs rescued by kind-hearted garbage guys? But how did teddy bears manage to look so chirpy even when they were glued to a filthy dumpster? And what on earth was that woman doing playing a cello on the sidewalk?

'I don't believe it. It can't be.'

Miranda? What in God's earth was she doing playing the cello at the entrance to the underground car park at Dublin airport?

'Stop. Stop. Mickie, stop.'

'Even the Virgin Mary couldn't stop here to give birth.'

Robert looked back but the huge dumpsters, construction vehicles and taxis had obliterated his view of the cellist.

'Why did you want me to stop there?' asked Mickie.

'Sorry. My mistake.'

Emotional stress meltdown? Robert shook his head and tried to banish the hallucination of Miranda, his very first girlfriend playing the cello at Dublin airport. Deep breaths, Robert. It was a trick caused by the polluted light, racket and stress that he'd seen Miranda playing the cello. At school she played the viola and the violin. He played the piano. It was when they were playing Schumann together at the age of 15 that he had launched into a jazz rendition which made the entire class laugh and howl. Robert couldn't care less. It was only a stupid school class and he hated Miranda. The teachers punished him even if they attributed his behaviour to 'teenage stroppiness'. Robert remembered it differently. That was the day he discovered his passion and gift for jazz/classical improvisation. Miranda didn't speak to him again until he was 17 when ...

'You're here,' Mickie announced. 'Just gimme a bell when ye're out.'

CHAPTER 54

Liz opened her eyes and quickly closed them again. It simply couldn't be true. She was having an 'out of body experience'. Here she was on the floor of Cafè Antoandrezi slumped into the arms of a young man who was the spitting image of Hans.

'What's your name?' she croaked.

'Hans.'

Liz moaned. She closed her eyes and heard the young woman asking Hans if they should call the ambulance.

'D'you know where you are?' The young man asked in German.

If she hadn't been hallucinating Liz would have answered: 'I spent most of my youth here. My name is on the plastic sheet that keeps the draught out.'

'Hans, I'm calling the ambulance.'

'No, don't,' Liz croaked. 'I'm sorry. I mistook you for somebody else.'

She had seen the tattoos on the young man's arm. He wasn't 'her' Hans.

'I'm so sorry. But I thought you were somebody I knew in a former lifetime.'

Hans and the young woman again exchanged worried glances hearing the words 'in a former lifetime'.

'I used to come here as a student,' Liz explained. 'I'm in that old photograph. But who put it up in there?'

'You mean the couple in the snow?'

'Yes. That's an old photograph of myself and my husband Hans. Or rather my former husband.'

'You're the woman in that photograph?'

'Yes.'

'But that's incredible,' said the young man.

'Yes,' said Liz, 'it is incredible how people age and no longer look the way they used to when they were in their 20's.'

'No, that's not what I meant. I'm so sorry,' said the young man. 'I should have introduced myself. I'm Hans' nephew - Hans Dietrich – Hans D.'

'You look exactly like him,' said Liz laughing.

'But this is amazing,' said Hans D. and then rushed over to tell the old man the exciting news. Any other young man, Liz thought would have said 'so that's why you fainted!'. But Hans D. wanted to spread the good news as if she were somebody who'd just risen from the dead. The elderly man did not share their excitement. He angrily threw his newspaper aside and marched out. Hans D. politely ran ahead and opened the door for him. He needn't have bothered because the old guy only growled at him.

'He likes to have the place to himself,' he explained to Liz.

'He reminds me of the grim reaper sitting there every midday,' sniffed Lena. 'Why doesn't he go and drink his wine in the graveyard?'

'Because he's a valued customer,' Hans D. joked.

'And one of these days I'm going to...,'

She didn't finish her threatening sentence because Liz had burst out laughing. This was one of the weirdest days she'd had in years.

'Lena, this is the famous Liz,' said Hans D.

'Famous?' queried Liz in her politest tone.

'Please, let me get you something to drink, to eat,' said young Hans D.

'I just want to know how that photograph ended up on that wall.'

'It's got quite a history,' answered Hans D.

'And maybe you could give her a quick synopsis within our lifetimes,' said Lena with a wide smile. 'Unless you want me to give her the two-line version.'

Twenty minutes later Liz had all the answers.

CHAPTER 55

On her way to Bella's Bistro Moira felt like yodelling in the rain. What a turn up for the books! She only dashed off those animal sketches to annoy Oscar or bring a scintilla of reality into his nutty arty studio. She was so busy trying to remember some of her satirical 'paintings' she almost missed the vaulted entrance to Bella's Bistro with an array of silver dog bowls plus the canine water fountain. This wasn't uncommon in Vienna – city of dogs. Some restaurants even had special menus for man's best friend. But not many sophisticated restaurants adorned their entrance with framed animal drawings from Moira's 'sketch archive'. The largest drawing showed a slobbering hound with the speech bubble 'ich bin hungrig'. This was the mistake all English speakers made - 'I am hungry' instead of the correct German 'ich habe Hunger' i.e. 'I have hunger'. Moira counted 10 of her old drawings! What had happened to Oskar the artist who in their dating days used to dance on her sketches to show her what he thought of her desecration of 'True Art'?

A smartly dressed waiter whipped open the door and invited her inside. The joint was jumping and there wasn't a spare seat to be had in this thriving restaurant.

Drool gushed against her teeth as another waiter glided by with four portions of glistening melon and prosciutto.

'Moira! Moira!'

Age certainly hadn't withered effervescent Bella. They hugged and laughed like long lost friends. Then in that stance so typical of all women they stood back and assessed one another.

'You look fantastic, Moira,' said Bella.

'You look even more fantastic, Bella,' said Moira and almost trotted out the Irish phrase she heard down the decades when she returned to Mayo. 'You haven't changed a bit'

But changed they had even if neither looked like ancient hags. As they walked through the restaurant the diners smiled up at them. The men looked straight into their eyes as opposed to London males who needed a degree in ophthalmology before they would gaze straight into a woman's eyes. Yes, this was definitely the Vienna Moira remembered. She felt her old age blues evaporating like morning mist. This was her kind of menu - tasty, crunchy, mature men and even more luscious food. Bella ushered her towards the kitchen area. The busy chrome and silver kitchen with the elegantly dressed cooks in yellow and black was a symphony in buzz, hiss, sear, fry, crackle. Hopefully they'd soon be sitting down to their reunion lunch. Unless of course Oskar had changed and was late for lunch. Also in their starving student days Oscar could sniff out a free snack better than a bear getting a whiff of a salmon ten miles downstream. Moira mentally checked herself. Stop thinking of people as they were 40 years ago.

'This time I am definitely going to kill him, Mauro,' Bella was saying to her manager.

'Calma, calma, Bella.'

'They ran out of gas in the middle of nowhere? This time I'm definitely going to gut and barbecue him.'

'With green salad on the side or a pikant Sauerkraut?' Mauro asked and laughed.

Moira didn't have to be told. Oskar was in the dog's house.

'I'd better find somebody to look after the kids,' said Bella.

'Anything I can do?' asked Moira. 'We can always postpone lunch.'

'I'm so sorry, Moira,' said Bella.

'There's nothing to be sorry about, Bella.'

Moira patted Bella on the back. Forget about hiking up Mount Everest in your bikini. Thirty-five years with Oskar and Bella was still able to forgive and smile! Bella was a real woman!

'What happened this time?'

Over a pre-lunch glass of champagne and a platter of mouth-watering hors d'oeuvres, Bella enlightened her.

'He hates driving.'

Moira nodded. Oskar hated everything that wasn't connected to his 'art'.

'What happened to-day?'

'Today Klaus drove him to the Wachau … at four o'clock in the morning. He wanted to get inspiration for his next range of masterpieces.'

Bella threw a withering glance at the messy masterpieces that glowered down at them from the walls in the 'gallery room' where Oskar gave his unique and rare lectures to diners who had paid handsomely for the 'dinner/talk/complimentary dog snacks'.

'Something about mid-Summer madness or late summer melancholia,' said Bella with a long-suffering sigh. 'He's been out sniffing the pre-dawn colours in Burgenland or the Wachau. Klaus drives him there. But today Klaus was supposed to look after my grandkids and take them to University.'

'Your grandkids are already going to University?' she asked.

It took a lot to shake Moira. But the fact that Oskar's grandchildren were attending University was much weirder than the artist scuttling around the Austrian countryside soaking up colours for an upcoming exhibition on Midsummer Madness.

'They'll be here any minute. They're dying to meet you.'

'Me?' asked Moira bewildered.

'When the grandkids were small Oskar used to babysit them in his studio. Babysit! He couldn't even spell babysit. He gave them paper and paints and told them to get on with it. They loved copying your animal sketches.'

'Oh dear!'

'They had no interest in Grandad's masterpieces but loved Frau Maria's work. They couldn't pronounce Moira.'

'Aiee!

'That wasn't the only thing,' said Bella. 'Ten years ago this place was bankrupting us. That's when Claudia our youngest suggested Dad do dog portraits for clients who had the deluxe dinner. Claudia had just started in advertising and of course knew it all at 19.'

'Didn't we all?'

'Then she tells him she earns more than him with her part-time job.'

'Low blow.'

'A true teenager! But Oskar wanted them to be proud of him. He did those dog portraits. Most times the poor creatures looked like a cross between a degutted bear and the makings of a Kebab. But after Oskar had given the owners' an arty lecture about the ephemeral nature of dogs' souls and how Darwinesque the dog's ears were – well, he became the hottest thing in town. Or rather the restaurant did.'

'And he hated every minute of doing those dog portraits?'

'Oskar always hated anything normal.'

'How did you do it? Cope with the art speak I mean?' Moira asked.

'We had a pact. I wouldn't bore him with my recipes. And he would cut down on the art talk. He never did. I'd give him my complex recipe for pasta alle sarde and he'd waffle about painting bleeding tomatoes to signify the blood of peasants toiling in the fields to grow the wheat for the spagetti that the rich owners would sell for a profit – blah blah blah.'

'The things we do for love,' said Moira laughing.

'Speaking of which. Heinz still comes in asking for you.'

'Heinz?'

'He never got over you.'

'Heinz?'

'Big teeth, gorgeous eyes, Professor, wittering about Kant, Sartre, Wittgenstein, never got over you.'

'How's Professor Witless these days?'

'Retired, four ex-wives, 30 portraits of you.'

They were still laughing when the door burst open and four kids rushed in all carrying blue and orange satchels.

'Grandma, we're going to be late for our lecture,' said the tallest girl who looked about 11.

'We won't graduate if we miss today's lectures,' said a very solemn girl.

'They take University very seriously,' explained Bella.

'Which University?' asked the bewildered Moira. Those kids looked as if they'd just graduated from the sandpit.

'The University of Vienna. Your Alma Mater,' said Bella.

'I see,' said Moira when in fact she didn't see at all.

'They're off to the KINDERuni,' Bella explained.

'A new type of Kindergarten?'

Moira was relieved. It was just kid stuff. She wasn't surrounded by a gang of geniuses off to University before they were even teenagers.

'No. It is NOT a Kindergarten,' said the youngest little girl who hadn't pranced around her like the rest of them. 'It's the enjoyable quest for knowledge at the University of Vienna.'

'Granny, we're going to be late.'

'Granny, we need to get our stamps today or we don't graduate.'

'Madonna Santa, I'm going to get you there,' said Bella picking up her mobile.

'What's your name?' the solemn little girl asked Moira.

'That's Frau Moira,' said Bella punching in another number.

'You're Frau Maria the painter?'

The kids rushed over to Moira with the eagerness of football fans meeting their star player and proudly introducing themselves: Bella's grandkids Sofia and Josef, their friends Lisa and Nina, the serious girl.

'I love your work, Frau Maria,' said Nina gazing up at Moira with a glow in her face that most kids reserve for puppies.

'Thank you.'

Was it any wonder she couldn't think straight? Kids going to University, Oscar gone awol, lunch postponed and four kids clamouring around her like crazed fans calling her Maria.

'Will you teach me please?' asked Nina.

'What...?' asked the bewildered Moira.

'How you get your dogs to laugh? I've never seen a dog laugh.'

'What lecture are you attending today?' Moira asked.

'*Did tourism exist in Ancient Rome?*' the four kids chanted.

Moira racked her brains. Tourism in Ancient Rome? She hadn't a clue. And she'd spent more time doing tourism in Rome than most Italians.

'It's the last lecture this year on our curriculum,' said Nina, showing Moira a Kinderuniwien 2008 booklet with 3 jumping kids on the cover.

Moira read the synopsis of the lecture about tourism in Ancient Rome. Today the kids would learn how mobile the Romans were long before cars, railways and planes had been invented. The Romans rode horses. That was all Moira knew. She hadn't a clue if the Romans had donkeys or if they conquered Europe hopping around on chimps.

'Have you been to any of these lectures, Bella?' she asked in desperation.

'Grannies can't attend OUR lectures,' Sofia announced proud as a pigeon who's just fought off a vulture.

'If they qualify, some journalists may attend our lectures,' Josef added.

'Frau Maria is a travel journalist,' Nina announced.

'They still have some of those magazines you wrote for,' said Bella

'Any chance I could sit in on that lecture?' Moira asked.

'You have to get a badge like us,' said Sofia.

'Frau Maria needs an adult badge,' Josef corrected her.

'We'll show you where to get one.'

'Granny, the lectures start in an hour.'

And that's when Moira had her brilliant brainwave.

'Bella, why can't I accompany the kids to the Uni? I can drop them off, chaperone them, see if I can attend this lecture. OK?'

Bella threw her arms around Moira.

'Grazie, grazie. I'll make you some lunch. Any preferences?'

'Surprise me,' said Moira with a smile.

CHAPTER 56

Mickie's first remark to the fiancée with four large suitcases was:

'You're staying with us for a while then?'

Madame ignored him.

'Why didn't you order me a proper taxi?' she snapped at Robert.

'This is a proper taxi.'

Whereupon the young Madame sniffed, looked around her and said:

'I thought Dublin would be a bit more advanced.'

'Just get in the cab,' Robert ordered.

Even the teddy bears on the back of the dumpster looked shocked at the sharp tone to Robert's voice. He was so furious with the way she had treated Mickie that he was ready to dump her right here and now at Dublin airport. But a mobile yelped and Chloe Me dived into her £600 bag. Robert knew the price because she kept repeating that it cost £2,000 in a shop but her friend had bought it directly from the designer.

'I'll call you back. I'm in Dublin.'

She clicked her mobile shut, got into the back and waved dismissively at Robert like Marie Antoinette sacking an apprentice cake maker. Robert banged her door and got into the front with Mickie. Why didn't he just tell her to piss off back to London and get the hell out of his life? Mickie wouldn't be surprised. Years of driving a taxi in Dublin he'd seen and heard it all.

'Got any more jokes?' he asked Mickie.

'I got a few great shark jokes,' said Mickie. 'Heard the one about the Kerryman and the sharks?' and he was off.

Robert was semi relaxed by the time they drove by a bus stop on the main highway between the airport and Malahide.

'Oh Christ!'

He could not believe his eyes. Miranda was now sitting alone at a bus stop playing a cello. He jerked his head around to get a better look but the hallucination was gone. He should have had that pint at the airport. He hated a quick pint but if he'd known that the stress of breaking off his wedding would lead to another Miranda mirage he'd have had several. For 2 years after his jazz break out at school all the schoolgirls had only one word for him. LOSER! It never bothered him. Young Robert knew his prodigy talent flowed from his fingers along the piano keys and blended into musical magic the way flour, eggs and a bit of butter metamorphosed into lip-smacking pastries given the right cook. At seventeen he had everything – genius talent and a guaranteed future in business after a few fun years at Oxford. He'd satisfy the pater's plan to graduate with a degree which he would do with nada problema because apart from his piano genius he also had a brilliant mind for maths. He had every intention of coasting right into a jazz/classical career after the gap year and fun at Oxford. The only time he ever had a doubt back then was when Miranda spoke to him for the first time since he'd 'wrecked' their school performance. She had plonked herself down next to him in the canteen one day and asked:

'Why aren't you applying to music school?'

'Don't need to,' would have been his usual arrogant response. Or – 'did any of the immortals have to do music school'? But he had never been that close to her before. He was looking into her bright eyes and his mouth went drier than sand in the desert.

'You're going to faff away the most important years of your life living it large at Oxford.'

She sounded just like some old lady on the telly. He laughed.

'I'm serious. You got the gift and you'd prefer to piss it away with your mates. With your gift you should care about music.'

'I couldn't live without music.'

She smiled and got up.

'D'you want to come to … '

They dated for six months saturated with exquisite music and lessons in sex. When she started at the RCM they drifted apart. Music and practicing took over Miranda's life. Robert was learning that no matter how talented you were you had to work at it. Especially in business at Oxford. Their hours conflicted. The few times they'd met since then they spoke about music.

'You were right,' he used to remind her. 'I'm a loser.'

'No way, you're not,' she used to say hugging him tight and patting him on the back.

'It's gone. The music part is dead.'

She only hugged him tighter and said: 'The music never dies. Everything else does but never the music.'

In a weird way she was the only one who completely understood how his music life had been devastated and destroyed by Dad's death.

'Good one, Robert,' he thought.

Miranda – a woman he hadn't thought about in years suddenly had all the answers. Maybe he should get her number, give her a call and ask her to explain why it was so bloody difficult to dump Chloe Me. Just say it, would probably be blunt Miranda's advice.

'I don't want to marry you ignorant, Nazi saluting bitch.'

'And we're here, lady and gentleman,' Mickie announced as he stopped, jumped out of the cab and stretched.

'Why has he stopped here?' snapped Chloe Me glaring out at the overgrown bushes and path that lead to Uncle Steven's cottage.

'That's Uncle Steven's.'

Chloe Me gaped at the cottage. That narrowing of the eyes into her best serpent look said it all. She would never set as much as a toenail near that junkyard. But Mickie had already pulled out two of her suitcases and plonked them down on the path. That was the only reason she jumped out of the taxi – to get numbskull Robert to order a real cab and book her into a five-star hotel if such a thing existed in Dublin. But Chloe Me's plans were scuppered when an old guy and three huge hounds raced up to Robert. Chloe Me hated dogs.

Boru was the first to notice Chloe Me. Followed by Finn and Molly he rushed over to welcome her to their home. Chloe Me bellowed at the one-eyed Boru, then viciously walloped him and Finn with her handbag while kicking Molly with her spiked high heels. Molly moaned pathetically and Boru and Finn moved closer to protect her. But Chloe Me kept on kicking and smacking the whimpering dogs.

'FUCK OFF YOU UGLY BRUTES,' she kept shrieking.

Robert stepped forward.

'You hurt a hair on their heads and I'll kick the daylights out of you. You're the real brute and not these lovely doggies.'

He sat down next to them, hugging and comforting the traumatized trio. Chloe Me looked contemptuously down at Robert and the dogs. She then opened her handbag, sprayed disinfectant on her hands as if the close proximity to the dogs was worse than catching cholera. Robert erupted with anger. Still hugging Boru, Finn and Molly he yelled over to her.

'YOU'RE WORSE THAN THE DEVIL INCARNATE. I'D PREFER TO MARRY A RABID CROCODILE COVERED IN SLUGS AND SNAKES THAN EXCHANGE ANOTHER WORD WITH YOU.'

Robert was puffing louder than a 19th steam machine. The worried dogs tried to calm him down by snuggling even closer and lavishly licking his face, ears and hands.

'It's ok, guys,' Robert kissing the heads of all three.

He stood up. Towering over the three dogs who gazed adoringly up at him Robert looked the image of a heroic conqueror facing enemy hordes.

'I'LL SPELL IT OUT FOR YOU. YOU ARE THE VILEST OF THE VILE, AN IGNORANT, NAZI SALUTING BITCH AND AN UGLY DRUNK. I WISH I'D NEVER EVER SET EYES ON YOU.'

Robert paused and looked down at Molly who was 'smiling' and holding up her paw. Robert took it and continued in an even more commanding tone.

'YOU'RE A BRUTAL BULLY WHO GOES AROUND KICKING AND HURTING HELPLESS ANIMALS. YOU'RE DUMPED!'

Now all the dogs were holding up their paws to him. They looked as if they'd clap and applaud him if they could. Robert bent down cooing and patting his pals. He didn't see that the brutal dog abuser was scowling into the distance with a hand over one ear and listening to her phone with the other ear. Uncle Steven had already picked up her four suitcases and put them into the car that Henry had rented. He ushered Chloe Me towards Henry's rented car which looked posher than the Queen's Rolls Royce next to Mickie's.

'I'm Uncle Steven. So sorry. I forgot to tell Robert I booked you into a suite at the Shelbourne. I'll drive you there.'

Chloe Me assessed the car Uncle Steven was pointing to. She installed herself in the back signalling that sitting up front next to the shabby uncle was beneath her.

Robert patted and kissed the dogs and promised them a barrel full of treaties and a swim in the sea.

CHAPTER 57

Liz was so stunned she could hardly speak. The upstairs flat that had once been Antonina and Andrezej's home had been transformed into the most dazzlingly chic restaurant.

'Unbelievable! Who did all this? When?'

All the walls were decorated with photographs Liz had taken. Each one contained memories of the happiest years of her life.

'How did they all end up here?' she stuttered.

'D'you want to have a closer look?' Hans D. asked.

'Let's all have some Gru Vee first,' Lena called over to them as she poured wine into three glasses.

Liz followed Hans D. over to the corner table. Instead of sipping her wine, Liz wanted to toss the entire carafe of chilled wine over her head and then ask for a bucket of ice to put her face in. That might wake her up and bring her back to reality. This had to be some kind of dream/nightmare? She closed and opened her eyes a few times. But wherever she looked she had a full view of all the walls covered with her photographs. Some had been reprinted into different sizes: huge, medium, normal. All were framed and some had strange decorations dangling over them. Why? Liz decided to concentrate on the mini banquet of canapés Lena had gone to such trouble to make for her.

'We know the stories behind these,' Lena said tapping the nearest photos. 'They're some of his uncle's favourites – Next Swan, Wild Geese, Sewer Stefan, no more corsets....'

Liz semi choked and spluttered up her wine. Lena jumped up with the intention of giving Liz the Heimlich maneuver. But Liz was laughing louder than she'd done in years.

'I was just remembering how it all started,' Liz said wiping away the tears of laughter. 'One night Martin was telling us yet again about the tenor Leo Slezak performing in Wagner's Lohengrin. The opera ends when Lohengrin gets on a swan and they glide offstage. But the stagehand pulled the swan out too soon and it just zipped by. Leo had a great sense of humour and told the audience 'he'd wait and catch the next swan'. Martin had already told us that a few hundred times. Some bright spark came up with the idea that the next time he told that catch the next swan story he'd have to pay for a round of drinks. And that would put an end to his swanning.'

Lena tapped a photo of Moira in front of the Votivkirche and cut-outs of geese, geese and more geese.

'Remind me again of the story behind that one,' Lena asked.

Liz sipped her wine and had another scrumptious salmon and avocado canapé before she launched into her story.

'It started one evening when we'd finished our term exams. We were all recovering from months of endless studying.'

'And getting nicely pissed.'

'We rarely got sozzled. We couldn't afford to. But the end of term was one of the few times we could relax and forget about learning. Then Gerhard began boring us with all the exam questions he hoped he got right about the architecture of the Votivkirche. That was bad enough but then Moira started on her Wild Geese epic. As if we all didn't know that the Votivkirche would never have been built if Count Maximilian O'Donnell an Irish descendent of the Wild Geese hadn't saved the life of emperor Franz Josef in 1853.'

'And that's when Martin said the next time Moira mentioned those geese, she'd have to pay for a round,' said Hans D. laughing.

'The beginning of our 'you'll pay a round the next time you tell us that'.'

'I know where you are,' Lena said and pointed to a large photo of Liz framed by pieces of film and camera lenses.

'And that's June,' Liz said quickly before Lena could ask her anything about photography. 'You have no idea how often she mentioned corsets.'

Liz pointed to cut outs of corsets and one made of whalebone.

'June drove us all mental by reminding us that we'd all be suffering from crushed ribs in corsets if Emilie Flöge hadn't invented the first bra. She was Klimt's lifelong friend but after he died everybody forgot Emilie the fashion genius.'

'That's my favourite,' said Lena pointing to a handsome man who seemed to be squatting in some sort of dark tunnel.

'Sewer Stefan, our film fanatic,' Liz laughed and pointed to the image of a sewer behind Stefan. 'He studied economics but also wanted to be a film critic and saw at least a dozen films a week.'

'And never shut up about 'The Third Man',' said Lena.

'A fantastic film. But Stefan drove us nuts repeating all the things the director had to invent since Mr. Welles didn't always turn up on the day. That's why he filmed those famous running shadows of Orson Welles on the war-torn walls. Stefan told us hundreds of times that Carol Reed had to film some of the famous sewer scenes in London and NOT in Vienna. Orson didn't like the stench and there were too many rats in Vienna.'

'But Stefan didn't have to pay for a round.'

'One mention of 'The Third Man' and he had to pay for three rounds. If he ever reminded us it had been filmed in Vienna in 1948 then he'd have to cough up a few more. But Stefan didn't mind. He did it because he loved the challenge of slipping in a few more details we didn't know about.'

Lena pointed to another photo which had bundles of garlic stuck to the frame.

'But Smelly Frieda the garlic lady didn't have to pay for a round,' Lena said. 'It was you and your friends

June and Moira who had to pay for the Gru Vee if you repeated her story.'

Smelly Frieda! Liz laughed even louder thinking how they all got it wrong about their friend Frieda the Finnish medical student. Every guy who saw Frieda nearly fell over himself trying to date her. She was gaspingly beautiful. But the minute the guy got close to her it was a case of gasping for breath and retreating faster than a rabbit down a hole. Frieda smelt higher than any dead fish filled sewer. The only time she didn't stink was when she ate her breakfast with them in the student canteen. One morning over breakfast they finally discovered why Frida reeked to high heaven. Frieda wanted to study and graduate. She didn't want every man in the Medical Faculty wilting with lust the second they clamped eyes on her. She rubbed garlic around her neck and stuck an old sardine down her back. That way she wouldn't smell it herself but everybody else would and leave her alone. The Three sometimes resorted to 'doing a Frieda' when they didn't want to break a nice guy's heart.

'How do you know all that?' Liz asked.

'Uncle Hans told us to learn the backstories so when relatives reserved a table we put them next to the right photos.'

'But who invested in all of this?'

'His uncle Hans of course,' said Lena pouring more wine. 'He always kept in touch with Antonina and Andrezej and came back here in '92 when they told him they were selling the building and seeing the world, first stop Buenos Aires. But they hoped the new owners would still keep the Café. Uncle Hans promised them he'd make sure of that and asked my lawyer Mum to check all the company details. The shock nearly killed them. Neo-Nazis using a fake company name wanted to use this as a meeting place and change the wine cellar into a duelling room with photos of Hitler and swastikas. Uncle Hans and his mates got together and made sure this would never be owned by Nazis. He told Antonina and Andrezej they had a much better offer for them and their Café would have more than a plaque to them. They went off to Buenos Aires and the rest is history.'

'And lived happily ever after?' Liz asked hopefully.

'They're still living very happily. Present tense,' Hans D. said as he refreshed Liz' glass.

Liz gazed around at all the memories. Her Hans had done all of this.

'This is a sort of museum now?' Liz asked.

'No way! It's one of the busiest bars and restaurants in Vienna. We're always booked solid for weeks.'

'But this morning ...'

'Downstairs is probably the only place in Wien where there's no Wi-Fi for mobiles. That's why the grim reaper comes while we're preparing for lunch. Of course, we have our own private wi-fi access.'

'But it must have cost a fortune to set all this up.'

'Which was no problem. Uncle Hans has disposable millions but doesn't want anyone to know how he made them. Lena and I know but we're sworn to secrecy.'

'I'll make us lunch,' Lena said. 'We'll have another few sips.'

'And then we'll blame the Gru Vee for letting Liz in on our secret.'

CHAPTER 58

'I'm going to be a vet when I grow up,' Nina informed Moira the minute they were in Mauro's cab. 'Did you know that rabbits can have baby bunnies while they're pregnant with the next batch?'

'And she never shuts up about the size of ants in different Schanigartens,' Sophie scoffed. Nina ignored her and handed Moira her copybook.

'I drew these during our lecture,' Nina said pointing to the drawings in her copybook.

'When she should have been listening to Professor Sonja.'

'I was listening,' Nina protested.

'You didn't know all the quiz answers.'

'Neither did you.'

'What was the quiz about?' Moira asked.

'Roman animals,' all three girls replied.

'Did they have donkeys?' Moira asked not having a clue what animals the Romans had.

'Don't know,' the three replied.

They were sitting in Mauro's taxi, the three girls and Moira in the back and Mauro in front with his little mate Josef. Moira took Nina's sketchbook and flicked through pages of cats, elephants, horses and mice.

They all looked so mournful they could have been on Noah's ark starving for food and waiting for a few crumbs to be tossed down from the clouds. Nina was a gifted artist but her creatures looked more solemn that Moira's Mayo relatives at a funeral.

'I can't make them smile like yours,' Nina said.

'We'll show you,' said the two other girls and snapped the sketchbook.

'No, you won't,' Nina shouted and grabbed it back. 'You two couldn't even draw a slug.'

'Girls, girls, girls,' said Moira, 'Cut it out. Behave.'

Silence followed as Moira transformed one sorrowful kitten into a cheeky cat chasing a mouse.

'Drawing is not easy,' she told Nina. 'But I'll give you a few tips how to cheer up your little zoo.'

They watched in awe as Moira showed them how to draw animals with grinning eyes and happy faces. Hoots of laughter echoed back from the two lads in front. The upbeat radio music also helped Moira concentrate on something she hadn't done in years.

'Now you try.'

The three started adding very inventive and funny changes to their drawings. Moira was suddenly reminded of the funny Wolfibeet labels she'd made for Robert's birthday jam and was overcome with guilt. She'd been so busy thinking only of herself she hadn't given him a thought.

'We're here,' Sophie announced as the cab stopped.

'But this isn't the Uni,' Moira protested.

'Yes, it is,' five voices contradicted her as they all jumped out of the taxi.

'You all know where you're going,' Mauro said to the kids. 'I'll show Frau Maria where to get her pass. Then she'll join you in the auditorium.'

The kids had already joined other pals and they all looked more excited than kids on their way to birthday parties. A bewildered Moira followed Mauro towards another building.

'I thought they were going to the University.'

'They are,' said Mauro pointing to a new building. 'That's part of the Kinderuni. I wish they'd had this when I was their age.'

Nur in Wien, Moira thought. Only in Vienna. Kids gasping to go to 'school'. What next? It was almost a relief to see only adults at the desks and offices where Mauro showed her how to apply to attend the 'Gab es im alten Rom schon Tourismus' lecture.

Ten minutes later Moira had her 'permit' with her name and embossed with 'Universität Wien'. She hugged it to her heart and proudly flashed it as she entered the new auditorium in the Kinderuni. Looking up at the rows of seats she saw that the girls were skipping up and down the steps with their mates. Josef was a few rows further away with his own groupies. Moira sat at the back and gazed in wonderment as the new arrivals rushed inside looking happier than kids at a football match. Shakespeare got that one wrong. This was not a case of:

'The whining schoolboy with his satchel
And shining morning face, creeping like snail
Unwillingly to school.'

The kids were having a whale of a time. They listened enraptured to the lecture even if one or two also played under their desks, some secretly blowing tiny balloons to and fro. A kid in the aisle across from her was flicking through a comic under her desk. But all the others gazed entranced at their professors listening to the most fascinating lecture Moira had heard in decades. The things she, the world traveller, learnt: The Via Appia was first built in 312 BC. The Romans had invented the road system and the zebra crossing (a rock in the middle of the road). Some Romans (no women of course) went on educational trips to Greece. Plinius the elder died during the Vesuvius volcano while trying to rescue friends. The fascinating lecture was followed by questions Moira could never answer about what Pliny had written. The first encyclopaedia! What did the Romans use to write messages to their armies all over Europe? She hadn't a clue but the kids did. The girl opposite Moira had stopped reading her comic and was eagerly answering a question about how many of Hannibal's elephants survived. Only one or maybe more! How and why was the Alexandria Library burnt? The kids again competed with another to be the one who knew most of the answers.

When the lecture ended most of the kids swooped down towards the professors and jumped around trying to get their attention. Moira lingered and watched. Like Mauro she too wished something this amazing had existed when she was going to school. She also had to digest the fact that on Saturday all the kids would be at their Graduation in Moira's old University where they would get their 'degree' in the glorious Festsaal. Moira sighed with envy. The only Graduation she'd been to was Robert's. None of The Three had pranced around in their robes and mortar boards when they got their degrees.

She slowly made her way outside to catch up with the kids. After that she would go back to the hotel, have a strong cocktail and then play the insulting Crumblies recording for Liz and June. Together they had to come up with a strategy of saving their beloved Robert from that two-faced ferret.

CHAPTER 59

June had finally located the Kult-Klo recommended by Jeanne at the opera underground station. This 'Culture Toilet' was a public loo with a difference. Strauss waltzes echoed nonstop inside and outside. Talk about 'taking the piss' she thought. It had revolving gates which opened after you paid the entrance fee. The 'entrance' walls showed a gigantic portrayal of the Vienna opera house boxes - a view June knew well from all the times she and Martin had been in standing room gazing up at them. And now people were paying to piss in front of a box painting accompanied by some of Strauss' waltzes. June looked at the other posters luring clients into spending a little bit even if they didn't need to wee. They had an old piano in the men's loo opposite a row of modern toilets. And while the guys were relieving themselves, they could gaze at the bottles of alcohol and glasses on the shelves over the loos. The private ladies' loos in the Kult-Klo had red velvet doors with large numbers exactly like the opera house boxes. June stood and watched the reactions of passers-by and tourists.

'It's an absolute disgrace to have that thing there.' She overheard a wrinkled oldie say to her friend as they walked by.

'Some idiots have no respect for opera,' her friend snorted. 'Stupid tourists ruin everything. Our city is almost unrecognizable.'

The two shuffled away sneering through their upturned noses. June felt like telling them to lighten up. Didn't they have any sense of fun? Couldn't they see that the Kult-Klo had nothing to do with real opera? If it had been there during their student days Martin and his mates would have jumped over the barriers, then played the piano with one hand and pissed into loos with the other. They'd probably have had competitions on who could give the longest, cleanest or innovative performance.

But one thing the krantig oldie had said was true. 'Their' Vienna was almost unrecognizable. June only had to look at the underground map most of which hadn't even begun when she and Martin lived here. In modern Vienna even dogs had cabs. June took the escalator up to the ground and lingered for a while gazing at her beloved Opera House. She had to resist the temptation to go in and ask if they had any standing room left for that evening so she could relive old memories.

'Stop it, June,' she told herself. 'You're worse than Wolfgang.'

A tram stopped almost right in front of her. She watched the passengers get on and off. That too had changed. Trams no longer had 3 high steps to hop or struggle up depending on the age of the travellers. You could now walk straight onto the tram. June joined the other passengers and was thoroughly enjoying her ride until she remembered she had no ticket. She got off and watched the tram slide away.

And there in front of her was the Postsparkasse. Normally she would have rushed in to bask in the wonder work of her favourite art nouveau architect Otto Wagner. But today all her attention was focused on the little park in front of the historical building. There were two placards of the adorable Jack Russell imploring dog owners to stoop & scoop. He was holding a funny notice in his mouth with the warning that dog owners would be fined 36 Euros if they didn't. Both cardboard signs were stuck into the park's grass. It was her lucky day. One was close by and the other one near a bench. June ran to the nearest one, pulled it up and put it under her arm. She hopped happily towards the second one, bent down and was releasing the little treasure when a hand clutched her arm and announced in a most authoritative voice.

'Sie sind verhaftet.' (You're arrested!)

June fell sideways with the shock and landed snout down in the grass. The doggie placard she'd yanked from the grass flew up in the air and landed a few feet away. The policewoman picked this up first and then walked back to June to make sure she didn't make a dash for it. It was only then she noticed that the 'criminal' wasn't exactly a teenager. She helped June get up and then asked if she was hurt or if she needed any help.

'You have some nerve,' June snarled. 'How dare you try and arrest me. I've done absolutely nothing wrong!'

The policewoman waved the doggie sign. June reached over and tried to snatch it from her.

'That's mine,' she yelled. 'It's for my grandkids in Australia.'

She reached out trying to snap the sign back but tottered sideways again. June heard the fabric ripping. All the safety pins that held this side of her 'new' dress burst open and pricked her upper thigh. Blood dripped down her leg. She yelped in pain. Her amazing masterpiece had been destroyed by the idiot who was now helping her to sit down on the park bench. The previous occupants - a cuddling couple - moved over. They had intended to stay out of curiosity but the policewoman told them to shove off.

The young policewoman – Polizistin Lanz couldn't have looked guiltier if she'd arrested her own great-granny by mistake. While June sobbed at the loss of her new look, the policewoman explained that June wasn't arrested. She was only trying to warn her that she couldn't steal the doggie signs. But if it meant so much to her, Polizistin Lanz would make an exception and give her one. June's tears slowly stopped. She came to her senses and started apologising.

'I only learnt about those signs this morning,' she explained. 'I didn't know it was illegal to steal one. That's the second one I've ever seen.'

'But you're Viennese, aren't you?'

'We'll always have Vienna.'

Polizistin Lanz looked baffled.

'It's a joke my husband always made,' June explained. 'I haven't been back for 10 years. These weren't around then.'

'So sorry for hurting you and my name is Lilian.' She shook June's hand.

June was now feeling sunnier than the sun, thinking how much mileage she'd get telling the Two about being arrested. Try and top that, old tin can ashtrays in the Uni. She wiped away the blood from her thigh and tried to close the safety pins.

'I'm so sorry.'

'It's my own fault, Lilian'.

'At least let me pay you to get it repaired.'

'No need, Lilian,' June reassured her. 'I'm on my way to the Webshaus to finish it on one of their sewing machines.'

'Webshaus? You know the Webshaus?'

June explained how long she knew the Webshaus.

Lilian was completely shocked.

'That's unbelievable! Every year they give the new police recruits a summer concert. Mine was 5 years ago.'

'Have you been back since?'

'You couldn't stop us. We fund-raise for our special concert and barbecues. The Webshaus has beautiful music, fab food and that dream of a garden.'

'Barbecues. Now that's new. Who's in charge of these special events?'

'Robert. He comes back twice a year. He comes in May to celebrate his dad's birthday and then again in July. But we won't be meeting him this year. He said his mother would be here instead. We're all looking forward to meeting her and thanking her.'

June was so shocked she couldn't even whisper: 'I do NOT believe it!'

CHAPTER 60

'You could do with a pint or two, matey,' said Mickie.

'Could you drive me back to that bus stop with the cellist?'

'You definitely need that pint,' said Mickie guiding his friend over to his taxi. 'And not at a bus stop.'

Robert explained. He wanted to know what Miranda was doing in the airport car park and then at the bus stop playing the cello.

'She always wanted to be a composer. But the weird thing was she liked the background noise in bars, football stadiums or rallies. Said it inspired her. She might have been filtering the new noisy Dublin through the cello.'

'And I thought I'd heard it all,' said Mickie as he opened the car doors to let the 3 dogs settle in the back.

When they arrived at the bus stop Miranda looked as if she was done for the day. She was standing with her cello upright in its case next to her.

'Hey there. How about a bit of Bach or Dvořák?' Robert yelled out from the car.

Miranda looked more shocked than poor Boru when she'd been battered by the Klo's handbag. The cello dropped sideways. Robert leapt out of the car and ran over to her.

'I didn't mean to shock you,' he said hugging Miranda.

There was so answer from the silent statue almost frozen in Robert's arms.

'I'll park on the side up there,' Mickie called out from the cab.

Still no answer from Miranda.

Robert gently eased her out of his arms to have a closer look. Floods of tears streamed down her face.

'I didn't mean to frighten you. But we saw you at the airport and then here.'

Sob, sob, gulp, sob. At a complete loss Robert again folded Miranda in his arms, patted her back, kissed her hair until the barking trio brought him back to reality. They looked as if they too wanted to know what the heck was wrong with Miranda.

'I wasn't playing the cello,' Miranda said wiping away some of her tears with the bottom of her dress. Robert offered her his shirt sleeve.

'You were composing? Let me guess. Miranda's Moo Moo mazurka? Quiet green fields smothered by bulls and cows farting? A Klickity Plonk Polka? You're going to the races to absorb the sound of horses' hooves?'

Miranda now sobbed worse than a wounded deer. Robert stopped trying to be funny and gently stroked her hair.

'Miranda, what's wrong? What happened to you.'

'The music, the music,' Miranda sobbed. 'I can't play anymore.'

'You hurt your hand?'

'No. My fingers are fine. It's the music, the music ……'

'The music, the music, go on,' Robert said in his most encouraging tone.

'The music died. It died.'

'No way!!! What did Miranda always tell me? The music NEVER dies.'

'I WAS WRONG, WRONG, WRONG.'

'The music never dies,' Robert repeated and waved over to Mickie to help him bring Miranda away from the bus stop.

'Mickie will take you with us to Uncle Steven's. He's got loads of hankies.'

'And when was the last time YOU played anything?' asked Miranda with hints of her old bossy tones.

'The day before yesterday actually.'

'And before that?' Miranda persisted.

'The night before that.' Robert declared in triumph. 'The music never dies.'

Miranda kicked the cello case and was about to run away but Boru got there first. The one-eyed dog stood on its hind legs and snuzzled her neck until she put her arms around him and sat back down on the bench. Not to be outdone Finn and Molly rushed over and sat on either side of her.

Robert was about to admit the truth. He'd given up music and was drunk as a skunk when he 'played'.

'The music didn't die then?' Miranda asked.

'No,' Robert lied. 'The music never dies. Now let's get you over to Uncle Steven's. This is Mickie.'

'Pleased to meet you, Miranda.'

'Where were you headed?' Robert asked.

'I don't know.'

'Everyone gets lost, sometimes,' Mickie reassured her. 'Don't worry.'

'I wanted to escape.'

'From what?'

Stubborn silence.

'Miranda, come on.' Robert sounded sweeter than sugar. 'Just spit it out. Mickie has heard it all before so what's the problem?'

'I hate fukking music.'

'So do we! Wait until you hear the lads imitating Elvis in our local.'

'Or Mickie playing his cuckoo instrument.'

'Ok. Ok. You win,' Miranda sighed. 'I couldn't stand it anymore so I quit 2 months ago. After years of playing suddenly I couldn't stand hearing a single note. I don't know why. This morning I just got on a plane with my cello. I've no idea why I picked Dublin. I just wanted to sit down somewhere new and play.'

'In the most deafening spot at Dublin airport? Pull the other one, Miranda. You're having me on!'

'No, I'm NOT,' Miranda yelled. 'I just wanted to play and NOT HEAR THE BLOODY MUSIC.'

Her angry voice echoed louder than the traffic and the three dogs jumped off the bench with the shock.

'And I thought ….' Mickie didn't get time to finish his 'I'd heard it all'.

Miranda had already plonked the cello between her elegant legs and was zipping through the Finale of Saint Saëns 'Carnival of the Animals' followed by a sizzling version of Bach Cello Suite nr 1.

Robert crossed his arms. He gazed at the revitalized Miranda, smirking prouder than a cat who'd gorged a pound of stolen scrimp.

At the end of the piece a beyond triumphant Miranda stood up, waved her bow in the air as if signalling to Robert 'BEAT THAT, BOZO'.

Mickie and Robert applauded and roared 'BRAVA, BRAVA'. Miranda bowed, kissed her bow and then blew kisses to her audience. Boru, Finn and Molly dashed over to express their appreciation. Miranda held out her hands and let the three slobber all over them.

'What did I say?' Robert was about to requote Miranda's 'the music never dies' but Mickie got there first.

'Could we invite Madame to a celebratory champers?' he asked leading Miranda towards his cab and ushering her into the front seat.

Robert placed Miranda's cello safely in the trunk and settled in the back with the dogs.

'Just as well you're not allergic to dog hair,' said Mickie in his normal voice. 'So where would you like to go, Miranda?'

'Anywhere you want.'

CHAPTER 61

Liz sat on a bench in the Volksgarten and gazed in amazement at the beauty of the Viennese roses. The layout of the benches seemed to be the same as she remembered when she first sat here recovering from the tragic loss of her camera crushed by the Soviet tanks in Prague in 1968. A group of tourists stopped in front of the roses to take close ups and selfies. Four children stomped on the 'forbidden' ground and tried to steal a few roses. The parents only noticed when the kids started yowling because they'd pricked their naughty hands. The parents immediately checked if any guards or gardeners had seen how the kids had broken the rules. They yanked the youngsters away while 2 adults patted back the earth that the kids had disturbed. Liz felt sorry for the kids. For them visiting parks with only wall to wall roses was about as boring as doing their homework.

Roses were definitely not at the top of Liz's favourites. For years just a mention of roses reminded her of how she had ruined her own life sitting during the storm on this very bench watching all the rose petals being pelted by the rain. But after lunch with Hans D. and Lena she still felt higher than a kite.

The couple next to her very discreetly poured red wine into small plastic glasses and put the bottle back in their bag. Liz wondered if it was against the law to drink alcohol 'al fresco' in Vienna.

Liz laughed remembering the framed photo of French Antoine with what looked like glasses of wine dribbling over his young face. She wouldn't have recognized French Antoine if they hadn't stuck a passport photo of him next to the dribbling wine montage. French Antoine was fascinated by the German names of wine such as 'Alter Knabe' (old guy), 'Nacktarsch' (nacked arse). When he was warned he'd have to pay for a round if he didn't shut up about wine, he told them he had changed to Austrian beer. By the time he had sipped his way through his glass of beer and bored them rigid about when, who, where and how beer had first been brewed even Antonina and Andrezi wanted to shove him into a beer barrel down in the cellar.

Nothing could stop Antoine trying to enlighten them about the origin of alcohol. Until they put their heads together and came up with a killer idea. The minute Antoine started on his bevvy history boredom Martin gave the Fad Four the signal to play the tango. Antonina and Andrezej loved to dance the tango. So did most of the students. Afterwards they all got a free refresher bevvy. In the first photos Liz had taken of those gloomy semi toothless, scrawny guys they looked more miserable than 4 drenched cats dying in a ditch. They were grieving eternally for their Jewish player friends who had been thrown out of the Vienna Philharmonic and murdered. They were always in mourning for the lives they would have had if the Nazis hadn't taken over all music and orchestras.

But after decades of sadness the Fad Four finally found happiness and success. It happened one cold spring evening when they were all studying for exams. Some were writing their assignments. June was fussing and tutting over an original design she had to finish for her exam. The Fad Four were enlightening Martin about the history of the baton which might come up in his exam.

Suddenly Sewer Stefan burst into the café yowling and yelping in pain because he'd dashed straight through the hard plastic dividers. The wallop had almost blinded him and he had to keep his eyes clenched. Antonina rushed over and tried to ease his pain with a little hot cloth.

'Are they here?' Stefan kept asking because he couldn't open his eyes.

'Are who here?'

'The Four. The players.'

'Why?'

'Are they here?'

'Of course they are,' everyone yelled.

'Now keep calm, Stefan, gently rub your eyes and you'll be fine in no time,' Antonina said. 'Then I'll bring you over to them.'

'Man, you sure got thumped.' Martin laughed when he saw the state of Stefan's face. 'You know you're supposed to come in sideways.'

'Just for once could you let ME get a word in sideways?' Stefan hissed.

'Certainly, your highness,' said Martin grinning at Stefan's elegant tuxedo.

'Have they got their instruments with them?'

'Of course, they do. Where d'you think they are? In the oven keeping them warm?'

'Zip it, clown. Are their tango outfits here as well?'

Antonina placed a glass of Stefan's favourite beer into his hand.

'Thank you, Antonina,' said Stefan, tossing back half the glass.

She patted the back of his tuxedo which was something he wore on many occasions in comparison to the other students who couldn't even afford a tie.

'Did you want something from them?'

'I got them a job.'

'A job? Tangoing in the sewers?' Martin couldn't resist asking.

'My sister got married today but the band she hired for the reception are still stuck on a train,' Stefan explained. 'Some last-minute disaster. Her wedding reception will be ruined if she has to resort to cheap records.'

'What a terrible disaster,' the students gasped ironically. Sewer Stefan's sister, an habituée of posh overpriced places never set foot in their special Café.

'But she loves the tango and her husband will pay anything to make sure it's a night to remember. I've got 2 taxis waiting outside.'

With Antonina's help the four almost leapt into their fun tango outfits which June had designed. Martin made himself useful and carried their instruments to the taxis. Stefan hugged Antonina as she helped him glide carefully through the divider. As promised Stefan's brother-in-law Felix paid The Fad Four more than handsomely. He also changed their lives by getting them other 'jobs' playing at events and concerts.

This finally led to recognition in both the tango and classical world. The Fad Four changed to the Fab Four. In the last photos Liz had taken of them they were smiling more broadly than four swans who'd met their life mates. The Café remained their local and they filled the wine cellar with cases of fine wines they got at glamourous events. Some were so exclusive even French Antoine was speechless. The Fab Four's music had also been recorded and was now played in the upstairs restaurant.

Liz sighed. Her Handsome Hans! What would her life have been like if she hadn't lost her mind that wild day in July, calling him a Nazi and blaming him for the loss of her babies? What if she'd moved to Hamburg with him? Liz shook her head. Dwelling on the past didn't achieve anything as she'd told June thousands of times. But at least now she knew what had happened to Hans after he'd moved to Hamburg. Hans D. and Lena had divulged their 'secret' after they had moved on from canapés to Lena's Cordon Bleu accompanied by local summer vegetables. Hans was now a writer. Liz had laughed out loud.

'What's he writing? The history of everything? But he's not exactly famous.'

'He's very famous,' Hans D. said. 'But not under his own name.'

'Why?'

'He writes children's books under a pseudonym. He's sold millions worldwide. But he doesn't want anyone to know his real name.'

CHAPTER 62

Lisa and Henry sat holding hands on Uncle Steven's patio. If all the birds in Dublin had landed on them twittering coocoo, coocoo they would not have been distracted from gazing entranced into each other's eyes. It was only when a hand picked up their empty cocktail glasses that the lovebirds noticed Uncle Steven.

'Up for another love potion?' he asked the two.

Lisa jumped up and metamorphized into a livid witch with her arms crossed and a glare in her eyes that rivalled that of the devil's.

'You invited that creature here? You invited that skunk here!!!!'

'Shall I refresh your drinks?'

'No. Not until you explain why you invited *her* to the races.'

'Ok, I'll tell you. But could you please get me a bevvy, Henry?'

'Sit,' Lisa ordered.

All smiles Uncle Steven settled into his usual seat. When Henry returned with a cool glass of beer he looked as if his joy was now complete.

'Thank you, Henry. Cheers!'

'We're listening,' Lisa snarled.

'Did Robert call you and tell you what happened here today?'

'No, he didn't,' Lisa snarled. 'Why would he?'

For the next ten minutes Uncle Steven told them how the bitch had clobbered Boru and Finn with her handbag and kicked Molly with her spikey high heels. He didn't spare a single detail of how the three doggies had been frightened to death by such horrendous cruelty. Henry put his arms around a sobbing Lisa, hugged her tight and kissed her hair. Uncle Steven paused, had some beer and then threw himself into describing how Robert the Knight had rescued and consoled the puppies while dumping the bitch into the deepest hole in hell. Lisa jumped up, threw her arms around her Dad and begged for his forgiveness.

'I'm so sorry, Dad for what I said earlier. You never do anything stupid.'

But Henry still looked perplexed.

'I'm still in the dark,' he said seriously. 'After she kicked your puppies how could you put her in my car and then drive her to that hotel?'

'I'd have preferred to toss her on a bonfire and I certainly hadn't reserved Madame a suite at the Shelbourne.'

Uncle Steven put his glass down and told his tale of that drive into Dublin, keeping up his act as chauffeur while Madame in the back scowled at her mobile.

'And what do think of Robert's new decision?' he asked in his new false sugary voice.

Madame continued scowling at her mobile.

'Has Robert told you of his new plan?'

Madame kept scowling.

'Have you seen his new apartment?'

Now he finally had Greedy Guts' full attention.

'A new apartment?'

'Robert is finally following his dream. He's taken the first step and downsized.'

'Downsized?' Madame's flinty eyes narrowed in disbelief.

'But hasn't he told you he's left his job?'

'He got a better offer?'

'No. He's focusing fully on music. He has huge talent.'

'In finance,' Missy Flinty snarled.

'Robert quit his job weeks ago. He's downsized to a little country flat for the two of you where he can practice and compose without annoying the neighbours.' He deliberately mentioned 'country' because he knew little Missy Pissy hated rural areas.

'The *countryside*. Never! And he would never downsize,' she sniffed.

'He has downsized. Luckily you have your own city flat and a job. You'll be able to support him.'

'Ridiculous,' she snorted haughtily. 'Robert has masses of properties and money.'

Uncle Steven stopped at a yellow light which annoyed Madame even more. She glared at him from the back with the hauteur of a despot expecting everything to go her way. Uncle Steven was ready.

'Robert doesn't own as much as a shed.'

'He'll inherit his mother's estate and their properties in Vienna,' she sneered with the arrogance of a fox flicking off a flea.

'No, he won't. They're in trusts for musicians.' Since he couldn't yodel halleluiah Uncle Steven savoured the moment just the way he and Martin had relished the rare gobstoppers they got as kids.

'That's rubbish. Says who?'

'We all do. I also helped Martin draw up his will. He only bought that old London warehouse for space so he and his mates could play symphonies and Mozart operas. Nobody expected the area to become so pricey. June will be moving out soon. And then it will be transformed into the finest Musicians' establishment in Europe. Didn't Robert explain that to you?'

'Explain what?

By the time Uncle Steven had finished spinning his spider's web of lies they were parked in front of the Shelbourne hotel.

'I DO NOT FUCKING BELIEVE IT,' snarled the little shit.

'I'm so sorry I upset you like this.'

'That miserable shite thinks he expects ME to support him. I DO NOT FUCKING BELIEVE IT. NO WAY!'

She was spitting in disbelief as she leapt out of the car and stormed up the entrance snarling at the hotel personnel to deal with her luggage. She didn't as much as glare back at Uncle Steven who was now basking in the delight of having saved Robert from that toxic reptile. After June had brought him up to date on how the drunk had behaved at the birthday party, he had come up with an idea of ridding their lives of the poisonous money grabber. His original plan had been to take the reptile for a 'private' stroll along the beach and divulge Robert's 'moving to the countryside' fib.

Uncle Steven stopped telling his tale. All was silent on the patio for a few minutes while Lisa and Henry tried to connect the dots.

'You invited her here so you could tell spin her some tale about Robert being poorer than a goat'?

'And drowning in debt.'

'But how did you come up with that idea?'

'Mrs. Casey was here one evening rambling about historical TV dramas when wealthy fathers used to come up with tricks to test men and see if they wanted to marry their daughters for love and not the money she'd inherit.'

He had driven the tarantula to the hotel to be absolutely sure she knew she'd been dumped. Robert had screamed out his 'dumping speech' so loudly the fish in the sea could have heard it. But Madame as always was paying more attention to what was coming through on her mobile earphones. She had paid no attention to what Robert was screaming. To her kicking a few dogs meant nada, nada. Uncle Steven knew she'd slime her way back to Robert by lying and weeping about being savaged by dogs as a child which had traumatized her for life. But when he told her that church mouse Robert would only have debts to scatter at their wedding, the scumbag pulled off her engagement ring and threw it at him: his cheap nephew could keep his bling.

He was about to show Lisa the ring which was worth quite a sum but was covered in kisses by three adoring dogs leaping all over him.

'Well, look what the cat brought in,' said Lisa rushing over to hug Robert, Miranda, Mickie and his wife Siobhan.

CHAPTER 63

Moira only noticed the tall, elegant man because he stuck out in the crowd of kids who were hollering and leaping around the campus grounds. The guy exuded an air of gloom that clashed with the kids' merriment.

'Opa,' Nina shouted and waved to Mr. Misery.

With a grandfather like that was it any wonder the little girl was as solemn as a statue and couldn't draw a smile on a cat? Moira wasn't in the mood for gloom. After the exhilarating lecture Moira felt as elated as any of those kids and wanted to jump up and down and run around the campus with them. When Mr. Misery finally spotted his granddaughter waving at him the guy's face lost its despondency. Mr. Elegant waved over to Nina. And that's when Moira spotted the ring. But this couldn't be Hugo. Not her Count Hugo. She wouldn't have recognised him if her life depended on it. But she would recognize that ring anywhere on the globe. The one with the family crest and the three rubies.

Moira felt her heart jump into her tonsils. She started groping for her sunglasses only to realise that she was already wearing them plus the baseball cap to keep the sun wrinkles at bay in her very Irish skin. She had refreshed her lipstick – but only because she was back in professional mode and was basking in the awe and admiration that the kids had poured over her. Thank God she was looking elegant and sweetly smelling of Chamade.

Nina ran up to her grandfather bubbling about the painter who'd looked after them. He listened most attentively to his young granddaughter. He smiled down at her and even in the throes of her rapid breath Moira noticed how all doom and gloom had evaporated from him. Her heart nearly jumped out her ears when he stopped in front of her and shook her hand. Those pampered hands hadn't changed even if the rest of him had.

'Ich danke Ihnen.'

The very formal 'Thank you'. Not a shred of recognition. Moira waited in a welter of excitement, a bursting heart and the urgent need to laugh out loud. How strange could life be! She waited as he took out his wallet, a very sleek expensive one suitable for the gentleman who always had everything. How sweet, she thought. He probably wanted to buy his granddaughter an ice cream from the nearby stall.

'Was schulde ich Ihnen, gnädige Frau?'

HOW MUCH COULD HE PAY HER? The very formal request to tell him what he owed her. OWED HER? He thought she was the 'hired help'.

How dare he stand in front of her with his open wallet looking like some throwback to the days when men treated women like property! End of her breathlessness and onset of ice-cold fury.

'Aber bitte,' said Moira in that Viennese dialect they all used to imitate when they felt like having a good old laugh. The English equivalent of a genuine Viennese dialect was like a mixture of a Kerry brogue with a New Orleans lilt. Nina looked most surprised but then started laughing.

'Please, it was my pleasure,' said Moira and gestured to Hugo to put his wallet away.

There wasn't the slightest scintilla of recognition in that face. Just confusion. What was a Viennese gentleman aristocrat to do? The help had looked after his grandchild for an afternoon. The help had to be paid.

'Such an amazing girl.' Moira continued in her newly acquired Viennese brogue. 'You wouldn't believe how clever she is. But I suppose you do.'

It was all for the benefit of this little girl to whom Moira had become very attached to in a few hours.

'I'll see you again Nina,' she said and patted her head.

'Really?' Nina gasped as if she couldn't believe her ears. She rushed forward and hugged her. Moira was so surprised she tottered back slightly.

'Bye now,' she said to both of them. 'I must be going.'

Before I throw up on YOU this time, Moira thought remembering the green vomit that she had sprayed over his mother all those decades earlier.

***

June sat on the bench with PC Lilian who was bringing her up to date on events at the Webshaus when Robert visited. June was just about to tell Lilian who she was when two women bolted out of the nearby Café screaming that their handbags had been stolen. Lilian gave June her card before rushing off. She still couldn't believe it. Robert had secretly come to Vienna twice a year to check if all was going well at the Webshaus. Why had her son lied to her for years? June wiped away some of the blood on her thigh. What a complete idiot she'd been and always was. Slashing a few old clothes and ending up with an outfit that a pack of cats could have put together. Clipping her hair thinking it would turn back her clock by a few decades. She sat on the bench thinking of all the stupid things she'd done. She had wasted all her design talents. Her daughters had married men from a distant part of the globe to get away from her. She saw Lilian come out of the Café holding the robber and putting him into a police car. June watched them drive away. She had a choice. She could sit here on the bench hugging the paper terrier with his Wurst and poo slogan until the cows came home or get her ass in gear and stop wasting more of her life. Lilian had left the other doggie sign on the bench. June picked it up. One for each of her grandkids in Australia.

Getting into the cab June didn't care if it was a flea taxi or a 'no lice wanted' car. She'd get to the Webshaus and find out all the secrets Robert had kept from her. Then she'd buy something normal to wear instead of trying to look like some nutty hippie denying she was hitting 60. She had no interest in the views from the cab. She looked down at the scratches made by the broken safety pins. They were swollen and looked like red warts. What next? Blood poisoning? The cab stopped outside the Webshaus. The glorious scent of grilled food and the sound of magical music drifted towards her. Laughter echoed loudly when the music had finished. Laughter had been omnipresent back in the days. So how had she, Liz and even the laugh a minute Moira forgotten how to laugh, laugh, laugh? She lingered outside gazing at the crowd of young people some with instruments, others holding sausages on sticks some cooked, some still raw.

'Frau June. You've arrived.'

June recognized Franziska the administrator.

'Why didn't you call? We've been expecting you,' said Franziska.

'Me?'

'Who else?' laughed Franziska. 'Robert called and told us you'd be here this week. But he didn't know exactly what time you'd pop in.'

CHAPTER 64

'Take your pick. Chicken, fish, beef, veg, soup, sauces. All yours.'

Uncle Steven stood in front of his open freezer still chockfull with the divine home cooked delicacies.

Two hours later if a platoon of starving elephants had invaded Uncle Steven's kitchen it couldn't have looked messier. The table, shelves and counters were covered with the empty food containers. The sink was piled high with plates, cutlery, bowls. Every inch of the cooker was covered with pots and pans. Empty wine and beer bottles lined the floor. The scent of luscious dining drifted out onto the patio where Uncle Steven and his guests were finishing their desserts, licking their lips and sipping their drinks. The 3 dogs lay sprawled out near their empty bowls, their eyes closed but lips smiling blissfully.

Their evening peace was suddenly shattered by Mrs. Casey racing up the steps onto the patio and shouting: 'You won't believe it.'

Even the dogs were thinking the same as the humans. *That's the first time I've seen Mrs. Casey run faster than a hare.*

Robert jumped up and sat Mrs. Casey down on his chair.

'It's on in a few minutes,' Mrs. Casey panted.

Lisa handed her a glass of water.

'What's on?' she asked.

'Cats catch criminals,' Mrs. Casey panted.

'Cats usually catch mice and rats,' said Mickie who had known Mrs Casey all his life. 'Criminal bats, maybe?'

'Turn on your tv.' Mrs. Casey ordered.

'Have you had lunch?' Uncle Steven asked wondering if Mrs. Casey had been hitting the gin bottle even if she was the soberest women in the district.

'They showed a preview at the end of the news. I wanted to make sure you wouldn't miss how Cats Caught the Criminals in your Auntie Moira's place in London.'

'Auntie Moira is in Vienna.'

'I know that,' Mrs. Casey sniffed. 'This is a TV programme about her place in London and cats catching criminals. It's on in a few minutes.'

'Into the living room people.' Uncle Steven ordered as he guided Mrs. Casey into the most comfortable armchair.

'Is she all there?' Miranda asked Robert.

'If Mrs. Casey says there's a programme on TV about cats catching criminals in London you can bet your life on it. Godmother Liz works in TV so maybe she did something with cats. But Auntie Moira doesn't even like cats.'

'Champagne anyone?' asked Uncle Steven.

'Yes, please' They all chorused with the exception of the dogs.

They had sipped their way through 3 bottles by the time the cat piece ended.

'Mrs. Casey. That was amazing,' said Robert standing up and applauding her. 'Can't thank you enough.'

'I've recorded it. We'll definitely watch that wonder again,' Uncle Steven said picking up the empty glasses and champagne bottle.

'Lord Henry snap to. You're still on duty. Dishes.' Lisa guided Henry to the sink and made him slip on a pair of rubber gloves. 'That's washing up liquid.'

Henry grabbed it and pretended to squirt it at her while chasing her out of the kitchen.

Miranda joined the laughter more joyously than she'd done in months. She knew there were a few oddballs in Robert's family. But he'd never mentioned Mrs. Casey.

'Can I help with the dishes?' Mrs. Casey asked.

'You're a guest,' Uncle Steven said almost shooing her out onto the patio. 'Dishes can wait. Robert, why don't you take Miranda and the dogs for a walk along the beach?'

'Couldn't we do the dishes first?' Miranda asked.

'My Lisa and her valet will do that. Want to bet?'

'He always wins,' Robert told Miranda, taking her hand as they walked towards the steps. The dogs had raced ahead and were barking back at them from the beach.

'I'm delighted Liz has gone back to drama. She must have spent months filming those cats.'

'I loved that bit about the lunatic pelting her husband with eggs and then twisting a string of sausages around his neck trying to choke him,' Miranda said.

'Or hitting him with the frying pan. So inventive. But they must have raided every garbage bin in Fulham to collect all that rotting garbage. YUK!! All those shots of excrement and wormy bones. But Liz always was a wonder.'

'I wonder where they got that idea for a cat drama?'

'Miranda, the only thing I know about cats is that Mozart loved them.'

'Did he have any?'

'I'm sure he did. Poor kitties. They didn't last long in Mozart's day with all those deadly diseases.'

'You're beginning to sound just like your dad.'

'Who was allergic to cats. But he's finally returned to Vienna,' Robert smiled at her and then gazed up at the sky.

'The stars are out,' said Miranda putting her arms around him and kissing him.

The dogs looked at the two embracing. By the looks of that passionate duo, they'd be playing on their own tonight.

CHAPTER 65

The Three walked solemnly and silently amidst the ancient gravestones in St. Marx cemetery. Liz's head was bowed much lower than her two friends who both thought it was her way of showing deepest respect for Martin's funeral. They were both wrong. She kept her head down because she didn't want her friends to see how happy she was. Pierre had emailed her that morning threatening to sue her for locking him out of 'his' house and giving all his organic veggies to locals. How dare they pick 'his' garden bare! She took a long, deep breath. She was in St. Marx's cemetery saying a final farewell to Martin. She would focus fully on the solemnity of the occasion for their dearest Martin's sake.

She'd have felt a huge relief if she'd been able to watch Moira mentally whizzing Count Hugo 'sans teeth, sans credit cards, money, shoes, ties, underwear, sans anything' to a shed in Fulham. He'd lose his arrogance after he'd hungrily chewed off his manicured toenails. Moira was thoroughly enjoying her fantasy of the filthy, starving count scrounging around the communal garden fighting with the rats, feral cats and foxes for bits of putrid food. But one look at Liz's solemn features and she remembered where she was. She dispatched the count back to his own luxury prison.

'Are you ok?' she asked June and took her arm.

She would tolerate another 30 minutes of putting on the act and then she'd check back with Bella and Oskar and get all the lowdown on married, divorced, or maybe widowed Hugo. But deep down she didn't care. She preferred thinking about what a hit she'd been with the kids. She was looking forward to seeing them all again at their Graduation on Saturday in her old Uni.

'It's just up there left of the Josef Madersperger's grave,' June said. Martin used to laugh and say how symbolic that the inventor of the sewing machine was buried only a few metres away from Mozart's.

Liz looked at the two graves. Mozart's had a tall, weeping angel and only a few flowering plants. Mozart fans had probably picked the place bare so they could make petal memories. Every inch of Madersperger's grave was covered with blooming plants. Who donated so much to his grave? His descendants, tailor clubs, sewing factories?

'We're here.' June looked very happy as she waved up to the angel that appeared on too many Vienna guidebooks.

'Why are so few flowers planted here?' Moira asked waiting for an immediate answer from the all-knowing Liz.

But by the look on Liz's face she was taking this scattering more seriously than June herself who had opened the silver box with Martin's ashes in it.

'Thank you both.'

June wanted this 'burial' over and done with as quickly as possible. Over brunch she'd come clean about the ashes. Hopefully the two would laugh at her pathetic plan of scattering bits of Martin all over their favourite places in Vienna. She'd also ask Liz and Moira to forgive her for gnawing their ears off wittering nonstop about Martin for the past ten years.

She bent down, ready to scatter the ashes but a low breeze blew half the dust right into her eyes. June yelped in pain, groped in her handbag for napkins while tears burst down her cheeks. Liz mistook this for more of June's staged mourning. When June collapsed onto her knees covering her face and sobbing, Liz laughed and picked up the empty silver box.

'For heaven's sake, June. Give it a rest.'

'I need a hankie, please,' June panted.

'You should take up acting in your old age,' Liz joked.

'Shut the fuck up,' Moira yelled and angrily pushed Liz the way she'd like to kick lousy Hugo.

Liz fell over and landed next to June. It was only then she noticed the red spots in June's eyes.

'All the ashes flew into my eyes,' said June mopping her eyes with the napkin she'd finally removed from her bag.

'So you weren't pretending to cry?' Liz asked.

'No.'

Liz burst out crying.

'I'm so sorry for what I said.'

The two hugged and kept on sobbing. Moira looked at the grass and remembered the signs 'Keep the grass' and 'Eat the grass' (some bad Viennese translations of 'Keep off the grass'). Martin used to say it was just as well people didn't eat grass. If they did Ireland would be bald and not emerald.

Liz and June were startled out of their hug when a bawling Moira with floods of tears streaming down her face dropped down next to them.

'Why did it have to be Martin? Why did it have to be our lovely, lovely Martin? Why is life so shite sometimes?'

***

Life wanted to hiss and snarl down at The Three weeping out their sorrow. Their tragic loss had been caused by the Grim Reaper with the scythe, not Life.

CHAPTER 66

'They now have all the observational evidence they need.'

If Babs had been announcing to the world that she had won millions on the lottery she couldn't have glowed more happily.

'Yes, we have,' said PC O'Reilly looking as happy as Babs. 'Those criminals will be in jail until they snuff it. And we've also got the glue lock guy.'

Sergei, Shaun and Phil were also seated around a new garden table. The communal plot which a week earlier would have won top prize for the filthiest dumping patch in London was now being transformed into a stunning garden.

'How can I ever thank you all?' asked Babs smiling down at Sweetie and BG who were cuddled together snoozing at her feet

'We're thanking you, Babs,' said Phil. 'Without you we'd never have had such luck. Cheers!'

They all picked up their cups.

'And thank you Moira and Liz,' said Sergei.

'Do they know you've already caught those criminals?' asked Babs.

'll email Liz after their funeral in Vienna,' said Sergei. 'She'll be thrilled to know we've been commissioned to do a drama series with more cats and criminals.'

They all beamed brighter than Christmas baubles. The bastards were now in jail and the only thing they'd kill in the next few years were the masses of cockroaches in their cells and the lice they'd be scratching until they were bald and toothless. The prison guards were making sure they'd always get hordes of those visitors. The bastards had nearly killed a sweet old lady like their own granny. They had tortured and killed hundreds of helpless animals. Those criminals would get more than what was coming to them.

'I still don't know how you all did it so fast,' Babs said.

'We couldn't have done it without those two,' Sergei said pointing down to the two cats.

'And without our Director Sergei,' Shaun said.

'And without Shaun's acting prowess impersonating you, Babs.'

'So, after you left me in Charing Cross Hospital, what happened?' Babs asked.

After they had set up the CCTV and the film studio inside Moira's flat Shaun and Phil installed tiny remote cameras to the cats' collars. After they'd been rewarded with multi treats, the cats didn't mind being ordered around the room while Shaun and Phil filmed them and checked the results. Later an ambulance delivered Babs (aka Shaun the aspiring actor about to enter his groundbreaking role) back home. Shaun/Babs tottered out of the ambulance. The para medics then installed *her* outside in *her* usual place with a mobile clutched in *her* hand.

The stars were out – or at least the few you could still spot in the polluted London night sky. Shaun/Babs was still outside babbling on *her* mobile, the kitties chased one another around the communal garden playing with the bits of food and bones that were being thrown from the 3rd floor.

'Stop throwing food into the garden,' Shaun/Babs yelled up.

'Shut the fuck up, you old cunt.'

It sounded exactly like the nightly exchanges between Babs and TD that Moira heard every night. PC O'Reilly, Phil and Sergei (who was now installed inside as director) were thrilled. Shaun had duped the neighbours. It wasn't long before the old Italian yelled down at them in a mangled mess of English and Italian where every second word was 'shit', 'prick', 'cornuto' and 'bastardo'. The trap was laid. Sergei was in the kitchen opening their beers when he heard Phil yelling at him to come quick and see what was being filmed. They couldn't believe it.

Two of the gang were slithering across the trimmed hedges thinking they were completely hidden. But their smirks were caught on a dozen cameras. The thugs whispered and held out drugged goodies to the two cats who slowly waddled towards them as if trying to decide if their goodies were better than the thrown-out food. Phil and Sergei almost passed out with excitement watching the live footage. PG waddled up to an outstretched hand. The criminal's smirk widened until

PG clenched his strong teeth into the swine's wrist. Years of practice picking up and arranging DVDs had come in very handy. A few seconds later Sweetie had copied her beloved and gnashed all her teeth into the other criminal's wrist. The two howled and shrieked and tried to pull the cats off their arms. Another thug was also screaming his guts out because he had tried to smother Shaun/Babs. As if they'd practiced for years the cats let go simultaneously. The criminals clutched their bleeding arms and started to run. But not for very long because BG and Sweetie had already jumped up onto their shoulders and were chewing their ears off.

PC O'Reilly watched gleefully as the gang danced and howled around the garden with all the cats' claws stuck deep into their skin. Phil was ecstatic to see how his super clever BG had surpassed all his expectations. By the looks on both the cats' faces they were having the time of their lives. The criminals finally spotted the men outside Babs' door and knew it was all over but not before Sweetie and BG dealt a final insert of claws into their necks. The criminals flopped like collapsed soufflés with the cats on their heads. The cameras hidden in the hedges, in parts of the grass and inside one fake bone had captured more than the team had expected in all their wildest dreams.

'We had so much footage it was a real treat editing it,' Phil explained to Babs. 'We spent the night editing the garden footage and all the videos you'd given PC O'Reilly. Amazing luck. We immediately contacted local newspapers and TV news. Never in a million years did we think they'd broadcast it so soon.'

'And I never expected them to slime out of their rathole that fast,' said PC O'Reilly.

'Those monsters wanted to show us how clever they were,' said Sergei.

'But they didn't. We won, we won, we won. And you, PC O'Reilly will go down in history.'

'And who's changing the garden?' Babs asked.

'Every second garden shop in London. That way they'll get free promotion when we're all being interviewed again on how we did it.'

Little happy tears sparkled in Babs' eyes.

***

Life smiled down at them. Life was pleased. It was only thanks to Life that those humans and two cats were now getting the happiness reward they deserved.

CHAPTER 67

A group of tourists who had travelled halfway across the globe to see Mozart's grave were trying not to lose their patience. They knew Vienna attracted a lot of Mozart fanatics and could understand why some broke down with sorrow. But they'd been waiting for 10 minutes. They couldn't take any selfies as long as those 3 weeping women were monopolizing the grave and ruining their view.

June was the first to notice the impatient tourists who looked as if they were about to click their heels like annoyed horses.

'Girls, I think we're being watched.'

Liz looked up but Moira's nose was still dripping and she held out a hand.

The tourists misinterpreted this as a begging for money gesture. They wondered if this was maybe a rehearsal for a modern production of Mozart's burial. He was so poor his 'wife' had to beg for the money to light a candle maybe? They didn't know whether to clap or not when June gave Moira a napkin instead. After she'd blown her nose Moira also noticed the tourists and got up. The Three linked arms and walked out of the cemetery. The tourists took a few shots of them in case they'd see this in some film later.

The Three spent the next hour strolling through the Vienna Woods before having brunch in a non-touristy Heuriger nestled between trees and rows of vines. After her first sip of Gru Vee June admitted her original idea was to scatter Martin all over Vienna and not only in St. Marx. That way she'd come back regularly to Vienna and probably get fined by the Waste Watchers. Then she brought the two up to date on how she'd been 'arrested' and had spent the afternoon at the Webshaus. Robert had made sure that all students would hear tales about his dad and the inspirational designer June without whom the Webshaus would never have existed. Franziska sewed her torn outfit and said it was inspirational. She wasn't kidding either because some of the barbecue guests wanted to know where she'd bought it. They'd love to buy one like it. Franziska also had one of the students style her hair so she wouldn't look like a half-shaved leopard.

Liz told them how she had lied about what happened 30 years earlier in the Volksgarten. June and Moira tried to comfort her by holding her hands. But Liz was topping up their glasses and telling them what Hans and their old mates had done for Antonina and Andrezej who were still seeing more of the world than Moira. Her Hans had also become a world-famous writer. She'd read a few of his short stories on the bench in the Volksgarten. One story was about 3 children feeding their skeleton horses by stealing carrots thrown away by the rich. It was set in 1860's

Vienna when birds had more to eat than most working families and their horses. Hans had also done justice to the women who had slaved on building sites where the Opera, theatres and the most glamorous buildings in Vienna now stood. She was so immersed in reading the stories she thought she was hallucinating when Hans arrived in the Volksgarten and sat down on the bench next to her holding a bottle of wine and two real glasses.

'I don't want to rain on your parade,' said Moira 'but I'm the biggest liar.'

How often had she had told them that Hugo hadn't sent her a single letter? Lies, nothing but horrible lies. He had written loads which her mother forwarded to her in Paris until she told her to return the letters back to Vienna. She was living with Louis at the time. Later she found out that Hugo had even visited Mayo looking for her. But her brothers told him that their sister was 'away with the fairies' and Hugo had a very lucky escape. By the time the brothers had told her this, she'd already set up her own travel business. Things were going amazingly well and she couldn't resist flaunting this by writing to him and telling Hugo she'd always remember their Spring of Love.

'But why were you so angry when Hugo didn't recognize you?' Liz asked. 'You'd never have recognized him if he wasn't wearing that ring.'

'Don't know.' Moira shrugged. 'Could be my old age denial.'

Liz didn't have time to ask what she meant because June was singing:

'For if all liars
Received a lock like this on their mouths,
instead of hatred, calumny, and black gall,
love and brotherhood would flourish.'

This aria from The Magic Flute which was one of Martin's top 50 favourites. Martin had also educated Liz and Moira about the scene where Papageno was given a golden flute by the three goddesses and then sang:

'Now fair wenches,
If I may - I'll take my leave'

The Three sipped their Gru Vee all thinking the same thing: Martin had taken his final leave.

'I love the finale to Don Giovanni,' Moira announced.

The Three smiled and sang 'Questo e il fin di qui fa mal'. Some of guests close by even joined in. Most people could relate to the finale of the Don after he was hauled into a scorching Hell to get what he deserved. Instead of the Don, The Three were visualizing the descent of that serpent Klo Me into eternal fires. Her name would never be mentioned again by any of them unless they wanted a good old laugh about how clever Uncle Steven was.

'What are we going to do now girls?' June asked.

'Go for a snooze in the vineyards?'

'And get bitten by mosquitos.'

'Get arrested?'

'I mean in the future. We're not getting any younger.'

'Yawn, yawn.'

'And we'll all be 60 before the end of the year.'

'Which we're all trying to forget,' Moira said.

Liz took copies of Hans' book out of her rucksack and handed one to June and Moira.

'Is there an English translation?' June asked

'You don't want to read the original?'

'I want to send them to my grandkids.'

'They'll love them,' Liz assured them.

'I want a new start,' Moira announced. 'But ..'

'She doesn't know what yet,' June and Liz chorused.

'Because I've got lots of choices.'

'We know. You can sell or rent out your flat now that it's famous. And Bella and Oskar are auctioning off your animals.'

'Some of my sketches,' Moira corrected them. 'But that's the past. I'll tell you when I've decided what to do next.'

'We've all got new and exciting choices. Weren't we lucky Robert brought us back to Vienna?'

Moira blew her nose, pretending she had a touch of hay fever. Let Robert tell them it wasn't his idea but hers. Enough was enough except when it came to another little glass of Gru Vee.

'The first thing I'm going to do is finish my Birthday Boy Film Project,' said Liz.

'Cheers Robert,' the Three clinked their glasses.

CHAPTER 68

That afternoon a group of walkers came onto Uncle Steven's patio as was their custom. They rested on the chairs, sipped from their water flasks and then left cooked delicacies on the table before resuming their walk. The walkers covered the containers with cushions to prevent the gulls helping themselves to the delicious meals. They didn't have to worry about the three dogs. Sometimes they also accompanied them on their walks. But not today. The dogs were exhausted from all the activity the previous evening. They were enjoying a little peace and looking forward to more fun when they all got back from that day's races.

The dogs were still snoring when Lisa quietly crept up onto the patio, clapped her hands and scared the life out of them.

'Got ya,' Lisa laughed.

Uncle Steven looked with love at his daughter who could always pull this trick off, something he never could. He sat down on the nearest chair, removed the cushions and licked his lips seeing the gifts that had been left by the walkers/chefs.

'Which one of Beethoven's sonatas starts with fresh air and sounds exactly like little horses skipping through the countryside?' Miranda asked Robert.

'And they're off,' Lisa said to Henry who was helping Uncle Steven put back all the cushions.

'Dad used to say that a lot of Mozart's works were inspired by the sound of horse hooves,' Robert told Miranda. 'Mozart was only 8 the first time he travelled to perform in London. He spent half his life in horse carriages travelling all over Europe. Imagine being stuck inside there for months, for years hearing nothing but the clipity, clop, clop, clop of horses' hooves.'

'The sound of horses' hooves is the food of love not clip clop,' Lisa informed her cousin.

'Absolutely,' confirmed the besotted Henry. 'I love the sound of hooves in the morning.'

Miranda felt like shouting that 'MUSIC was the food of love' and would have finished the opening lines of Twelfth Night with 'Play on'. But she knew they all needed a little rest from playing. The night before after watching Cats Catch Criminals while tossing back too much champagne they sat on the patio celebrating Liz's drama and improvising everything from Dvořák to Mozart with the help of the dogs pounding pans with their paws and Mickie getting full use of his cuckoo whistle while Siobhan played the flute. The cuckoo whistle didn't appear very often in classical music so they played several versions of Strauss' Im Krapfenwand'l Polka which would have been nothing without the cuckoo. It had been the most glorious evening.

Tonight, Miranda would relax with the others on the patio. Robert had come up with a fantastic Summer plan. They would visit several little islands off Finland, listen and relax to the sounds of the summer seas and make love under the midnight sun. But before that Robert was taking her and Uncle Steven to Vienna. They'd celebrate with The Three, play classical and jazz in the Webshaus and say a final farewell to Martin.

CHAPTER 69

The first stars were shining in the sky over St. Marx. Only the sounds of sleeping birds could be heard in the locked cemetery where people were banned from entering after 20.00 hours.

But somebody had broken the rules. A man stood near the angel on Mozart's grave. It was Martin shaking himself like a man who's woken up from a long sleep.

'About time,' he heard a group say behind him. 'You took your time.'

Martin blinked at the sight of what looked like Mozart, Beethoven, the Fab Four and all his favourite composers and players dressed up in wigs and costumes.

'Can't always be on time. That's life,' Martin said walking towards them.

'No this isn't life. It's death,' the group recited happily. 'Where you get what's coming to you.'

'Is this a dream?' Martin asked.

'Dream on, laddie. You've been dead for ten years. Remember the barbecue?'

'We were all having a laugh,' Martin told them.

'Mainly because you were hopping around dressed up as the bat from the Fledermaus.'

'Exkuuuzee mois,' Martin said in a most offended tone. 'I was singing the finale. And if I say so myself giving a stunning performance.'

Martin paused. He was about to list all the famous tenors who had sung the hilarious Bat but they could also be here among the ghosts of St. Marx.

'But then?'

'When I flopped backwards in my costume with my wings out wide, they all thought I was still acting and went on dancing.'

'But you'd walloped your skull against a stone and died laughing.'

'End of bats and opera,' Martin sighed.

'And a new beginning,' the Fab Four chanted.

'Which would have started years ago if your wife hadn't locked you up in all those boxes.'

Mozart and Constanze stepped forward and hugged Martin.

'I'm thrilled to meet you, batty fan,' said Mozart taking Martin by the hand.

Strauss II put his arm around Martin. 'We were all crying the day you died.'

'Because your Fledermaus has a funny ending where everyone dances and nobody dies?'

'Because we all admired you for never giving up on your conducting dream,' said Mozart handing him his baton.

'I've died and gone to loony land?' Martin murmured to himself as he heard meowing all around him. Then a huge Labrador leapt up and put his paws on his shoulders.

'Elvis. My little Elvis.' Martin kissed and hugged the doggie of his teenage years in Dublin when they all idolized the real Elvis. 'I've definitely lost the plot.'

'No, you haven't.' A horde of kittens and cats smiled up at him.

'You're no longer allergic to them,' Elvis doggie told him.

'You're sure?' Martin asked as two dazzlingly beautiful cats suddenly appeared on Martin's shoulders and kissed his cheeks.

'That's Shoppin and Klara,' doggie Elvis informed him. Martin heard the cats meowing a piece by Chopin which Clara Schumann loved to play.

Martin turned to the Fab Four as he saw horses dancing in the background.

'Is this some kind of loony bin? What on earth is happening here?'

'Being dead can get boring, so we keep ourselves entertained with music, singing, dancing, animals. Or if we want to, we can zip off all over the globe or stay here and hold our own concerts. What's your favourite piece?'

'Changes every week,' said Martin laughing.

'Join the club, Maestro Martin.'

'Who would you like to conduct first?' one of the Fab Four asked.

'Mozart of course,' another Fab Four answered.

'Thank you all,' Martin gulped and happily looked around at all his dead favourite people.

'Shall we tango, Martin?' Constanze asked and pulled him away from Mozart.

'She can't get enough of it. Tango wasn't around in our days,' said Mozart signalling to a group of Argentinians who had joined them postmortem.

The Fab Four hugged Martin before Constanze hauled him away for the tango. They whispered to him that he would receive *their* special gift later.

'We're taking you over to Café Antoandrezi later on.'

CHAPTER 70

'You're amazing,' Liz congratulated Hans D.

He had again transformed the upstairs restaurant. Now instead of tables and chairs it had a long buffet groaning with the most delectable selection of delicacies, the likes of which they'd never seen in Vienna as students.

Hans D. smiled and rushed off to help the waiters who were pouring wine into carafes and arranging the glasses.

'My nephew is a real star,' Hans said.

'And so are you,' Liz said. 'How did you manage to invite so many from the old days?'

'You mean our young days?' said Hans kissing Liz's hair.

The two looked like newlyweds, holding each other tightly with one arm and using the other hand to sip and nibble. June looked over at them and couldn't have been happier. She couldn't wait to tell Robert how Liz had been sitting on the bench in the Volksgarten reading Han's book when he sat down beside her with a bottle of wine and 2 real glasses. A case of More Love at Second Sight!

Earlier that evening before any of the old friends had arrived, they sat down together and discussed some of Hans' stories. June and Moira had already zipped through a few and thought they were absolute winners. The story that touched them most was about children who had died in 1860's Vienna and returned as ghosts to work during the night to help their parents who slaved so hard to feed them before they died. The little ghosts would also laugh and play more than they had when alive, pushing one another through the walls or racing around on donkey ghosts. They understood the story about the ghosts of three happy kids skipping up and down the spire of the Votivkirche, the church where Hans used to sell the Christmas trees. It was in memory of his and Liz' lost babies.

In other stories he wrote about groups of kids returning during the day as birds. They'd amuse themselves and have fun seeing who could shit most on the wealthy aristocrats strolling by. Other days they had fun with the Emperor and his entourage who sat in luxurious carriages being pulled by dozens of horses. It was the Emperor's duty to just glimpse at the buildings and assess if the work was being properly done by half-starved men, women and children. If the carriages paused in front of workers they always had to bow to his majesty. Instead of the Emperor's wave, the starving workers would have preferred beer and sandwiches in return. This never happened until the day the ghost kids leapt around on the backs of the horses making them fart so loudly that it looked as if they were having a farting competition. The workers were the only ones who could see and hear this and they clapped and clapped. The Emperor and his entourage misinterpreted this as a sign of adoration for his Empire and from then on rewarded the workers daily with leftovers from banquets.

'Hans and I are doing a TV adaptation of his stories,' Liz said. 'We're starting with the one set in the 1860's when the Ringstraße was being built. Could you believe it that Vienna was teeming with more squalor and slums than all of Victorian London? Hans has definitely made up for the lack of an Austrian Dickens.'

'Your stories are so moving,' June told them. 'There's a plaque near our home when the whole area was wall to wall warehouses. It has a black & white photo of hordes of men lining up for hours waiting for a 'call up' job. If they got the job they'd get paid for shifting all the tea, spices and lord knows what else into the warehouses. Not even Dickens wrote about them.'

'You know what she and Martin achieved?' Liz asked Hans.

'We're talking about Hans' stories, not Martin,' June said and shuddered a bit wondering if Wolfgang was invited. If he was she'd tell him the minute he mentioned Eugenie and the word aliens he'd have to pay for 222 rounds. If he didn't lighten up and stop whining about Eugenie and her Planet of Goodness, she'd give him a bottle of wine and tell him to piss off to Eugenie's grave and have a few with his alien pals. But she could never be that cruel to Wolfgang. It was thanks to him that she realized what a remembering Martin pain she'd been for the past 10 years.

'June, are you still designing costumes?' Hans asked.

'I'd love to,' June admitted remembering all the work the students were doing in the Webshaus.

'We're going to need loads of poor kids' 19th century costumes when they're slaving or playing their ghost games,' said Liz. She sounded so perky she reminded June of Frizzie Lizzie the student telling them what her next photography project was.

'Play on Mozart,' June said also perkier than a clown.

'Forget Mozart.'

'That's exactly what I'm planning to do,' June said. 'Ten years ago Martin and I were planning to change our penthouse into lodgings and practice rooms for music students. But they already have enough of those in London. With all the new refugees I now think it would be much better if they had other choices along with music. If they want to be chefs, actors, builders, designers, photographers they need to be trained.'

'And they could practice by designing and sewing all the costumes we'll need for our productions,' Hans said.

'Where will you be filming?' June asked.

Liz and Hans laughed.

'What's so funny?'

'A period TV drama series is not something you can produce overnight.'

'You've also worked in drama, June?' Hans asked.

'I've listened to Liz educating me about it for decades. From script to action, crew, costumes, props, financing, directing, catering, producing, photography, you name it.'

'A period drama is definitely more time consuming and challenging.'

'Will you be filming in Vienna or London?'

'Too soon to say. But there are loads of derelict locations in London that could pass for 19th century poor places,' said Liz. 'But that's the future. Right now it's party time.'

June didn't have time to agree before Moira rushed over to join them.

'I just saw your photos, Liz. Who put up all the decorations around them?'

Liz nodded towards Hans.

'How did you remember all those stories? I'd forgotten most of them.'

'You were trotting the globe, remember?' June joked.

'Maybe I can explain,' Liz suggested. 'When we spent all our student years here all we did was study and … and ..?'

She waited for Moira's answer.

'Waffle.'

'Go to the top of the class. We had no wifi, no phones, no laptops.'

'We were like our old grannies repeating the same stories over and over again. But even I'd forgotten why the Votivkirche was built,' Moira said.

Liz and Hans held each other even closer.

'I love your stories,' Moira told Hans. 'All those details about real working horses. Today, you mention the word horses in Vienna and the first thing anyone says is Lippizaner.'

'And she's off,' June said to Liz.

'Only because Liz was always wittering about the amount of horse dung in London. At the end of the 19th century there were thousands of horses in London. During the night hundreds of workers had to get rid of their droppings.'

'And where did that waste go?' Liz asked.

'The Thames?'

'Did women wear pattens in Vienna?' June asked.

'Pattens?' Hans asked.

'Those high iron things women had to strap under their shoes in Victorian days to avoid all the horse crap. Back when dresses came down as far as their shoes.' June explained. 'But when they went to church on Sunday they had to take them off at the door so they wouldn't sound like a pack of horses clattering down the aisle.'

'And every time I wanted to remind them about pattens they told me to zip it,' said Liz glowing up at Hans.

'Maybe you can weave that into your drama,' Moira suggested. 'And maybe I could help with the horses.'

'You're hired,' they all said.

'You could also play a granny sweeping up the dung shit horse apples.'

'Or batter you two with my pattens.'

'Liz told me how Cats Catch Criminals could never have been produced without your help,' said Hans.

'Would you really like to work with us on this drama, Moira?'

'Love to.'

'Now she's finally decided what she'll do in the future,' June said to Liz.

'*She* was already thinking of working with horses in Vienna,' Moira informed her friends. '*She* was also thinking of giving drawing classes. But if you need an art director - *She* might be available.'

'I can't wait to tell Robert,' said June.

'Tell him we could do with some of his musical invention.'

'I wonder what happened to Smelly Frieda!'

'She was here last year,' Hans said. 'I happened to meet her. And before you ask she's still as stunning as ever. She told me her daughters said their generation didn't need garlic.'

'Things change,' said Moira waving over to the first guests Oskar and Bella. 'Some people don't.'

Oskar would always be first in line for the buffet. He waved over signalling that he'd join them after he'd had a few nibbles. Bella rushed over and hugged them all.

'Thank you,' Moira told Bella.

'For what?'

'For the most amazing lecture I've ever heard and the best afternoon in years.'

'The kids think you're the amazing one.'

'When can kids ever be trusted?'

They both laughed and clinked their wine glasses which Lena had filled for them so they wouldn't have to stand in line like Oskar and Count Hugo who smiled and waved over to them.

'Will you be going to their graduation on Saturday?'

'Wouldn't miss it for the world,' said Moira and joined the queue at the buffet.

Two hours later there wasn't a crumb left on the buffet. The tables had been put back but much closer together to make room for a small dance area. One table had changed into a wine bar where one could top up with red, white or rosé. Beer was also available and Oskar manned the barrels. The entire room echoed with the clinking of glasses, laughter and catch-up chat until Hans D. hopped up onto a table and jingled two bottles together to get everyone's attention.

'Hear ye, hear ye,' he said in a most exquisite Viennese accent. 'You can now lose a few calories by dancing the night away. By popular demand the first dance ain't the mazurka or the waltz … but … ?'

'THE TANGO,' they all shouted.

Hans D. pressed a button on the wall and pointed to a large photo of the laughing Fab Four. The beautiful music of their youth drifted out. They were all so overcome with happiness they listened in silence to the first round and then Hans D. clinked his bottles together and ordered them all onto the dance floor.

They tangoed, waltzed, rumbaed and cha-cha-chaed. Their hearts danced like wildfire especially when they thought they saw Martin with cats on his shoulders standing next to the Fab Four outside the window. None of them ever mentioned they had visions of Martin kissing kittens with his arms around the Fab

Four. When June imagined Martin outside with the kittens, she waved him in, waltzed him over to the wine bar, filled two glasses with Gru Vee.

'Thank you, love,' she murmured to the wine. 'Zum Wohl.'

And Life, Love and Laughter went merrily on.

www.ingramcontent.com/pod-product-compliance
Lightning Source LLC
Chambersburg PA
CBHW032225010726
47494CB00002B/354